THE
UNREASONABLE
ADJUSTMENT

G J Ravenhill

Copyright © 2023 G J Ravenhill

All rights reserved

The characters and events portrayed in this book are fictitious. Any similarity to real persons, living or dead, is coincidental and not intended by the author.

No part of this book may be reproduced, or stored in a retrieval system, or transmitted in any form or by any means, electronic, mechanical, photocopying, recording, or otherwise, without express written permission of the publisher.

ISBN-9798371307149

To Betty.

Finally.

PROLOGUE

"US says $134bn Treasury bonds seized in Italy are fake — or are they?" Financial Times June 2009

On the 3rd of June 2009, two Japanese men were caught on a train near Chiasso smuggling US treasury bonds worth $134.5 billion into Switzerland. The bonds were hidden in a case with a false bottom. The men were travelling from Italy to Switzerland and were never charged with any criminal offence by the Swiss, Italian or US Governments.

Conspiracy stories sprung up on the internet claiming that the North Koreans or China were involved and one even believed that the Japanese government had instigated the operation to offload the bonds on the open market to help their economy. The American Secret Service claimed the bonds were fake and had not originated in the states. The Italian government refused to claim they were fake until it was confirmed by Washington, thus fueling speculation and myth.

Whether the bonds were real or not is pretty irrelevant to those with a criminal entrepreneurial disposition. Stan Tennant had exactly that kind of disposition. He wasn't bothered about conspiracy theories or myths.

Stan just wanted the $134.5 billion.

CHAPTER ONE

May 2010: The Emergency Department, Winchester Hospital, southern England, about an hour away from London.

It had been a steady day in The Emergency Department. There were a few patients being treated for various accidents, breathing problems, and an elderly lady sitting up on her trolly shouting at everyone who walked by that she wanted her mother.

The day was about to change. As soon as the ringing shrill from the red phone started it fractured the relative calmness of the emergency department. An ambulance crew were speeding their way towards the hospital with an extremely ill patient, a severe car accident victim or something equally as devastating.

"Nick get yourself to resus there's a shooting coming in," ordered the co-Ordinating Sister, the red phone still held to her ear.

Nick, momentarily stunned, looked at the sister,

"A what? A shooting?" Nick thought he heard what was said, but just needed to clarify.

"Yes. Male, about thirty-five, bleeding heavily from his chest, no exit wound evident, BP 80/50, pulse 150, sats 85% on 02, has recently amputated fingers on left hand, a cut in the shape of a G on his forehead, multiple burn marks on feet and appears to have had his nails removed from his toes. Family behind ambulance, were not at scene. Police escort with ambulance."

Shocked, Nick looked at the Sister as she scribbled gunshot on a piece of card and placed it on the floor plan of the ED department in front of her. She turned and whispered to Nick,

"He's a bloody mess, Nick. Not likely to survive. Probable homicide. Keep anything he brings in, clothes, watch, wallet, anything, as the police will want it."

Nick nodded. The adrenaline began to power through his body as he regurgitated the words, 'Homicide, police.'

Nick had never been involved with a patient who had been shot. In fact, he'd never heard of a gunshot victim coming to the emergency department. He could understand if this was London or Birmingham, but here? It never happened.

"How long Boss?"

"8 minutes." The Sister picked up another phone to put a code red out to the team.

Nick strode into the resus room. All three bays were empty, their contents on show as the blue curtains were open. The bays were prepared, ready and able to accommodate any emergency presented to them. Nick decided to commandeer the middle bay and switched the monitor on at the rear of the bay.

Monica entered the resus room, her neatly ironed light blue scrubs, and blonde hair tightly tied up, projected professional nurse and competence.

"I'm with you Nick,"

Nick smiled, relieved that it was Monica as she was one of the most experienced nurses in the department. Nick had been a nurse for a couple of years, and knew his stuff, but working with Monica was a godsend.

The two nurses began doing a quick sweep of the bay, making sure everything was hopefully available and working.

"You got the keys Nick?"

"Yes."

"Open the drug cupboard, we are going to need quick access."

"We need blood too,"

"Being sorted. You had a gunshot before?"

"Nope, only stabbings. How's that foot of yours, Nick?" Monica didn't look at Nick as she asked, she was busy preparing a tray ready for any cannulation or injections that may be required.

"Oh a lot better thanks. Not sure what was going on there."

"Probably just your shoes!" She looked down at his highly polished brogues, "Don't know why you don't wear trainers like everyone else!" Her concentration returned to preparing the bay.

"I know, I'm just a bit old-fashioned I guess."

The crashing of the doors and sudden chatter came nearer to the resus room and voices became suddenly louder as a trolley was rammed into the resus area and into the bay, with Nick and Monica standing either side. Out of nowhere a couple of doctors, surgeons, anaesthetists, and the two ambulance crew were helping Nick and Monica transfer the patient off the ambulance trolley and onto the ED assessment trolley. As Nick cut through the material of the man's heavily bloodied shirt, Monica attached cardiac leads to his chest, and unattached the oxygen tubing from the portable canister to the built-in supply of the bay.

"This man is going to need surgery quickly!" A voice boomed from out of nowhere.

There was a lot of blood, and amazingly the man was still alive, drifting in and out of consciousness.

"Hello sir, you're safe now, you are in hospital" Nick calmly spoke as he wrapped a blood pressure cuff around the man's blood-covered arm.

Monica lifted the monitor and sat it at the bottom of the trolley ready for it to be pushed to surgery.

The man opened his eyes and coldly looked through Nick, the life in his eyes slowly drifting away.

"What's his name?" A doctor asked,

"We think Frank." Replied one of the ambulance team.

The doctor tried to talk to Frank, but he was too sleepy. The monitor he was attached to bleeped, but no one took any notice. They didn't need a machine to tell them how damaged this patient was.

Frank suddenly pulled the doctor close to his mouth and mumbled something through his mask, whilst coughing blood into it.

"Suction!" The doctor quickly ordered, as Monica, one step ahead of him sucked the blood from Frank's mouth.

"Say again Frank,"

"Tell my wife," he had a thick accent that was difficult to understand. It wasn't an English accent, maybe Spanish or Italian "Tell her she knows what to do."

"She knows what to do?" The doctor replied, hoping he heard Frank correctly. He was fully aware that he probably wouldn't say anything again.

"Ok, he's crashed."

Monica leant over Frank and started chest compressions, her arms thrust down on his chest, her gloved hands soaked with his blood.

Screams suddenly filled the resus room as two

women ran in, looking like they had just come from a party due to their elegant dresses. Nick managed to cradle both women to stop them from going anywhere near the mess of a possibly dead Frank.

"Frank!!" one of the women screamed. "My husband!"

She slumped to the floor as the other woman crouched down to hold her in her arms.

Frank had died.

The emergency department had been locked down as soon as Frank arrived in the ambulance. Police had shut off the resus room and Frank's body lay still and quiet, a single sheet covering his corpse.

"Nick, just come with me to talk to the family," The doctor who had spoken to Frank requested.

Nick nodded and followed the doctor to the small relative's room.

Inside sat the two women and a child, a toddler of about three years old, playing on the floor with some coloured plastic bricks. In the corner stood a police officer nodding to the doctor as they entered the room.

The doctor introduced himself and Nick explained to the women what had happened to Frank and what the medical team had tried to do to keep him alive.

The women grabbed onto each other and howled, the noise cut through the room like a female fox screeching out for a potential mate in the dead of night.

"The last thing he said Mrs. Giordano was 'Tell my wife she knows what to do,'" The doctor disclosed to the two women.

Nick didn't know who the two women were but presumed that the doctor was talking to the wife as she was the woman who fell to the floor.

Through blubbing tears, the other woman looked at the child playing on the floor. She leant down and whispered into the boy's ear,

"My darling, Danny We will avenge your father's death. The Grimshaws will pay for this in this life and the next. We will never forget, I promise." No one heard what she said to the boy. She kissed the boy's dark haired head and put her arm around Frank's crying widow.

CHAPTER TWO

Twelve years later

"That's a stupid amount of money!" Nick stated with a mixture of jealousy and disgust.

On the large, wall-mounted TV, a man, who apparently came second in the last Olympic games 400 meters, wearing a blue tracksuit, held one end of a giant cheque, the other end held by a beaming woman dressed smartly in a dark suit, her glasses perched on her auburn hair. On the cheque, written in bold letters:

'Seventy-Eight Million Pounds'

"£78 million! Come on Nick Goldsmith! That would be fantastic! You need to buy a ticket!"

Nick scratched his head through his thinning greying hair, "Liz, I've told you the odds......"

"Are stacked against us!" Liz finished his sentence. A sentence that he would say tediously every single week.

The couple sat on their old, brown, yet very comfortable, sofa. Liz's smooth, shapely legs draped over Nick's lap as he sat bolt upright looking somewhat uncomfortable whilst watching the news on their TV. Liz was a fairly voluptuous woman, her ample thighs weighing heavy on his legs. Gently he massaged one of her manicured feet seemingly without effort, as he did on most evenings.

"Could do with that cash though. It would solve a few problems. But then again, I guess it would cause a few too."

"Like what?!" Liz was disappointed, though not surprised, that her husband could see the negativity in winning such a considerable, life changing sum of money.

"You'd need security with that much money."

"You'd need a bloody big wardrobe for all my new shoes!"

Nick flashed a sarcastic smile, "Liz I'd be dead within a year with that much cash. I'd eat and drink my way to heaven!"

"On our yacht!" Liz leant forward and picked up her glass of wine up from the glass-topped table next to her, "No work. Just shoes and jewels!"

"I'm tempted to buy a ticket now." Nick boisterously exaggerated his impression of eagerness.

"Get one tomorrow, Nick!" Liz pushed, "Oh and I could get Botox as well!"

Nick looked at his wife's face. It was full, fresh and happy. An inviting face with large blue eyes still as bright and alluring as they were when he first fell in love with her.

He kissed her cheek, "I love you,"

"And I you."

"Good. You don't need Botox, you're perfect the way you are," he whispered gently.

"I know darling, but never mind all that, just make sure you get a ticket. There's a love."

Nick eased her legs gently off his lap and stood up slowly. He was tall with relatively broad shoulders but a bit of a stomach that he had tried to shift for years. His love of beer and chocolate was far stronger than his need and desire to lose weight, "I will! Then I'm going to win and pay for someone clever to get rid of this bloody disease!"

Liz looked at her husband as he stretched his arms steadily into the air. The disease had started to take more of him in the last year. He'd become slower, more unbalanced and his anxiety levels were through the roof. She knew that they were about to enter a tough time in their lives and although it was farfetched to think they could win the lottery, they had to hang onto a dream. A nice lottery win would help them live when it was time for Nick to leave work when it became too challenging. They still had to eat and clothe themselves, never mind a mortgage that had a painful ten years left to pay.

They both had discussed, researched and planned how their future may pan out ever since that wet, Thursday afternoon, almost ten years ago. Liz and Nick waited, apprehensively sitting in a small box of a room that was probably once used for storage. Opposite them perched behind a desk sat an uncomfortable looking neurologist, his head analysing Nick's medical notes. Eventually, he muttered that he believed Nick had Parkinson's disease.

Their lives changed that day.

Liz and Nick both knew that Parkinson's disease was a degenerative disease that eventually would result in probable disability. How long? They didn't know. They were fully aware that it was a one-way ticket, so they had to get on and enjoy life and to a degree they had done just that. But the thought of the future always hung around like the smell of rotting fish.

Practically, their main concern was money. Ok, Nick may qualify for a bit of a pension on the grounds of ill health, but there were complicated bureaucratic hoops to jump through. State benefits were out due to Liz earning a few quid and they had no savings of note. Just like most couples in the same situation, they weren't going to be on the breadline, but it was going to be hard and major changes would be needed in their life.

Nick had tried to stop thinking about his impending future a couple of years after diagnosis. But the fear of the unknown was overbearing and constantly rattling around his mind. The pills he had been prescribed did their job, kept him moving and earning, but they had side effects and would eventually stop being effective. Over the last year or two, his ability to do his job had declined, and he had nearly run out of medical options.

Unfortunately, his deterioration accelerating, evident with his slowness and stiffness getting worse, resulted in simple yet important mistakes. One of his most debilitating symptoms was fatigue. He knew that no employer would give him a couple of hours to sleep when and where he needed to. Nick was fully aware that any further decline would not be accommodated by his employer and no further reasonable adjustments would or could be made to his working life.

He couldn't hide his errors anymore, it was perfectly obvious he was struggling. This pressure building up inside him and his paranoia led him to think he was being watched, scrutinised and judged by his colleagues and managers. He was fed up subtly asking for help that mostly never came, or if it did a co-worker would assist with a deep sigh as it interrupted their own work. Ok, most people were helpful and supportive, but unfavourable support by a few of his colleagues had an enormous impact on Nick.

Finding himself trapped between the pressure of trying to stay employed and fighting a disease that slowly revealed new symptoms on a seemingly daily basis, Nick knew that his working life could end in one hell of a mess.

He would need a plan B, and quickly.

CHAPTER THREE

Within forty minutes of leaving work, Nick was nearing his local pub. It only took a few minutes to walk the short distance to the pub from his house. He hadn't been in a pub so early in the day for years, not since college; constructively filling the long gaps between lessons. The large, shingled car park at the front was unusually empty, just a couple of vans were parked, one of which obviously belonged to a plumber due to the giant tap painted on its side. As it was only just gone eleven, Nick was not surprised that the car park was not busier. He walked along the path that dissected the pub garden, up to the wooden doors that were the pub entrance. As he pulled open the door and crossed the threshold, he was hit by a wonderful sense of calmness and fluidity in his movement as he made his way to the deserted bar. The ease of his gait and openness of his stride was a rare occurrence these days, only achieved by all the stars aligning, his medication working and being stress-free. The decision not to struggle at work for the rest of the day, temporarily enabled Nick to feel like the usual sensation of his limbs normally weighed down with lead piping being replaced with the lightness of carbon fibre.

The pub, The Bull, was quite large, with decor circa 1984 and needed a paint. At the front of the pub, a covered wooden decking held several tables and chairs, commonly occupied by smokers even in the depth of winter. On the grass in front of the pub and decking were scattered pub benches, slightly warped in the heatwave of last year's summer. Unfortunately, the drinks were a little on the pricey side. But it was convenient as it was an easy walk from Nick's house. Plus the inflated prices kept the local beer boys out. Not that it was posh, far from it, but it kept the rowdy party drinkers away, pricing them out, economically forcing them to stick to the cheaper boozers in town. The Bull attracted families, couples, and locals, a mixed bag of punters chatting, having a laugh and having a decent pint.

Nick's only gripe was during the hot summer months there would be kids playing everywhere and dominating the calm environment. Whilst attempting to have a quiet drink in the garden serenity would be shattered as all you could hear was the delightful sound of children shouting and screaming, their parents relaxing, oblivious to the noise they had brought with them whilst they enjoyed a drink in the sun. The end of the school holidays were always celebrated by

Nick as the kids finally returned to school. He could then have a beer in the now child-free garden, counting his lucky stars that he didn't say "I want to be a teacher" to the careers officer when he was fourteen. Although he had been abused working as a nurse it wasn't as bad as a classroom full of thirty unruly kids!

Reaching the bar, he stood and looked around. It was empty. Later in the afternoon it would become busier, as it always did, with a constant trickle of customers. The lounge was fairly long, with a dormant fireplace surrounded by a large black fireplace, and a few posters advertising food and future pub entertainment. One slot machine stood near the front door, ready for someone to feed it any change they had in their pockets. The tables and chairs were quite old in style, but they were comfortable and a mixture of different size tables encouraged large groups or couples to enjoy the environment.

"Usual?" the owner (Nick could never remember his name) came through the back door drying his hands on a tea towel, peering over his thick-rimmed glasses.

"Please." A barman remembering what his customer drank was always a good start.

"Not working today?" the landlord put the towel down, placed a straight pint glass under the copper handle and pulled.

"Something like that," smiled Nick, "finished early".

"Sounds good to me." he put the full glass of beer on top of the wooden bar in front of Nick.

Nick gave him a tenner, took his change, and carried his beer gingerly to a small round table in the far corner of the room. He plonked the pint down on a beer mat, chuffed that he had managed to carry the glass of beer successfully without collateral spillage.

Nick liked The Bull. It was steady most of the time but had busy moments, giving it a bit of an atmosphere. Going for a couple of pints was becoming harder for Nick as he found it difficult to carry more than one drink at a time. Due to his Parkinson's, his right arm was stiff, and you need a little bit of shock absorption in your body when transferring drinks from the bar to a table, which he lacked. Whatever was in the glass he was holding in his right hand would end up leaving a trail along the floor. So, if he was in a round with some mates, he'd have to give them the money to get the drinks on his behalf. This resulted in the inevitable teasing and banter from his friends and so to prove the point during one Sunday drinking session that he wasn't being lazy, bought and carried a round of beers. When he handed over several quarter-full pint glasses with the landlord walking behind him carrying a mop and bucket, the bar banter suddenly ceased.

Comfortable in his chair, Nick pulled out his phone and started reading the news. Years ago he would have sat in the pub reading a newspaper, but those days had long gone. He wasn't bothered, he quite liked the phones these days with their camera, messaging, and the internet. He could bet on horses, buy and sell shares, check football scores and even order a beer in some pubs. What more was needed in life? Coincidently, it is far easier to catch up on world affairs via a mobile phone than trying to fight with a broadsheet especially when you have Parkinson's disease.

Glancing up from his phone, he watched as a woman marched confidently through the bar door. He had never noticed her in the pub before. She was about five foot five, with dark black hair tied up in a loose ponytail, green combat trousers, Dr Martin boots and a dark top. Some sort of sweatshirt or hoodie.

His eyes followed her to the bar. She stood at the bar and waited to be served. It appeared the landlord knew her and had served her before,

"Hi Sam," she said, and then, for some reason, her arm suddenly shot up in the air, "Beer is shit!" she smiled as she brought her arm back down.

Nick had to look twice. The girl's head twitched, and her hand covered her mouth briefly, trying to shut herself up.

"What you having Jess?" the landlord did not even wince at her criticism of the pub's beer.

"Cider, pint please."

"Sure."

"Clinton!" she snapped.

Nick continued to watch the peculiar exchange playing out at the bar in front of him.

"Cider's crap too!" the girl shouted, apologising straight away.

Nick laughed slightly louder than he meant to. The sort of laugh you do and quickly regret when you see someone slip on ice then suddenly realise it's a serious situation because they haven't attempted to stand up again.

Hearing laughter, Jess spun around at once and stared at Nick. Her dark eyes looked angry, stripping any comedy from the situation.

Her head twitched.

Nick's head dropped, and he quickly looked back at his phone.

"I can't help it you douchebag!" she called over; her arm jumped again.

"Sorry, I didn't realise." Nick embarrassed, lifted his pint as an apology.

"Well be careful. Not everyone's perfect."

"I know. I'm sorry."

"Idiot!"

Nick uncomfortably smiled in acknowledgement. He felt his face radiate heat and knew that he had turned a bright shade of sunburnt red. Jess appeared to be a very confident and a strikingly good-looking woman which only added to Nick's discomfort.

Jess sauntered over to him and placed her glass on his table. She sat down on the stool opposite him.

"It's Tourette's," she said, sipping from her glass.

"Yeah, I guessed eventually. Look I'm sorry,"

"You weren't to know," her head began to twitch, she looked up and shouted, "Dumb drinker! Big Boobs!"

Nick ignored the outburst, "How long have you had Tourette's?"

"Too long. Started with small tics and then went mad."

Nick started to laugh.

"What's so funny?"

"Boobs? Can you say that?" Nick smiled.

"Hey I was a kid of the '90s! That's all we ever heard! Boobs and Oasis!"

"I'm Nick by the way. How come I've never seen you here before?"

"I only come in when it's reasonably empty. When it starts to get busier, I tend to make my excuses and leave. As you've experienced, I can become a bit confrontational." she smiled, "I'm Jess."

Suddenly Nick's alarm went off on his phone. He reached into his pocket and took out two pills, both in their aluminion blister pack. He opened the packaging, dropped the pills straight into his mouth and swigged them down with his beer.

Jess inquisitively peered straight at him; her head twitched.

"I have to take them at certain times, hence the alarm to remind me. Pain in the arse." he took a further sip of beer to ensure his pills had gone, "Another drink?"

Jess nodded as she swigged at her pint very quickly, "Ronald Reagan! Give me a minute I've just got here!" She took another gulp before asking, "Should you take pills with alcohol?"

Nick stood up, "I'll take them with anything! I have Parkinson's disease so need to take 'em at certain times. I'll get you one anyway. I need another."

"Bit young aren't you?" She looked up at him. He had a funny face, a bit plump, had small eyes, and he hadn't shaved for a couple of days.

"Early-onset young bastards Parkinson's disease. Had it for ten years. Same again?"

"Yes please!" her arm jolted into the air, "Deaf Muppet!"

Nick went to the bar. He could hear Jess behind him, her muffled noises and the odd profanity breaking the silence of the empty pub. Once the first drink had been poured, he took it back to the table, and then returned for the second.

After finishing her first pint she picked up the newly delivered cider. Jess eventually spoke, "It's only when you know you've got Parkinson's that you can tell something isn't right about you,"

"When my dyskinesia kicks in you'll know about it."

Jess smiled and took a large mouthful of her drink, "What's dyskinesia?"

"Moving about all the time, involuntary, dancing like a snake, unable to stop moving," Nick shuffled in his chair, "It's when I can't stay still – dyskinesia,"

"Michael J Fox!" Jess stood up suddenly and did a Nazi salute before sitting down, "Must drive you mad!"

"Could say that. Like you I guess, I can't help it." Nick was amazed that she had just performed a Nazi salute in the middle of a pub.

"You working?" Nick asked.

"Oh yeah!" again she stood up and sat down, "I'm a novelty high-class escort! You know, a niche experience! 'Course I'm not working! I have Tourette's! Who on Earth is going to hire me?" Jess smiled, "I'm actually a carer, well sort of, for a mate, he had a stroke."

Nick smiled, "I'm a nurse."

"Sod off!" Jess would have spat her cider out had she just taken a sip.

Nick paused. "Ok that was you was it not your Tourette's?"

Jess nodded.

"Why do you say that Jess?"

"I can see the shake in your hands; I wouldn't let you come near me with a commode never mind a needle!" Jess laughed loudly.

"I got moved to admin. My career ended far too soon. Bastards!" Nick picked up his pint and took an unsightly swig, "Been stuck in a mind-numbing job for too long, planning my escape,"

"Least you're working still and getting decent cash,"

"I guess so. I don't have much of a tremor by the way."

"You do when you pick that glass up,"

"Yeah, I guess so. Sort of. It's not that straightforward."

"Sort of? Your hand visibly shakes when you pick your beer up, love."

Nick smiled. He liked her directness.

"I'm guessing you wouldn't get a job with the bomb disposal unit!" she chortled into her cider.

"Good plumber though. Great with a sink plunger!" Nick mimed unblocking a drain with a plunger.

Jess laughed out loud again. A strange deep laugh that demanded attention.

"So why are you in here so early? Day off?"

"No. I got very annoyed at work. One of my problems with Parkinson's is I get foot cramps, or dystonia as they call it in my feet, and it totally stops me from walking. It's my foot twisting painfully and I can't put any pressure on it." Nick twisted his foot upwards and inwards to demonstrate to Jess. "In effect, I end up walking on my ankle!"

"So that happened today?"

"Yes. I eventually got to the office after being stuck in the corridor for thirty minutes and thought, sod this I'm off, I can't do this anymore. I need a pint!"

"Crap."

"Yes, not nice."

"You going back later in the week?"

Nick sighed, "I think I've had enough. I can't do it anymore."

"That's sad. What will you do?"

Nick shrugged, "See if I can get ill health retirement I suppose,"

"Nick, you're so young though."

"Argh, thanks Jess." He smiled, "I don't know; I'll chat to my neurologist and get some advice."

Jess's arm twitched into the air.

Nick and Jess sat and drank most of the afternoon and early evening in The Bull. The conversation flowed and Nick enjoyed Jess's honesty even though she could be a bit brutal at times. More people came into the pub as the day went on and Jess was quite pleased to see that although she got some strange looks, no one got bothered about her language and outbursts.

As a nurse, Nick had never looked after a patient with Tourette's, but he had seen the odd documentary about the condition. He remembered one documentary screened when he was a kid at school that had been on prime-time television. It was in the days when there were only four channels, and everyone watched the same programme. The following day all the kids at school pretended they had Tourette's. The playground was full of kids effing this and effing that. That week became a nightmare for the teachers, and school kids started legends about it that would last for years to come. To quell the uprising the school invited someone with Tourette's into an assembly to give a talk. Nick always remembered the man saying that hardly anyone with Tourette's has swearing as a tic. None of his fellow classmates listened and continued to laugh at each other swearing for no apparent reason.

"Have you learnt anything since you got Tourette's?" Nick asked Jess, the beer and cider were well and truly flowing now.

"Yes," she took a sip of her cider, "yeah, I have. Sambuca should be avoided at all costs," she laughed, a bit tipsy, "at the very least, if you can't say it, you shouldn't drink it."

"I agree Sambuca is evil! No, but really? Has your Tourette's changed you?"

Jess put her glass down and thought about the question, "We are in this shit alone," she smiled, a sad smile, "no one knows how you feel, how your feelings get hurt, you have to hide because it's not obvious at first you have it. The apologies I have to give about something I can't help! Why do I apologise for something I can't help? I haven't changed, my tics are a part of me. It's who I am."

"Yes, I can understand that. I've had to

apologise for being slow, dropping coins in a supermarket checkout queue. Christ, I've even apologised to a bloke behind me in the cinema because I was moving about too much!"

"Hell, I'd kick off if someone in front of me was moving about all the time!" Jess laughed. "So what about you? You learnt anything since you've had Parkinson's?"

"What have I learnt?" Nick looked up at the smoked-stained ceiling of the pub, "I think I've learnt a great deal."

"Like what?"

"Ok then. Doctors don't have a clue about a lot of diseases. Pills aren't always the answer. People are not very nice, life is short, and no one wants to hear you moan unless they are getting paid to listen! Then they tell you what's right and wrong as they know best!"

"Hey is that all?" Jess said sarcastically, her head twitching.

"Oh yeah and the beer in this pub is overpriced!"

"All the other local pubs have closed down over the years. No competition around here! Prints his own money that bloke," she pointed her glass toward the publican behind the bar, "bastard!"

"Bastard," Nick stood up. "Same again?"

CHAPTER FOUR

"Listen Xavier," said Stan, "I want those bonds in the UK! I don't care who else wants them, I want them here."

The line went quiet. Stan stood in the middle of his cell, the wrinkles on his large forehead multiplying as he frowned. His cell had a homely feel about it, with artistic black and white pictures on the wall, a bookcase full of novels and an art deco green antique lamp, on top of a dark wooden table.

"Xavier, you guys fucked it up in 2009 and I know I can get the job done and deliver."

"Stan, we are not saying you can't deliver. We know you can but…."

"There are no buts. I can move that kind of money quickly and safely."

"Ok, Ok Stan. Let's talk at the meeting with the others."

"I have your backing Xavier?"

"Yes, of course"

"Good."

Stan ended the call and placed the mobile phone under his mattress. He was fully aware it wasn't a good hiding place as it was the first place the prison officers would search in the event of his cell being "spun". Stan though knew that his cell would not be searched and therefore he was happy to keep his phone where he could get at it quickly. Stan was about to start one of the most rewarding jobs in his long criminal career and he needed to be able to communicate quickly with his colleagues.

The call from Xavier was positive. Another crime boss was on his side and would back him at the next meeting.

Everything would start to fall into place.

He knew it would.

CHAPTER FIVE

The birds in a nearby tree started their intrusive chatter at some stupid, early hour and then the annoying happy banter of dustbin men on the street provided clues for today's weather prediction. It was going to be a cracking spring day. The sun was about to earn its keep and fulfil its contract with a vengeance. It had been such a crappy wet winter; no snow, just damp, dark and cold. Early spring had not been much better, the continuous rain destroying any inspired hope from a flowering snowdrop. The brightness of this morning had awoken those forgotten feelings of optimism that had been hibernating for far too long.

Roger stared into the full-length cheval mirror that stood proudly at the bottom of his double bed. The bay window of his room accommodated maximum light engulfing his room with warmth and hope. The heat he could feel from the sun in his bedroom reminded him he was alive, safe and everything was going to be just fine.

Roger was about six foot tall, still had a full

head of scruffy grey hair, and a great cheerful, cheeky smile, which drooped on his right side. He looked good. Jeans, a white short-sleeved shirt, trainers, gold chain around his neck. Man, he felt good. He smiled at his reflection, gave himself a nod of approval and left the room.

It was an old terrace house, probably Victorian, and through the winter had been resentfully cold. The rickety old windows would knock on a windy night accompanied by the roof creaking, occasionally losing the odd tile.

Going downstairs and into the kitchen Roger opened the cupboard and took out the equipment and liquid food he needed to feed himself via his stomach tube. His stroke had taken away his ability to swallow and hence the tube gave direct entry to his stomach for the nutrition and liquid he needed. It had taken a while to get used to it but now it felt normal.

Of course, this curse of 'nil by mouth' meant he never experienced the taste of his meals. He could not enjoy the spiced heat of a curry, the tartness of gooseberry or the bitterness of a Brussels sprout. To Roger, this was a bit of a liberty really and he often asked God what the hell had he done to deserve such shit?

God never replied.

After Roger had tube-fed himself breakfast he decided to go out. Due to an element of anxiety, he had to consciously push himself to go into town at least a few times a week. As Jess was dying upstairs from her consequential hangover, he thought he'd take the opportunity to pop out and get some parcel tape and packaging for her. She was always selling clothes online. He slipped his coat on and locked the door behind him.

Roger walked with a stick. It was for precautionary support. He didn't want to end up on the pavement looking like a right idiot, but it had taken him a while to get his head around the idea of actually using a stick. He believed he was far too young to have an aid. His attitude swiftly changed following a visit to the Emergency Department one night with a potentially broken arm after falling. Sitting in a hospital cubicle, feeling embarrassed and sorry for himself, his pride subsequently backed down and he surrendered to common sense.

Slowly but surely, he made his way to the High Street. His fitness was fine, and he could walk quite a distance, albeit a little slowly.

Finally reaching the post office he was annoyed to see some idiot had parked their yellow motorbike right in front of the doorway, so he had to sidestep the wheel to get in. He begrudgingly joined the back of the usual long queue as it snaked from the counter to the front door.

While waiting, he dabbed the spittle that had accumulated in his mouth, away from his lips. He had to have about five hankies with him and whenever he arrived home, they were often drenched after a day of constantly wiping his mouth. Roger often thought it would be a laugh to have his pockets picked. He often imagined Oxford Street at Christmas, a pickpocket standing outside Selfridges screaming, "What the?" As the crook looked disgusted at the state of his thieving hand covered in saliva, having just tried to steal Roger's wallet. Instead getting a handful of dirty handkerchiefs!

The post office queue sauntered along very slowly. Roger sighed, regretting he had joined the queue in the first place.

A small, delicate, yelp suddenly drew his attention to counter number four. Looking over he could see a man wearing a motorbike helmet putting a bundled pack of £5 notes into a scruffy black rucksack.

The post office was being robbed!

Roger looked on in amazement. Who would rob a post office at this time of day when it was so packed? Are they stupid? Everyone in the queue was startled and dumbfounded by what was going on. It appeared that the robber was holding a gun wrapped in a brown paper bag and pointing it at the counter window. Roger automatically thought it was probably a banana as the scene was becoming comical.

As quickly as it had started it was over. The cashier had given the robber quite a few bundles of different denominations of notes and having pushed them into his bag, he turned to leave.

Roger smiled to himself, "Please don't tell me that yellow, Honda motorbike outside was his getaway vehicle. Jesus Christ!"

The robber scurried past the queue of increasingly nervous customers and left the post office. For a split second, Roger's mind switched to pre-stroke mode, and he considered tackling the thief. Instead, the reality of his current life forced Roger to step back to let him pass. He also remembered that sometimes being a hero wasn't worth the effort. There was no way he was playing hero today. He'd been involved in too many scraps restraining prisoners as a prison officer. On one occasion he wrestled with a prisoner who was threatening a governor with a sharpened toothbrush. The prisoner was restrained, and with the weapon safely on the floor, Roger had managed to get his nose broken by the prisoner's efforts to resist. After the incapacitated con was unceremoniously popped back into his cell, he received a call over the radio from his superiors asking if he could do a double shift?!

"Don't worry Roger I've got a spare clean shirt you can use!" he remembered the senior officer saying.

There were no thanks for his heroics that day, or any other day come to think about it.

Roger made a conscious effort to remember everything about the robber as he staggered past him. The outstanding feature he noticed was the "I Love Honda" sticker on the back of his helmet. Underneath in small writing, someone had scrawled 'Danny.'

"Shit. This lad was a professional!" Roger grinned at his sarcastic thought.

Immediately after the thief left the post office everyone sighed with relief as the ordeal had ended. One or two customers had started to cry, and some started calling for the police on their mobile phones. One man boasted that he had filmed the whole robbery on his phone. Roger, in the middle of the chaos, decided he'd better wait for the boys in blue and give a statement. They'd have the robber in the back of their car by the end of the day. This was an easy nicking. A 'mortgage payment' as any respectful prison reception officer would say, welcoming and booking the same old faces returning repeatedly, back to prison.

The police arrived quickly. Roger was impressed. Unfortunately though, after the crime and when the robber had buggered off. A young woman seeing Roger had a stick offered him a chair she had sought out from the back office. Roger happily sat down. After what seemed to be an hour a tall, tanned man, with cropped hair, in a smart grey suit, approached him with his notebook open and a pen in his hand.

"Hello sir, I'm Detective Inspector Craig Bullen, and I need to take your name and address and if there is anything you saw that may be interesting to us?"

Roger nodded.

"Okay, so if I can have your name and address first please Sir." the lack of enthusiasm was glaringly obvious from the Detective Inspector's tone.

Roger started to unfold his letter board that he kept in his pocket. It wasn't actually a board, it was a piece of A4 paper that had a protective transparent covering. It had all the letters of the alphabet on it and numbers from 0 to 9. Roger pointed at the R then the O, Followed by the letter G.

Roger could feel the officer's disappointment in getting the witness who could not talk. Out of a room full of willingly, talkative witnesses he had picked the short straw.

"Sir, I'm not being funny but is this going to take long?!"

Roger looked at him and smiled and quickly spelt out,

"No, it won't"

"You need to do that a bit slower sir, I didn't get that!"

Roger pointed at the letter N then the O, then the I and T.....

"NOT what?" the inspector looked agitated; he looked over to his colleagues who were trying to write down as much as they could from the people they were interviewing.

Roger continued to spell "won't,"

"NO IT WON'T."

When the policeman returned his mind to Roger, he could only see Roger's finger point at the N and then the T,

"That doesn't make sense at all sir." DI Bullen ripped a sheet of paper out of his notebook and gave it and the pen to Roger,

"Just write your name down on here mate," the Inspector snapped, obviously stressed at the slowness of the situation.

Roger looked at him. Shook his head knowingly and took the pen and paper. He then proceeded to try and write his name. He then gave the piece of paper and pen back to the policeman,

DI Bullen glared at the paper, "Sir that's just a scribble! Doesn't say anything!"

Roger shrugged his shoulders. He had learnt to become quite calm in these situations. His speech had been affected and he had difficulty in writing due to his stroke, so if you wanted to communicate with him you had to watch him point at letters on the spelling board and add a pinch of patience. Roger had learnt not to get agitated by ignorance and not to persevere if the other person was not even trying. Sometimes he would escalate the pain by playing on the situation, just to wind up the already angry ignoramus, sending them into a whirl of frustration and discomfort.

Roger stood up, shrugged his shoulders and smiled at the police officer. He then walked out of the post office. DI Bullen, acting like a fourteen-year-old who had just been told his girlfriend couldn't stay over, screwed up the piece of paper in his hand.

Outside in the fresh air, Roger looked up at the sky, there was not a cloud in sight. It was a beautiful cloudless day. Before his stroke, he would've loved to sit outside a pub and drink a nice cold pint of anything.

But that was not going to happen. Ever.

He decided to walk home. He had failed to get the packaging and tape for Jess and was secretly annoyed with the copper's attitude. Roger tried to live with his disability, and he did a decent job. But sometimes the lack of awareness that people had would cut through the defensive armour he had built up over the years.

When he arrived at the top of his road, he saw what looked like a yellow motorbike, half-hidden by shade down the side of a house.

He stopped and stared. Coming out of the gate he saw a man who must've been about 70, get to the bike, kick the stand back and push it through to the back garden.

"Did you get much Danny?" the old boy shouted.

Roger smiled to himself as he continued his walk. Even though the thief had made every mistake in the book, it seemed he may well get away with it. If the police didn't have time to listen to Roger, then it's their loss. Just because he was a dribbling, mute, tube-fed bloke, did not mean that he should be discounted as an important part of this world.

A police car sped past him with sirens blaring. He saw the car whizz past the post office and then the thief's hideout and eventually disappear into the distance. If Roger still could shout, he wouldn't have even bothered to yell "Wrong way!". The beautiful day had been scared by another nail in Roger's belief that he was still part of society.

CHAPTER SIX

Liz shouted up the stairs to her husband,

"What's the plan, Nick?"

No answer.

"Nick, have you taken your pills?"

No answer.

"Nick?"

Nick yawned, loudly. "Yep and I don't know!"

"Oh. Well, you need to ring work anyway."

"No, they know I'm off sick. I'll take a few days off and think about what to do."

"I'm just going to the shop to get some bits, do you want anything?" Liz was still at the foot of the stairs.

"No. But then again, I know, get me some chocolate please Liz."

"Yes darling, love you!" she called up the stairs.

"And you."

Liz closed the front door behind her as she left.

Nick had to dig deep to get the motivation to move and pushed himself out of bed before his hangover took hold. After taking his morning pills he managed to get dressed. Liz had left a pre-buttoned-up shirt, so he just slipped it over his head. Doing buttons up had been an issue for some time now so he had to sort out what to wear the night before with Liz. He had a slight headache but was keen to get on with his day.

He had his future to think about. He would investigate the possibility of ill-health retirement for a start. He'd have to contact the union rep about it, though he wasn't convinced they ever knew what they were talking about. Nick had been trying to avoid early retirement due to his worsening disability, as he knew deep down, that he needed to keep on working. Work was important to him, although he hated what he was doing, it gave him a sense of purpose, he could chat with people, and it was a reason to get his lazy arse out of bed in the morning. But he was struggling now. He was experiencing debilitating fatigue, insomnia and his concentration was terrible. These symptoms along with the physical challenges that Parkinson's disease had, resulted in a constant battle of trying to function properly at work.

Nick was not the sort to stay in bed all day waiting for a miracle cure to come along. There was no cure for Parkinson's disease and probably wouldn't be within his lifetime. He knew early on in his diagnosis that he needed to fight and keep moving. He was fully aware that one day his body wouldn't allow him to move, never mind enable him to challenge the disease anymore.

This awareness of his disease progression was buried deep in his mind, unfortunately, the knowledge had a habit of clawing itself out of his grey matter to rudely remind him of his destiny.

But he was not going to give up on life until that day came. With bravado his saying was "Never, Ever, Give up...Ever!" Sometimes though he just had to.

His current job was mind-numbingly boring. It didn't motivate him, it de-motivated him. All he did was tap numbers into a bloody computer. He had originally become a nurse to help people, to get a bit of job satisfaction. Not to be some suited manager's dog's body. For some months he was finding the job harder and harder to do; tapping the wrong numbers in, deleting data by mistake and sending half-finished emails as his fingers jumped onto the send key unexpectedly. Knowing that he was making mistakes in a mind-numbing job was eating away at him every day. The stress of trying to stay at work was ironically pushing him out of work. Nick needed to find something he could do, that was worthwhile and satisfying to him.

Unfortunately, his anger with the uselessness and frustration of his current job often surfaced and exploded at parties and family get-togethers. It wasn't wise to start asking Nick what he did for a living after he had downed a few beers unless you wanted him to drone on about the suicidal numbness of his role in the health service. Liz would often look over at him at a party chatting drunkenly to a stranger, arms flailing as his Parkinson's became worse with excitement and frustration. She quickly learnt that the combination of flaying arms, beer and hospital speak was a major signal it was time to take her husband home.

There were things in nursing he could have done that he felt would be useful to patients and satisfying to him, but every suggestion he made was rejected by some unknown faceless entity in Human Resources. They claimed they'd explored all possible reasonable adjustments that could be made to enable him to do his suggested roles, but they were not possible. The job in administration was the only suitable option. Doors had been firmly closed for his career.

Nick had to move on from his job. He had to get away. He had become a stressed, bitter, synthetic dopamine-fuelled, deteriorating bore. His life had to change.

His first move was a doctor's appointment. He had to buy some time and get a couple of weeks' sick leave. That would be easy.

Next, investigate how he and Liz would survive with one less wage. He guessed he wouldn't get much even if he qualified for ill health retirement but was lucky to have it as an option in his pension according to the 'short of empathy' woman in the HR department. Nick knew he was stuck between complete boredom mixed with probable physical collapse by attempting to carry on working and skid row if he was deemed too unfit to continue by his employer.

"Be positive! Never, ever give up."

He needed a job that he could physically do that was useful, rewarding and achievable. This unfortunately was where it all went wrong.

Ok, so a large employer could move you around departments if you were to become disabled until you quit, and that was cheaper and less controversial than sacking the disabled employee – for being disabled. But to get a new role with another organisation was nigh on impossible. For someone new to employ you without any knowledge of your work ethic or experience, hands shaking and constantly moving, twisting and jumping whilst being interviewed, was probably going to result in a firm "No."

"You've slipped back to negativity again! Be positive!" he muttered to himself.

Nick went downstairs. His dyskinesia had kicked in. Nick sat down on the living room sofa and picked up his iPad trying to keep it still as his arms began thrashing around. He checked his emails, looked at some mindless, time-wasting, fun internet sites, peered at the news and even searched "what jobs do people with Parkinson's disease do?" It came up with the thought that Hitler may have had Parkinson's disease which was someone he didn't want to have anything in common with!

Nick stood up, he needed to get some air, pick up his sick note and see what was going on in town. It was a lovely sunny day, and he fancied a stroll. He'd avoid the temptation of the pub. As much as he loved sitting outside a pub on a sunny day it was probably unwise to spend two weeks on sick leave in the boozer. He would fight all his urges and dig deep to stop himself from having a quiet pint in the sun.

Having left his house Nick eventually reached the road that ran alongside the park. On the other side of the park, he was surprised to see about three or four police cars speeding along the high street. They were obviously in a hurry, sirens shouting at people to get out of the way. He looked as they came up towards him, and motored past. He'd never really seen so many police cars together in this part of town. It must have been important. Bank job he thought. Murder? Major drug Swoop?

Nick strolled onto the grass of the park and decided to sit on one of the benches near the clubhouse and absorb some vitamin D. Relaxing, he looked out upon a vast expanse of green grass, muddy in places, supporting six football pitches. At the top of the park, coming out of the gap in the trees he started to watch a bloke on a bright yellow motorbike. The bike whipped over the park leaving a long trail of churned-up grass in its wake. The rider had a black bag over his shoulder and the most hideous purple boots on. That was a bad look. The bike went about 100 yards past where he sat, and left the grass, moving onto the road to continue its journey having just dissected the park.

"Douchebag!" Nick remembered Jess using the same expression last night, and it seemed to fit the bill today. Then he wondered if that was who the police were after. He thought better of it as to why four cars would be needed to apprehend the rider of a hideously bright yellow motorbike.

Nick's curiosity was dismissed by his phone alarm vibrating through the material of his jeans pocket. Time for his pills. He had become used to the bitter taste over the years and was skilled in the art of not needing liquid to swallow them. Taking the bright yellow tablets would hopefully mean he was prepped and oiled up for another four hours.

The emphasis on "hopefully."

CHAPTER SEVEN

A sudden banging from the room above prompted Roger to look up towards the ceiling as he tidied up his morning hydration ritual of plastic syringes and feeding equipment away.

"It wakes," he thought to himself, as he heard plonking and shuffling noises coming from upstairs.

Roger put the kettle on. He always made her a coffee in the morning. He had done so for many years and now it had become second nature.

Black with three sugars is how she liked it.

Jess clonked her way down the bare wooden stairs and into the kitchen. She had a bright pink towelling dressing gown on and her big black boots with laces dragging as she lurched along the floor.

Roger looked around, "She's going to go arse over bollocks if she doesn't start tying 'em up." he thought to himself. She never did though.

"Morning! Guess where I was most of yesterday and last night?" she asked, excited and a bit too happy for the morning, no matter how sunny it was.

Roger shook his head and hunched his shoulders.

"Pub." Jess smiled, "Got very drunk!"

Now that may seem a little odd for someone to be cheerful about being "very drunk" and appear not to have the worse hangover ever in the entire world. But you can rest assured she would soon be suffering. In time, once this excitement had passed, the pain and sorrow of her hangover would take hold. She would eventually pay the price for her long drinking session.

"Met a bloke, Ugly! Big Nose Nick! He has the Parkies, didn't shake much, but wouldn't keep still. Muppet!" she twitched her head several times, "And then his wife came down, she was nice, looked tired though. And then we all went for a curry! What was her bloody name?" she took a sip of coffee.

Roger shrugged his shoulders.

Jess slowly put the mug of coffee down on the kitchen table, "I don't feel well." she eased herself up from the table to leave the kitchen, "I'm going back to bed Rog. Oh yeah, her name was Liz" she delicately made her way to the stairs, "She wasn't going to come then she did. You been out Rog?" She didn't wait for a reply.

Jess went back to bed.

Roger sat down at the kitchen table. It's funny how the main focus of their house was the kitchen, yet he could not eat or drink. He hadn't had a drink for over a decade. Ten years plus since his world turned, crashed upside down and blew up into shreds of "what could have been?" and "I should have."

Roger was on duty when his life suddenly took a different path. He was a prison officer and had just closed the cell doors to the cleaner's cells on the second-floor landing, and walked back to the office. He had an hour left of his shift. Sitting at the main desk was Dave, his mate and colleague for years. Dave had taken him under his wing when he started in the service as a wide-eyed junior prison officer, showing him the ropes. Life as a prison officer was a bit different then. The screws had a bit of control and received a bit more respect from the guests staying at Her Majesty's jails.

Roger sat down at his desk in the office situated on the corner of the landing. Dave had put a cup of tea and a prison chocolate biscuit on the table for him. Roger bit into the biscuit, pulled out a newspaper from a drawer, suddenly went dizzy, tried to look at Dave, who was engrossed in the sports pages of his newspaper, attempted to talk to Dave, but nothing came out, and then Roger hit the floor.

Conscious, confused and scared.

Roger was having a stroke.

Since that moment he had not eaten a thing and not said a single word. The last item of food he had tasted was the cheap, flavourless chocolate of the biscuit Dave gave him. The last words he ever said were "Cheers lads" to the prison cleaners. His speech was gone, his swallow gone, and his life gone. Never was he to stroll around a prison landing again. Never was he able to say, "Can I have next Monday off boss?" Or "All right Mickey stop that mate, I'll get the nurse," to an inmate who decides to 'cut up' and self-harm with a smuggled razor blade, slicing open his wrists. He would never be able to ask, "Fancy a pint?" Or be spontaneous with "Mind that!" Or whisper to someone, "I love you."

From that moment Roger would never be able to do a champagne toast, have tomato soup, enjoy a curry, sip a cup of tea or even the simple delights of eating that first ripe peach of the summer or appreciate the unexpected satisfaction of a lager shandy on a hot August Bank holiday.

In a split second, everything in Roger's life changed. There was no argument that his working life had ended. Now being retired may seem great, good public pension, not getting up in the mornings, escaping the bullshit politics, but let's face it, no one really wants to stop working in their middle years unless it's due to a major lotto win. Never mind all the consequences that come with having a large stroke, the loss of speech, swallowing, balance, weakness and being fed by a tube.

One tiny little clot, probably from his heart, decided one day to go AWOL up his blood supply to his brain and then, due to total stubbornness of travelling up an ever-tightening tunnel, was forced to stop as it couldn't get any further and it was too late to turn back. This biological traffic jam blocked the blood transporting all the magic stuff to an important part of Roger's brain and wham! Shit! Where did my life go?

So, for the last ten years, he hadn't had a proper job. Who the hell is going to employ him? He can't talk, eat, or drink and he continuously dribbles. Six months after his stroke, a mate suggested he could be one of those human statues in Leicester Square, painted silver, acting like a soldier ready to charge, waiting for that £1 coin to be tossed in a bucket so that he could finish the move. This was so-called laddish banter, his friends trying to lighten the situation that their pal was stuck in.

"But the dribble falling from his gob, would surely ruin the magic of his World War One Tommy statue impression?" caused great hilarity as his workmates sat around him in the visitor's room at the rehabilitation hospital. Roger decided never to see them again.

Roger had done some "disability training" at the job centre after being medically retired from the prison service. He laughed to himself that he didn't need training to be disabled. This led to a go at entering data for a local insurance firm. But he got tired, the need for any sort of level of concentration was too much, and his employer soon realised that employing a disabled person like Roger, was not all it was cracked up to be. The classic middle manager tactic of being 'managed out' forced Roger into the sunset.

He became down, he was depressed, and he was lost.

A canny social worker, realising that Roger needed physical help at home and was in a psychological mess suggested he put an ad in the local rag for a carer for a few hours a day.

The carer could help him with some stuff around the house and also be a bit of company for him.

That advert was answered by Jess who became his carer and eventually moved in. After she had gone through the initial learning curve of Roger not being able to talk, using a letter board and the dribbling, they both became good friends. Jess quickly learned to understand his gestures and body language. Asking Roger to spell out every word on a letter board can take a long, long time. Their initial conversations tended not to flow. Jess would get bored and trying to be helpful she would finish the finger-pointing to Roger's sentences,

I am R...." Roger pointed at each letter on his board.

"Roger! I am Roger."

"I am really f....."

"Friendly!"

"..Fucked off with...."

"The government?"
"You!!"
"Me? Why?"
"You finish my s...."
"Sentences!?"
Silence.
"Oh, I see! I am really fucked off with you, you finish my sentences!"

This often resulted in Roger getting frustrated, Jess's Tourette's would kick in as she became more stressed, and before you knew it Jess would have stormed off and Roger had ripped his letter board up!

But slowly and learning together they became really good friends. In reality, she didn't need to help Roger get dressed. He could do it himself with a bit of a struggle and he wanted to keep some element of independence. He was proficient with his feeding tube that went into his stomach, and he was mobile around the house. The issue of what she did and didn't do was never brought up; instead they both enjoyed each other's company. They became just ordinary people sharing a house. Just having each other nearby was equally important to them both.

Jess always told people very quickly that she had Tourette's. They would say it was ok, be accommodating or laugh at her sudden outbursts and movement. But then it would become too much for them. It was too much for her too. She'd try so hard to control her tics and shouting, to keep her mouth from swearing, but that just ended up with Jess becoming more and more stressed and using more offensive and odd language. She'd eventually blow up with atomic tics and a battery of swear words firing from her mouth like cannons going off on a battlefield. This would end in Jess feeling remorseful, shocked and sad at her own behaviour, pushing her down a deep, dark depressive hole.

She reluctantly went to an interview once but as soon as she shouted out "Muppet!" to the question, "what do you do in your spare time?" She knew the job wasn't hers. Even though she had begun her opening gambit by declaring her Tourette's and written it on the damn application form.

"Disability aware employer? My arse!" It was only true If you were disabled and quiet, tic free and especially free of tics that involved the odd swear word! Seen but not heard was the policy of most "disability-confident" employers. Why bring her in for an interview if they knew you had Tourette's and would have serious potentially uncomfortable symptoms?

Over time Jess's Tourette's hadn't improved but hadn't become any worse. Roger never ever blinked an eye if she had an episode. He just carried on doing what he did, totally ignoring Jess's tics and occasional obscene shout-outs. As months and years drifted by, Jess became more confident and popped into the pub on her own, when it was quiet, the owner slowly getting used to her. Her time with Roger had improved her life massively, allowing her to grow and be Jess rather than that girl with Tourette's.

Jess's understanding of Roger and how he had been before his stroke and how the stroke turned his world upside down, enabled her to empathise with him but not to pity him. He'd always say it was "one of those things." And stoically just gets on with life.

They both had their own different disabilities, but they also wanted to live. Not just to live a normal life, but to live a life that would outshine and discredit all those before who had doubted them. Surely there was something they could do. Just because a man has a stroke, or a woman has twitches doesn't mean that it's game over. They didn't want to spend the rest of their days pigeonholed as benefit scroungers. They wanted to do something, be something and achieve something.

Soon they would get their chance.

CHAPTER EIGHT

Stan Tennant, whilst sitting in his prison cell, reading his usual newspaper, suddenly looked up. He was sure he'd just heard on the radio that a post office had been robbed in broad daylight by someone who had purple boots on and a bright yellow motorbike! If that bloke got nicked and ended up in prison, he'd have a torrid time for being the stupidest villain ever. Stan chuckled to himself.

Stan had a busy day in front of him. He had a big meeting tomorrow and needed to be on form. The Chiasso fiasco of 2009 with the failed attempt to smuggle bonds worth $134 billion was about to pay dividends after too many long years. Stan intended to lead the project on behalf of the criminal syndicate his team were working with. He had a feeling he was going to hear positive news after he justified why he knew the spoils of Chiasso should be administered in the United Kingdom. He had the storage, security and distribution set up and he was not going to allow any of his colleagues to change his plan.

The robber with the yellow motorbike had

given him a few minutes of light relief. But tomorrow was the most important meeting of his life. There were some immensely powerful people in the meeting and Stan knew he'd have to be on form to get his way. Moving the bonds had failed once before but it could not fail again.

CHAPTER NINE

The post office robbery that Craig attended with his team of police colleagues had bothered him. It was not the fact it was an armed robbery, he'd attended many intense crime scenes. Thankfully, there were no injured victims or worse still, deaths. It was that one witness who couldn't talk and the realization that he had wrongly dismissed him so quickly, that had freaked Craig out. Craig could not envisage ever being in such a dreadful situation. Imagine losing your voice, and not being able to verbally communicate with people. He found his whole encounter with the mute man quite disturbing, wondering how on earth a man could lose his voice. Regrettably for Craig, he had to leave the witness as he did not have the patience to face him. He was too stressed and irritated by the witness's slowness. Over the subsequent days, the guilt of dismissing the man left a nasty scar on his conscience. Unfortunately, in mitigation to his unprofessional behaviour, Craig was a worried man and the deeply entrenched anxiety he had was starting to affect his day-to-day life.

Six months ago, the skin on his leg started to jump and twitch. He could see the skin on his upper thighs slightly bounce as he sat in his shorts after a game of football. It lasted about three minutes and then stopped. He thought nothing of it. Brushed it aside. Perhaps he'd over-pushed it during the game? He knew and felt he was getting too old for a fast game of five-a-side football. He could feel the pain in his knee joints as he ran around the small football pitches in a sport that really didn't give players time to rest. He could do it twenty years ago, and he smoked then! But now it was starting to hurt a little and he was not enjoying the physical side of it. He was still fit and could chase the odd shoplifter, but they were normally unfit drug addicts falling over themselves trying to escape capture with a stolen item from a shop. His Five-a-side football league included lads half his age who were strong and very fit. So, he convinced himself that the funny leg thing was his muscles telling him to slow down.

His wife, Mandy, would have googled it by now and had him diagnosed with some strange tropical disease that he'd probably caught in a swimming pool whilst on holiday in Spain. Craig knew it was a bad idea to look on the internet, he knew it was pointless and would just worry him more. Put anything to do with strange body stuff, any symptom and you could almost guarantee that "cancer", or "horrible death" would be top. If it was not cancer his internet search would come out as some strange sexual fetish. So, he didn't bother trying "twitching thighs".

Craig got to see the doctor, the doctor believed it was probably just a nerve that was inflamed. Craig was fine and relieved by the diagnosis. It was the football after all. No cancer! He bought Mandy some celebration flowers on the way home, and then went to bed in preparation for his night shift ahead. He had agreed to be involved in an overnight stake-out and knew it would be a long night. Mandy slipped next to him. She knew how to get her husband to sleep for his first shift of nights.

A week and a half later his muscles in both thighs started jumping again. He was in bed reading, Mandy asleep next to him. He had to get out of bed as it was bothering him, not with pain, just that it was not 'right'. It didn't stop for about ten minutes this time.

That afternoon Craig had a phone call from his GP. She had spoken to a neurologist who said it was worth seeing him, and there was a "99% chance it was nothing".

Craig was a little concerned that he needed to see a neurologist. What did a neurologist have to do with his legs? He thought they were experts in brains. What could it be? If the odds were 99% that it was nothing, then what kind of diagnosis could it be in the remaining 1% of jumping skin symptoms?

Stupidly, and ignoring his own advice, he searched for neurologists to see what they did, he came across various diseases like Multiple sclerosis, Parkinson's Disease, supranuclear palsy, stroke, shit! They were scary diseases. His friend's mum had MS, and she died after spending years in bed. He never saw her but knew she was upstairs at his friend's house when they were playing on a computer in his front room.

But, like anyone else he'd have to wait for answers. As hard as it was, there was no point in guessing what it could be, if anything at all.

◆ ◆ ◆

That morning sitting in his car, a police van parked behind him, outside a suspect's house, he couldn't get the thought of the mute witness and his mate's mum out of his mind. He took a few deep breaths, got out of the car and shouted at the officers who were climbing out of the van.

"Come on let's go!"

Seconds after the front door to the terrace house was knocked through Craig stormed into the house and ran straight up the stairs. Crashing into the first room he shouted at the man, half asleep, dazed and about to try sitting up in his bed, his shocked face did not know what the hell was going on. Waking up and becoming aware that his bedroom had become full of police, the man smiled. Not a broad grin, but a satisfied smile. He put his hands above his head.

"Danny Giordano, I'm arresting you for the robbery of the Silver Street Post Office. You do not have to say anything, but it may harm your defence…."

CHAPTER TEN

The challenge that Stan and the coalition of criminal gangs had now, was how to get the bonds to their next destination? The Japanese Yakuza wanted to hide them in a consignment of food, the Italian Mafia considered sending them via a private jet and Stan was yet to pitch his plan. They weren't drugs, so not sniffable by a cute-looking dog at Heathrow. The bonds also wouldn't jump out on scanning equipment like an explosive device would at Dover's or Heathrow's customs. The bonds were just old pieces of paper. The only way they were going to be found entering the country was by a lucky stop by a customs officer or an informant.

Grassing was probably the biggest risk, and it was still not fully understood why the original smugglers of said bonds were stopped ten years ago on a train in Chiasso. One man paid the price for the failure, a supposed grass who managed to move his family from Italy to England. Stan had personally seen to his execution as ordered by his then bosses the Grimshaw brothers. But it was known that it wasn't 100% certain that he was the main grass, and he didn't disclose any information whilst being assisted to tell the truth. This involved Stan encouraging open disclosure by slowly amputating fingers amongst other violent acts.

In the previous month, the bonds had left the depths of the Roma Bank, their home for over 10 years, and been placed in a safe in the back room of a restaurant in Rome. They were ready to go anywhere in the world thanks to the Italian mafia brokering a deal with the Italian powers that be. $134 billion in US bonds, including ten so-called Kennedy bonds with a value of $1 billion each, were waiting for the second attempt to get them out of Italy.

The main meeting to decide who was going to run the operation had just started. Some of the heads of crime families and gangs were in the same room, some joined via satellite link and those who were incarcerated used phones from their prison cells. There were multiple translators on hand if needed but most of the attendees spoke English very well. They all knew each other and met once a year if they were free to do so, in a luxury hotel in Monaco. Stan hadn't attended for a long time due to his prison sentence but would always have a trusted representative at the meeting.

The meeting Stan Tennant had been preparing for was very productive. He had become used to meetings via his phone whilst in his cell, but he did miss the experience of actually being there so that he could read everyone's body language. Coming to its conclusion and after Stan had answered a myriad of questions, the consensus was that the bonds would be moved and administered in London as per Stan's plan. Stan was going to organise their transfer and he was determined not to fail. He was going to move the bonds very simply.

Stan walked out of his cell and onto the prison landing. He had a broad grin on his face.

Stan had an idea.

CHAPTER ELEVEN

Roger opened the front door to go into his house.

"Roger where's my coat?" called Jess as she heard him enter.

Roger hunched his shoulders, he had no idea. Jess was looking under the jackets hanging up in the hall. She seemed to be getting agitated.

"Where the chuff is it? Muppet! Muppet! Kermit is a green puppet!"

Roger walked past her and sat down at the kitchen table. On the table was his letter board,

"Living room?" he spelled out on the board.

"Yes, I'll check again" Jess went into the living room. "Found it!"

Roger looked at her as she came out of the room wearing her coat. He twisted his hands over to show his palms, indicating "What now?"

"Pub!" Jess replied, reading his body language, "Coming?"

Roger nodded. He got up from the table and picked up what looked like a school kid's lunch box. He opened it up to make sure he had a syringe, a small bottle of water, a pouch of liquid food, and some other spare parts, just in case he needed them.

They both left the house together.

The pub had a few drinkers in by the time they arrived, but it was still comfortable and not intimidating. Jess ordered a pint of beer for herself and took it to the table. She liked to sit out in the far corner of the pub, where she was out of earshot of other customers. Roger joined her. Placing his box on the chair next to him.

Jess sipped her beer and stared into space. Roger pulled out his handkerchief and wiped the descending saliva away from his chin.

He opened his folded-up spelling board that had been in his jacket pocket and started to tap out some words.

Jess was not paying him any attention. She was lost gazing into the pub, not looking at anything just taking it all in. She didn't often have much calmness in her day due to her tics. But now and again her mind and body would slow down, relax and become peaceful.

Roger waited for her response to the question that he had just tapped out on his letter board. None was forthcoming. She had not taken any notice of him at all.

Roger pushed her shoulder a bit harder than he wanted to, spilling her beer onto the table.

"What the...?" Jess sharply asked, hurriedly trying to blot up the beer from the table with a beer mat.

Roger shrugged his shoulders. He pointed at the board and started to tap his letters again.

Jess jumped up and then sat down again. Her calm moment was over,

"Well, I'm bored as well Roger! But that's just the way it is!" she took a sip of what was left of her beer and then plonked the empty pint glass onto the table.

"What do you want to do about it? Get a life! Ronald Reagan and Nancy!" she was starting to get annoyed.

Roger began tapping out the words again.

"Rob a bank." The hold-up at the post office had sparked a thought in Roger's mind. Ok so it was illegal, and he'd end up in prison, but he knew he'd do a better job than the robber he encountered. It would be exciting. He relished the adrenaline rush it must create.

"Yeah, great idea Rog! Stick up! We could be Bonnie Margaret Thatcher and Clyde!" Jess was at risk of exploding as her twitches hit back reminding her in no uncertain terms that she did have Tourette's.

Roger nodded.

"Get lost, Roger! Have you been talking to that mate of yours again?"

Dispirited, Roger looked at Jess's pint glass. He blew into his cheeks and switched his gaze up at the yellow, nicotine, stained ceiling. The pub smoking ban had been in force for years, but it was obvious that this landlord had not painted his ceiling since then.

"I know it's hard. I cannot dream of what you go through." she put an arm around him, "but robbing a bank isn't the answer. Thatcher milk snatcher! At least we get a few delivery jobs off your mate. That's exciting. Maybe we can do some more for him? Or even branch out?!" She smiled.

Roger smiled back and winked at Jess.

"What made you think of robbing a bank?"

Roger turned, pulled her arm off him and looked at her. He re-flattened his letter board and quickly tapped out a string of letters.

Jess read it aloud as he formed words and sentences,

"I am bored. I need some fun. Take some risks. To live!"

Jess threw her right arm in the air, bringing it down as quickly as it went up like an eager child who thought she knew the answer to the teacher's question before realising she didn't and was about to make an idiot of herself.

"Not being funny Rog, but robbing a bank probably ain't the way to cure your boredom! Hitler! Why don't you do some abseiling or sit in a bath of baked beans for charity like any other normal person?"

Roger sighed and again hunched his shoulders. He started to use the board again,

"I'll get away with it,"

"Are you taking the piss?" Jess whispered, looking around the pub just in case someone could overhear her crime-planning mate.

Roger shook his head, "No one notice a disabled man. People ignore what they don't understand. Look right through us."

"What do you mean they won't see us", her head nodded a couple of times.

Roger slowly tried to explain the robbery at the post office and although it involved the most incompetent looking hold up man in history, he seemed to have gotten away with it. He also told her about the utter contempt the police officer had in communicating with Roger.

"We are disabled they don't see us. They look straight through us, or stare so hard they can't figure out what's going on. No one really gives a shit. Don't know how to speak to us, hear us, chat with us." As with most conversations with Roger, he missed out words to save time.

"You're mad!" Jess laughed, "So you would go up to a bank cashier's desk, bring out your letter board, tap in "This is a hold-up?" The cashier would stare at you and loudly shout, "How much do you want to take out love?" And then politely and discreetly move all the slips and leaflets from her counter as you dribbled on them!"

Roger stared at her angrily; she wasn't taking him seriously,

"Why are you not working? Why do you have no boyfriend? Why do we go to the same places every time? Cause people know us. Feel safe. But go somewhere new and people can't handle us. I dribble and shuffle and you're unpredictable with your tics!"

"Thanks, Rog. You know how to make a girl feel wanted,"

"It's true. People go away when you start to shout!"

"I get embarrassed for them!" Jess snapped.

"My point."

Jess sighed and said under her breath,

"I know I can't get over being embarrassed about myself or being embarrassed because they are embarrassed."

"I haven't got over how I've become."

The two friends sat quietly reflecting on their thoughts. They both had feelings of being outcasts in society, of being left behind as life rolled by. They'd both tried in their own ways to kick start life, but as ever money, and others' belief in their abilities were absent.

Roger broke the silence. His fingers darting, tapping letters around his board.

"I walked the landings of prisons. People in there were all different. There were idiots. There were druggies, and there were criminal masterminds, the best at what they did. But all were in prison as they all got caught. We had the odd bloke in a wheelchair, done shoplifting and got caught, but we never had a disabled bank robber."

"Because disabled people are not Muppet! Muppet! stupid." Jess took a large mouthful of her beer.

"Exactly. No one will expect me to rob a bank!"

"Hold on Roger. What about it's breaking the law? Teddy Roosevelt! Teddy Roosevelt! Hitler! You've banged these thieves up! I don't want to break the law with one of your old colleagues closing my cell door at night!"

"The law is unfair. All bastards. What about when we do those deliveries? They are illegal!"

"As I've said, Roger," Jess said quietly, lowering her head to her chest, "I don't know. Ronald Reagan! And I don't want to know! As far as I'm concerned, it's all above board!"

Roger and Jess had been delivering parcels to various lawyers and solicitor's offices in and around London. They'd done it several times, working for Stan Tennant, and were informed the parcels contained financial and legal papers.

"If it's a crime then frankly delivering the odd small package to a lawyer's office in Mayfair, ain't exactly the crime of the century!" Jess looked at him sternly. "Anyway, it probably isn't even a crime!"

Roger nodded. It got them out of the house but the novelty of going to London in a posh car, supplied by Stan and with a suited driver, had worn off. On a couple of occasions, Roger had insisted on wearing black leather gloves when handling the envelopes or parcels just to wind Jess up, pretending that it was serious contraband. He had no idea if it was or wasn't, but expected it was all 'bent' knowing who he delivered them for.

"I'm just bored. Bored of benefits, bored dribbling, bored being ignored,"

Jess smiled "we're all bored" she stood up, twitched, and walked to the bar.

Roger wiped the dribble from his chin.

CHAPTER TWELVE

Liz was tired. She sat at her desk and looked at Edith as she was being pushed in her wheelchair across the atrium. Edith's head had slumped forwards in a very uncomfortable-looking position. Why the carers couldn't understand how to make someone comfortable in a chair was beyond her. The carer, pushing Edith, was trying to text on her mobile phone as they trundled by, not taking any notice of anything else, especially Edith.

Liz had worked at The Rose Care Home for eight years. She was the office manager, receptionist, bit of a cleaner and general organiser. AKA dog's body. Liz used to have two colleagues who worked with her in the office. After each of them left within a month of each other, they were never replaced. For two years she was told by her boss that their posts would be advertised soon. They never were. Her boss though was on her second Mercedes. The white one, two doors, that flies like shit off a shovel.

Over the eight years, she had worked at The Rose, she had seen and heard how badly the residents were treated. Not necessarily through lack of kindness, but mainly due to lack of awareness, knowledge and lack of staff. Liz always claimed that the carers were paid too little to do the important job they had.

"How dare our society pay people who look after the country's elderly such crap wages!" but no one ever took any notice. Liz knew that by the time a person realised how bad care was in some nursing homes, it would be too late. As they would be the frail resident receiving the poor care.

Liz often moaned at Nick at the end of the day that it was strange that it was being forced down our throats that you get what you pay for by bleating CEOs justifying their millions. Yet when it's our loved ones we don't mind paying those who look after them as little as possible!

Nick had started to worry Liz. She knew how important work had been for him and to think about leaving a job he once loved would be difficult for him to take. She had supported him through every battle he had had to stay in employment and was sorry to see that maybe now Nick had come to the end of his working days.

She also worried about money. How were they going to get enough money for them to survive? Ok so they wouldn't be absolutely broke but their lives would change. They'd have to drink less wine and justify buying stuff as opposed to just getting things without really thinking about the costs. Their lives had been good, but unfortunately, not through anyone's fault, their lives were going to change.

"For Heaven's sake," she sighed as she leaned back into her office chair.

Her sadness at her potential future instantly disappeared as her office phone rang. Liz picked it up and before she could say anything Nick started laughing,

"Hi, babe. Fancy a pint after work? I'm gasping,"

Liz smiled to herself, a stiff drink would go down a treat, "You bet your hat!"

"Meet you down there then." Nick hung up without saying goodbye.

Liz sat back in her chair and watched as one of the residents flew through the atrium on his disability scooter. He narrowly missed her desk as he whizzed by.

"Oi!" she shouted at him laughing, "This ain't chuffin' Brands Hatch!"

◆ ◆ ◆

Later that day Liz saw Nick walking down the path to the pub door. She trotted up behind him and put her arm around his waist, surprising him. Nick laughed as both entered the pub through the open glass-fronted door.

The pub was quiet except for Roger and Jess who were sitting in the corner and a couple of lads at the fruit machine. Nick noticed that Jess seemed more animated than the last time they met and the chap she was with was just sitting there staring into space.

Nick waved over at Jess, who waved back and ushered him over. He gestured he was going to get a beer.

"You happy to sit with those guys Liz?"

Liz looked around the pub her eyes stopping at Jess and Roger, "Fine Nick, but we are not getting hammered again tonight. I want to be back earlyish."

Nick ordered the drinks and turned to Liz, "Agreed."

Nick picked up the pint of lager and passed Liz her usual glass of wine. He walked with Liz over to the table.

They both sat down on the two chairs opposite Jess and Roger and put their drinks down on the table in front of them.

"Guess what? Hitler! Muppet! George Clooney! Now there's a man!" Jess seemed a smudge ticked off, "Guess what this idiot wants to do?" if there had been people in the pub they would have turned and glared at Jess as she was getting a little loud.

Roger put his finger across his lips and indicated firmly that he wanted Jess to shut up.

Nick interjected, "Hi Jess. Who is this? Are you going to introduce us?" Nick extended his hand towards Roger.

Roger took and shook his hand.

"This is Roger, I told you about him. Clinton! He can't talk, had a stroke, blah blah! And he's a Muppet! Clinton inhale!" she got louder as she said the last sentence. "And he's a great mate!" the more excited she got, the worse her symptoms became.

Nick raised his eyebrows to Roger, "Hi mate, I'm Nick and this is Liz, my wife."

Liz and Roger smiled at each other.

"So what's going on Jess?" Nick whispered.

All four leant in closer to each other to shield the outside world from Jess's reply,

"He" she pointed at Roger with her thumb, "wants to rob a bank." she leant back.

Nick smiled.

"Sorry I didn't hear that. Say it again."

Jess leant back in, "Roger wants to rob a bank."

"Yep you did hear," nodded Liz.

All four of them shuffled back into their seats and said nothing. Jess, Liz and Nick took sips of their respective drinks.

Roger looked at them, disappointed by the lack of encouragement.

Jess sat upright on her chair, "He's bored apparently." she smiled, "You know, go and get a hobby or something Roger!"

Roger smiled. He was bored. Bored of not

being able to talk, bored of dribbling, bored of spelling everything out, bored of attaching a syringe every few hours to get some food into himself. Yes, he was bored. Bored and totally bored.

"I can understand boredom. Hey, I'm bored!" Liz empathised.

"Why are you bored?" asked Nick, turning to Liz and looking bemused.

"I'm bored of working for idiots. I'm tired of doing the same thing every day."

"Do you want to rob a bank?"

"No of course not. I just want to do something!"

"That's a relief."

"So what do I do?" tapped Roger.

All three looked at each other.

"Get a job?" asked Nick.

"He has tried, Hitler! Jess nodded, "It's the constant dribbling though, puts off employers."

Roger shook his shoulders in an effort to laugh out loud. He had once done a bit of work for his brother bagging fruit and vegetables up for him on his market stall. The second bag full of tomatoes did not go down well with the woman who bought them, something about a long line of spittle on them. He lasted about sixteen minutes.

"Volunteer somewhere?" suggested Liz, "What did you do before the stroke?"

Roger pretended to turn a set of keys.

"Cook?" asked Liz.

"Screw!" said Jess

"Carpenter?" asked Nick.

"Prison officer! A screw!" Jess sighed.

"Oh," Liz took a sip of her wine. "Can you do voluntary work at the prison, you'd have so much to give?"

"You do know he can't speak? Has a tube to get food through and is the slowest walker ever!?"

"Oh right, guess it's hard."

Silence descended on the foursome as though they were all thinking about what Roger could do. But frankly, they had no idea. Nick broke the peace,

"There's no money in banks anymore."

"No, I guess not, all online." Liz agreed.

"Dealing drugs would be the best" Jess laughed, "No one's going to search a bloke who's dribbling! Come to think of it, no one's going to buy drugs from someone flaying their arms about or me, swearing and twitching!"

All four grinned at Jess's blatant discrimination of the dribbling community.

Nick stopped laughing and echoed Jess, "No one's going to search a man who's dribbling?" he looked at Liz.

"No you're right, he'd get through customs every time." Liz chuckled.

Jess stood up and gave a Nazi salute. "For those about to rock! Mrs. Doubtfire!"

Roger put his arm on her arm to try and calm

her down, but this just aggravated her tics. If a stranger had done this, she would have punched them hard. But she knew Roger wasn't being condescending, he was just trying to help.

Nick said again, "No one's going to search............you might have something there Jess!"

Roger took his arm off Jess, who was biting on her sleeve to stop herself from shouting. Her tics were uncontrollable and had the sensation of a sneeze about to happen that cannot be stopped or the most frustrating itch ever.

"Oh, so you want to go into drug smuggling now Nick?" Liz was cross at her husband's crassness.

Nick looked at her sternly, "Of course not, I'm only joking!"

Roger smiled. Undid two of his middle shirt buttons and pulled out the feeding tube that was in his lower stomach. He pointed to the end of it. Indicating that he could put stuff in it.

Nick sniggered. Liz slapped his arm.

Jess stood up, then sat straight back down and shouted, "I love Smack!"

"Yes, I agree!" Liz acknowledged Jess's tics, whilst also presuming and hoping that she wasn't a heroin addict.

Nick laughed, nearly choking on his beer. Clearing his throat, he stood up, "Just popping to the gents."

"I don't think my husband would make a good

criminal," Liz laughed, "I don't think he's stolen anything in his life!"

"I used to as a kid," Jess chipped in, "You know teenage stuff, make-up and whatnot."

Roger smiled. He had never stolen anything from a shop. Some of his mates used to until one was caught and then sent to a young offenders' prison. That was enough to put Roger off from a teenage life of petty crime.

"I was too honest," Liz replied, "I once got asked my age trying to buy a bottle of vodka. Instead of saying eighteen, I said my true age, sixteen, and obviously wasn't allowed it! I couldn't even lie!"

Jess chuckled and asked, "Can you lie now?!"

"Only when I tell him about the price of my shoes!" she looked to the other side of the pub and saw Nick walking towards them, "Oh here he comes, change the subject!"

Nick suddenly stopped and held onto the back of one of the chairs. His right foot had twisted up and contorted into a very painful position.

"What's he doing?" Jess covered her mouth, whispering to Liz.

"Oh, it happens now and again. It's dystonia, like a cramp. He's probably late with his pills again." she waved at her husband acknowledging his situation, "It'll ease down in a bit."

"Oh yes, he did tell me about this" replied Jess, remembering the conversation with Nick.

Nick stood embarrassed in the middle of the

pub, holding onto the chair trying to look as normal as possible. But he didn't look normal, and the stress of his situation only made his foot twist into ever-painful arrangements.

Jess got up and walked over to Nick, "Not a good look Nick!" She smiled, sounding slightly concerned.

"I know." Nick eased himself down on the vacant chair. His twisted foot raised slightly off the floor, "It'll sort itself out in a minute."

"Nightmare." Jess sat down next to him.

"This isn't so bad, but when it happens outside someone's house, and you can't move and it appears you are loitering for no apparent reason, you feel like a right criminal or even worse a pervert!"

"I can imagine."

Nick lifted his leg and tried to straighten his foot. It wouldn't move.

"There's no rhyme nor reason to it."

"Liz said you might be late with your pills?"

"No, I took them. They are probably wearing off."

"Christ, if this ever happened whilst you were crossing a road!"

"Thanks Jess, that's a pleasant thought."

"You know the film Genevieve when the girl drops the ice cream on the zebra crossing?" Jess started to giggle, "You could have a Genevieve moment stopping traffic!"

"Oh great Jess!" Nick tried not to laugh. He

remembered the scene in the old film. A little girl drops her ice cream and her brother is trying to pull her up as she tried to scrape it off the road. Meanwhile stopping the car, Genevieve, from continuing in a race, the driver, Kenneth More, shouts and curses at the girl! "You've managed to give it a name too – a Genevieve moment" he seemed pleased that a symptom, a painful one at that, had been named.

"I love that film."

"Me too." Nick stood up, and shook his affected leg, "Think we can walk now!"

"Good."

The four sat and drank, well three of them drank, for most of the evening, and staggered out at closing time. Jess's tics improved massively as the beer flowed, and Nick always felt "looser" and his dyskinesia improved after a drink or seven. He often felt a bit uncomfortable and a bit of a fraud in pubs. He'd had Parkinson's for some years now and he knew that after a drink or two in a relaxing environment, he would look like any other middle-aged man. He certainly didn't look like he had a degenerative disease. He was told he looked well and some people would say he didn't look like he had Parkinson's disease. But his leg movement hidden under the table, his stutter and slurred speech, the stiffness in his hands that moved slowly picking a pint up or his multiple mistaken photographs on his phone as he'd pressed the wrong button due to his poor dexterity often gave the game away to what was really going on.

He would suffer the next day, as the relaxing effect of the alcohol would disappear replaced with the stress of a hangover destroying his body with the stresses and strains of the disease.

CHAPTER THIRTEEN

Stan, alone in his cell, started making plans to smuggle the bonds back from Italy. It had to be done simply and efficiently with no drama. Those who knew would be those who needed to know. Those who knew and didn't need to know would, unfortunately, have to pay the price. There was far too much money for emotions to get in the way. The job had to be so tight that nothing would escape out into the world of the ever listening and watching police.

He had someone in mind who would do the job for him. He'd used this person before to smuggle contraband into the UK and trusted him. They would need help, but that could be sorted. It needed to be conducted using the most unremarkable people he could find. It was usually the demeanour and body language of the smugglers that gave them away. The ones that were searched and subsequently caught looked nervous before going through customs at airports. They would pace around, sweat and look uncomfortable. His thoughts were to use people who wouldn't obviously portray such traits. He needed smugglers who could hide their fear and not give themselves away.

Older people had been used as smugglers, mainly for transporting drugs on cruise ships. But since a couple got caught with £2 million of cocaine in their suitcases, the industry belief was that they were too risky to use.

Stan climbed into the lower bed of the bunk and looked up at the mattress above him. He was content with his plan and satisfied it would work. He just needed to recruit the right smugglers.

He had in mind the perfect person. Someone he could trust. Someone who would not let him down.

CHAPTER FOURTEEN

Over the next few weeks the four met up several times, usually in the local pub, and sometimes just for a quick brew in each other's houses. Nick was becoming a little less stressed and managed to get a couple of months off work so that he could relax and start to explore his options. Fortunately, the mild weather mixed with no work promoted the perfect scenario to have a beer or two in a pub garden and just think about what to do.

Half asleep, Nick scraped his hand across the bedside table blindly searching for his weekly medication box. He filled up the individual compartments with his medication every Sunday. A week's worth of morning medication at a time. He hated doing it; it took ages to drop the correct pills in the correct place. But if he failed to do it on a Sunday it meant that he had to get his morning pill when he was half asleep from the packets. Not an easy task to get anti-Parkinson's pills out of the most cumbersome, foil-lined, Parkinson patient-proof packaging without having taken your morning anti-Parkinson's medication first!

His probing hand eventually came across what felt like a weekly drug box. He pulled himself up and opened the lid relevant for that day. Throwing the pills into his mouth straight from the box, he picked up a cold cup of coffee that was left over from the previous night and swallowed all the pills. Sighing deeply, he eased himself back down on the bed. His head was pounding – really pounding.

"Who ordered Tequilas?" Nick covered his head with his hands. No one answered. No one was there. Nick would always suffer after a big session. But add in any kind of shot, wine or whiskey to the evening and he would awake at death's door the following morning. He would remind himself of the golden rule of not mixing drinks before having his first beer and always vowed just to stick to beer. But drinking anything over three pints and voila! The devil would join him in the pub and easily persuade him to say "yes" when offered a cheeky shot.

Liz had been up for a good hour. He could hear her downstairs clattering about. She had put the vacuum cleaner on resulting in the most irritating, earsplitting and painful racket. Hangover or no hangover.

"Oh Jesus." Nick slipped back down the bed and pulled the duvet over his head. Liz never had hangovers. He knew that within twenty minutes she would be upstairs cleaning, the vacuum cleaner banging into the side of the bed, driving him deeper into hangover oblivion.

Parkinson's and hangovers did not mix. Due to the stress on his body from too much alcohol, his symptoms were often exacerbated, causing him to feel much stiffer and slower. The secret of getting through hangover hell was understanding that there was no way out of the darkness. You chose the path and you have to endure it. Fighting was futile and maybe you should have believed the warning written on the drug box not to drink alcohol with the medication. So, Nick played the game, hid under his duvet and endured the torture of house cleaning that Liz had commenced. Sooner or later she would break him from his hangover and insist he helps. But that was not yet. Tough resistance would be called for in that situation. But he knew it would all be in vain, and his fight would fail.

❖ ❖ ❖

Roger pulled out his feeding tube from under his shirt. He sat at the small, pine kitchen table and started to push water into the tube with a large 60ml syringe. He then put his liquid medication into a cup, crushed a pill with two spoons (he could never find his pill crusher) then put the resultant powder into the same cup as the liquid. With the same syringe, he drew up the concoction and pushed it up the feeding tube. He followed this with another syringe full of water.

He had done this nearly every day since his stroke. It took a while to get used to it, but he was proficient at it now and it had become his normal life. He hadn't swallowed a thing since the stroke other than his own saliva causing a sudden bout of lung-drowning coughing.

Roger still had nightmares about the tube they put down his nose when he was in the hospital about a week after having the stroke. He remembered the "chubby fingers" that the nurse had when she tied the tube to his nose to secure it because he had been pulling the tubes out in his sleep. He hated that 'overweight, tube-inserting nurse'. But she probably saved his life. The tube was vital for fluids and nutrition as he was unable to swallow normally. Roger was grateful for her help, but she could have been a tiny bit gentler, or maybe another thinner-fingered nurse could have placed the new tube up his nose.

Ironically, it was a relief to have the operation for the permanent tube that was inserted into his stomach. His nose was getting sore from the temporary nasogastric tube, and it was constantly in his line of vision, taped to the side of his cheek.

Jess, head bowed, went into the kitchen. She

didn't look good. She had wrapped herself in her duvet, gingerly creeping into the room. Her black hair was a complete mess and tangled as if she had been on a log flume in a hurricane. Her face was pale, and her darkened eyes cried pain, squinting as she shuffled across the room.

Roger jumped when he saw how ill she looked. She looked frighteningly terrible. Jess sat down at the table and rested her head on the tabletop. She didn't say a word.

Roger started to tap out a sentence and then realised she wasn't paying any attention. He tapped her on the shoulder. She didn't move. He tapped her shoulder again and she slowly, delicately pulled her head off the table, with one eye half open she looked at him like a cat at the vets about to be spayed.

Roger smiled nervously. Jess stood gently up, then pulled herself from the chair and disappeared, slowly, back upstairs.

Due to the lack of intelligent conversation or any conversation for that matter, Roger decided to go out. He had to go and 'chat' with Nick. He had a proposal for him. He should have told him earlier but felt the time wasn't right. He really needed to do it today. He liked the bloke; thought they were cut from the same cloth. He felt they had stuff in common: their lives had been thrown upside down, both were hungry for more and both were fed up with being unseen by the world. Frankly, that's why he got on so well with

Jess. They were all on the same page fighting the same foes.

CHAPTER FIFTEEN

As the door opened Nick smiled, "Hello mate, nice to see you! Shit, I was rough this morning. Oh how's Jess?" Nick looked pretty fresh considering he had had the mother of all hangovers earlier in the morning. "To be honest, Roger, I think I'm still pissed."

Roger put his thumb down, indicating Jess's condition, like a Roman emperor condemning the gladiator to a torrid death. Roger then pulled an over-exaggeratedly sad face and then smiled.

Nick laughed.

"Well come in. Liz isn't here at the moment. She's had to pop into work."

The two men sat in the living room at the back of the house. Roger parked himself down on the sofa and felt himself sink about a foot into the soft material.

"You'll never get up now!" Nick looked down at Roger, "Cup of tea?" Nick quickly thought about what he had just said, "Oh shit Roger I'm sorry mate, my mistake, I totally forgot!"

Roger nodded. He pulled out his letters card, opened it up and pointed to the letters,

"Yes please."

"No sorry mate, I shouldn't have said that, I know you can't, Roger I've been looking after people with feeds for years. It's easy to forget I guess when you're not with a patient."

"One sugar." tapped Roger.

"What.....?"

"One sugar."

"Yes, but you can't drink it Roger!"

Roger grinned, "One sugar!" he tapped out again, a little harder than last time emphasising his request.

Nick left the living room, "Ok, ok, I'll make you a cup of tea."

Nick returned with one mug of tea and plonked it on the table, then returned for the other mug. He was walking quite slowly and appeared stiff, shuffling as he walked.

Roger pulled out a large syringe from his inside pocket. Nick winced when he saw it. The barrel of the syringe looked as though it had had oil in it at some point. It was filthy.

Roger put the tip of the syringe in the mug and drew up some of the tea. He then proceeded to put it down his tube.

"What the?!" Nick looked at Roger's face grimacing with concentration as he continued to slowly push the contents into his stomach, "But you can't taste it Rog!"

Roger laughed without making a sound. He closed the tube clamp and grabbed his spelling sheet, "I can taste it in my mouth."

"Really?"

"Yes really," tapped Roger, "Lovely cup – bit hot." and proceeded to laugh again.

Nick sipped his tea. Roger was right, it was a bit hot.

Slipping the syringe back into his coat pocket, Roger picked up his alphabet letter sheet and started to point at some letters.

"Drug dealing. You seemed interested the other week?"

Nick laughed, "Yes, who really is going to stop a dribbling man who can't talk? Who the hell is going to search my bags, with my dyskinesia, arms flying around, sweating, shaking arm and dodgy walk?"

"Agree." Spelt out Roger.

"And Jess? Hell, you wouldn't go anywhere near her!" Nick laughed, "Who's going to approach a woman with uncontrollable tics that get louder and louder as she gets more stressed?"

Roger smiled.

"I'd be flaying my arms about unintentionally kicking the sniffer dog that has just nailed me by sitting down by my side or I'd come through customs looking like I was still hammered from a week in Ibiza!" Nick stopped suddenly. "You do know I was joking right?"

Roger smiled.

"I would never smuggle drugs or anything come to think of it! I've never broken the law in my life! I didn't even go through that nicking phase when I was a kid."

Roger continued to listen.

"Ok a speeding ticket. Bastard was hiding behind a bush where 40 became 30. I had to do one of those speed awareness days. It was horrendously tedious! I'm taking the fine next time, can't sit through that rubbish again! I've never done anything like stealing or anything.....I mean I've smoked a joint or two, but nothing stupid. You know normal stuff." Nick gabbled.

Taking a long sip of tea nick asked, "Why do you ask?"

Roger tapped, "Wondering if you were serious?"

Nick, "Of course not. Sorry, I didn't want you to think I was a criminal or something. I guess being an ex-prison officer you know a crook when you see one!"

"Spent my life working with criminals." Roger's index finger flowed over the letters on his board, "There is not a criminal look."

"No, I suppose there isn't."

"I smuggled once," Roger admitted, pointing slowly at each letter.

"You what? I thought you were a prison officer?"

Roger raised his eyebrows and opened his

arms and hands to indicate "So?"

"Well, you're supporting the law aren't you? I mean I'm sure there are some bent prison officers taking drugs into prison." Nick stopped. "You smuggled drugs into a prison?"

"No." Roger firmly tapped, shaking his head.

"So what then?"

"Financial stuff." Roger tapped out.

"Financial stuff?" Nick was confused, "Oh right cash?" He suddenly thought of money laundering.

"Bonds."

"Bonds?"

Roger nodded.

"What do you mean bonds?"

Roger wiggled his fingers on both hands miming typing on a keyboard.

"What?" Nick was bemused, "Computer? Oh, look on the computer?"

Roger nodded.

"Hold on," Nick got up and went to the bedroom. He picked up Liz's tablet and turned it on, "Shit, what's her password?" Nick sat down with the tablet, trying to remember her password. He guessed a few obvious Liz type passwords, some words or phrases that she may have used but nothing. "Passwords! I can't tell you about the number of passwords that I have at home and work! I end up writing 'em all down. How secure is that?" Nick tried another combination once more and the screen opened.

"Excellent! Lucky guess!"

"Right........ok here we go, b o n d s" within seconds there was a list of possible websites about bonds. "Ok, here we go, Bonds definition..... Bonds are units of corporate debt .....companies as tradable assets. A bond is ....as a fixed income .... since bonds traditionally paid a fixed interest......to debt holders." Nick continued reading without saying the words. Finishing he looked at Roger, "So they are like IOUs."

Roger shrugged and rocked his left-hand face down to indicate "sort of".

"Shit." he carried on reading, "When did you do this? After your stroke?"

Roger shook his head, "Way back."

"How, What, why,.....come on, what happened?"

"Prisoner paid me," Roger tapped, "From Switzerland." he paused, "Years ago"

"Why bonds?" Nick couldn't see the reason why you'd "smuggle" a piece of paper out of a country.

"Tax," Roger pointed quickly at the letters on his communication sheet.

Nick nodded, acknowledging the reason. "Must have been a lot of bonds?"

"50 mils" tapped Roger.

"50 million quid!? Yeah right."

"And 1.75 million in Euros strapped to my body,"

Nick laughed, "How much?!" he stood up, "Bet you got a few quid? Million-odd Euros stuffed down your trousers!" Nick bent over to try and see what Roger was tapping in response,

"Yes. Into Heathrow, then the bonds went to Germany and the cash stopped in the UK."

"It's like something out of a film Rog." Nick sat back down, "Does anyone else know?"

"Jess. Delivery job for the same bloke,"

"What? You still work for him?"

Roger started tapping,

"Sort of. We work for a man who gives us stuff for lawyer's offices. Papers."

"Illegal?"

Roger shrugged his shoulders. He expected they were, but really didn't care. He and Jess got a bit of cash for it, and it only involved dropping off an envelope at the front desk of an office.

"Does it pay?"

"We've only done it a few times."

"Can you still go abroad and smuggle in a case full of Euros?" Nick asked, "No no I'm only joking, bet there's even more risk now with all this technology and x-ray machines. Never mind the sniffer dogs! They can sniff out anything these days."

Roger hunched his shoulders. Both men disappeared into their own thoughts for a few minutes.

"What an adventure." Nick smiled, breaking the silence.

Roger subtly nodded in agreement.

CHAPTER SIXTEEN

Long before Roger had his stroke, he found himself battle weary and broke. He had just endured a mind-boggling, head cracker of a divorce. He agreed that he and his now ex-wife Cheryl, shouldn't be together, but to break up so recklessly, so maliciously, so horribly, was not what he would have desired. To be honest, Roger believed that deep down Cheryl would not have wanted it either. But her solicitor was out for blood money and bore her legal way deep into Cheryl's head.

"If I'm entitled to it. I'm having it!"

"But I'll be broke Cheryl!"

"My solicitor said...."

It got messy.

They'd known each other since school. Not as friends, but they were in each other's classes. After college, he went off to do his prison officer training, ended up at Brixton then moved back home after a couple of years away. He worked at the local prison, made a few quid on the house sale and moved back from London with a good deal on a house quite close to his work. He had bumped into Cheryl in his local pub. In the days when you could smoke, he'd be at the bar, smoking and chatting to whoever came in to buy a beer or sit near him.

She recognised him first. Roger had to think deeply back to his school days before the penny finally dropped remembering her from his class. She was in the pub out with her friends, all dressed up, blowing off steam after a hard-working week. She hadn't changed since school. Her blonde hair was much longer, cascading down her back, but her cheerful face looked the same, her pure white teeth complimenting her still flawless skin. She and Roger spent the evening chit-chatting about school, the laughs and tears. Roger fell in love straight away. And that was that. They married six months later. Then three years had passed and bang! She had found someone else.

Lying in bed one Sunday morning, Roger stirred from his deep sleep and saw Cheryl sitting up in bed, staring, looking into space. They'd made love the night before after an unusually bad Chinese takeaway.

"You all right babe?" he yawned.

"I don't love you anymore Roger."

He walked out of that relatively short marriage, with nothing. He gave up in the end. Cut his losses. He'd realised both his and Cheryl's solicitors were bleeding him dry.

"Life's too short. You have it all. I ain't interested!" these were the last words he said to Cheryl.

Work was much tougher after the breakup. He worked on the second floor of B block in the local prison. It was a tough jail. A lifer's wing, young offenders, health care and remand. Remand was the hardest. People waiting to be sentenced, scared, and acting tough, some were frightened shitless, some shouldn't have been there, some were detoxing, and some were getting stoned. About three-quarters had been in before and just wanted to get on with it – a gym, three meals a day and a catch-up with old mates, yelling through the cell windows at night:

"'Allo Billy!"

"All right Dickie, where you been?"

"Well, I managed to be on the out for a month – broke back into that shop again and here I am!"

"Maybe you need to move on from that shop!"

"Where are you anyway?"

"On the corner of the 'twos'. I'm sure I've been in this cell before, I recognise the smell!"

There was always a trail of rubbish following the walls of cell blocks where prisoners had dropped their empty crisp packets and cigarette butts out of their windows. A tide line of criminals doing time.

The young offenders' wing was the noisiest, most threatening, saddest block in the prison.

Kids who had screwed up, joined gangs, made the stupidest of mistakes or just let their teenage angst get the better of them. Young men whose lives would change forever. Drugs, poor backgrounds, following in father's footsteps or the strong lure of cash-rich, seductive gangs.

Roger sometimes worked in reception in the young offenders' wing. when they were short-staffed. It gave him a break from B wing. In the evening, a prison van would bring kids who had just been convicted or remanded by the courts. Most of the time they were local kids, but every now and again you'd get a van full of London lads. The London prisons were full up or locked out and the authorities redirected them to other nicks where there were spaces.

"Ok, where am I Guv?" they'd say as they strutted into the reception area.

Once told they were still none the wiser.

"Never heard of it Guv!"

The odd fight would break out in reception, but nothing like in the young offenders' wing. He didn't mind reception; at least it was relatively quiet. The landings were full of loud music, kids shouting out their cell windows at each other, cutting deals or intimidating their neighbours.

"Oi! Cell 2, send us up a bit of burn."

"You what Jimmy? You still owe me for last night!"

"Don't worry, I'll pay you in a minute! Cell 2 you got any burn then?"

"I hope you ain't robbing Peter to pay Paul Jimmy?"

"You what? Who is Paul?"

There were some big strong guys in the young offenders' wing. At the other extreme, some tiny kids that although were eighteen looked about ten. Every one of these small ones Roger knew would suffer, until at least they had proved their worth. Some did. Quickly.

His normal place of work on B wing was different. The prisoners on B wing were lifers and long-term prisoners. They were just doing their time. Of course, it had its problems, the odd fight, drugs, hooch and other issues that any group of people would have if they were cooped up for years together in tiny cells.

There were a couple of famous criminals. Big names from tabloids who had committed murder. Any sexual offenders were on the sex offenders' wing. The odd one did appear in the normal prison population, but they were soon found out and quickly moved off the landing before they had a kettle full of boiling water mixed with sugar thrown in their face.

Relationships were formed between the prison officers and the inmates. Not overly friendly but a sort of mutual level of respect. The officers needed to get through their day, and their careers, and the prisoners needed to get through their own days and sentences. Prison officers did though have to be wary of manipulation and doing over-the-top 'favours' for the inmates. It was easy to be blackmailed or threatened into doing something stupidly risky.

Stan Tennant ran B wing. He wasn't the senior prison officer; he was a gangster from London. Not your typical gangster. He was very well-spoken, polite, and a model prisoner, but he ran the landing, if not the prison. His reach was long. He was locked up for killing one of his own men about 13 years ago. It was the only thing the police could get him for, and Stan always denied he'd done it. Most people believed him. They knew he'd killed a lot of people or had them killed, but not this murder. But it stuck and he ended up in court receiving a big sentence.

He still ran his criminal outfit, which was part of a larger European, if not the world, crime organisation. The Headquarters for the UK branch was in Manchester and Stan was its boss. Because of his position and notoriety, he'd done 8 years in a category A prison before being moved to his current prison. Stan was working his way to release and therefore was the model prisoner, although if you were stupid enough to dig deeper, you'd have realised that things were not as they seemed.

Stan Tennant had a good relationship with officers and the prison governors and managed to manipulate them in certain directions. He also gave them the heads up if something was going on in the prison that could upset the balance of life behind bars. He didn't grass, he just steered. But it was well understood by prison officers and officials that supplied information was only on Stan's terms. Prison officers would ignore the odd bit of trouble that was caused by Stan, letting the natural order of things sort day-to-day life out. It kept things quiet and moving along nicely. Everyone liked 'nice' and 'quiet'.

Roger had formed a good, professional relationship with Stan. Roger would chat to Stan, just quickly at first, not asking any personal questions, just passing the day. He felt they did get on and there was a mutual understanding of doing things the old school way.

Roger though, was about to unwittingly overstep the line.

CHAPTER SEVENTEEN

As time went on, with months of very subtle grooming, Stan got to know increasingly more about Roger. He knew he had just had a bad divorce, that he was skint, roughly where he lived, his car, the pub he went to, his work in the young offenders, his work history, his goals, his favourite TV shows, his football team and other seemingly insignificant information. Just titbits that Stan would accumulate over months and years.

Eventually, as time went on Stan started to use the information in a way that would threaten Roger's whole way of life. Roger would also realise that he had seriously broken his own rule of not fraternising with the customers of HMP Estates.

You never think it will happen to you hey?

The realisation started for Roger when he felt he was being followed or watched. Just walking along a street he'd feel eyes upon him from cars or doorways. He'd look out of his bedroom window at night and there'd be a car with someone in it, just parked up from his house.

Waiting.

It felt unsettling, uncomfortable and a little unnerving, but he couldn't guarantee he wasn't being just a little bit over paranoid.

Then one evening in the pub, a young woman who looked like a student from the local university, wearing a jumper, a long dark flowing skirt and brown boots popped a pint in front of him at the bar.

"Er, what's that?".

"It's a pint Roger."

"Yep, I can see that but why are you buying me a drink?" he smiled at her, "Surely you're not cracking onto me? I'm old enough to be your father" Roger laughed.

"No, not at all." she picked her brown handbag off the bar and headed for the exit.

"What? Why?" Roger turned around on his stool and watched her as she opened the pub door.

The woman stopped and turned, "Stan wanted to buy his mate a beer," then she left the pub.

Roger was stunned and felt a chill shoot down his spine.

He knew at that moment his life had changed. He knew that he was about to tread a path that he didn't want to go down. He knew the King's shilling had been forced into his pocket and he would struggle to give it back.

❖ ❖ ❖

Stan opened his eyes and looked up at his cell ceiling. He had had a pleasant night's sleep, except for some idiots who started shouting out of a window on the third floor at 4 o'clock that morning. He would have to sort that out. Couldn't be woken up at such a stupid hour. Very impolite.

He climbed off the top bunk and had a morning pee, followed by his normal ablutions. He flicked the switch on his kettle and sat on his chair to watch the news. There was no one else in his cell; he'd sorted that, preferring to have a single 'suite'. On his record was written 'single cell only'. One Governor of a prison did try and double him up claiming that the Home Office was screaming out for space as the courts were overflowing. It lasted about an hour and not long afterwards the governor found himself unceremoniously working in HMP Dartmoor. Stan managed to retain his single-cell status from that day.

At 08.30 Stan heard keys turn in his cell door, and his cell door was opened.

"Thank you, Mr. Varley," he called out to the officer.

"Morning Mr. Tennant," came the reply, "Lovely day,"

Five minutes later a large, muscular guy, wearing the same prison-issue clothes as Stan entered the cell with a tray of food. A blue plastic bowl, a carton of milk, a box of cereal, a banana and two slices of toast.

He placed it on the table, "Breakfast Mr. Tennant." he quickly left the cell not waiting for acknowledgement from Stan.

Stan was still sitting on his chair and pulled the small table nearer and began to eat his breakfast. He liked the order of prison, the routine, he knew what and when things were going to happen. He didn't have to think about how his day was going to go. This allowed him time to purely focus on his business.

It was challenging work once upon a time to run a business in prison, but over the years this had become easier. Mobile phones were getting smaller and there were a great deal more avenues for getting information into and out of the jail. He could even hold visual, virtual conference calls with colleagues all over the world, even if they were locked up themselves. The business he worked in had reacted and overcome the challenge of having "senior management" such as Stan, locked up in prison. There were procedures in place to keep the business going if one of the bosses was locked up and it included access to mobile phones and computers. The most important aspect of dealing with the risk of executive incarceration was of course cash. To do their job they needed cash. Everyone had a price; it was just a case of finding that price. A business model built on bribery and extortion coupled with extreme violence resulted in mountains being moved.

Stan felt a presence in the doorway of his cell as he chewed on a spoonful of cereal.

He looked up and saw Roger leaning with both arms up on the frame, "Thanks for the beer Stan," Roger said, voice lowered.

Stan turned round fully, his spoon still in his hand, "you deserve it, you work hard."

"Why am I being followed Stan?" Roger asked. He didn't want to get involved but knew that he was being dragged in.

"You look after my welfare in here, I think I should make sure you are ok outside." his voice was monotone and dry.

Roger looked at him. He could be looking at any middle-aged man, balding, with glasses, and a thin face. He reminded Roger of his uncle, an accountant. Didn't say much, dull, reliable, blunt and introverted. But he knew that Stan was an enormously powerful dangerous man.

"Stan, I appreciate your help but I don't need this right now. Please do me a favour and let me be."

"You need a holiday Roger." Stan stated, turning back round to have another mouthful of cornflakes, "Switzerland is nice at this time of year."

"Stan, I'm not getting involved. I am not doing anything for you or anyone else." Roger tried to stay calm.

Stan continued to eat his breakfast.

"Stan... Mr. Tennant, this can't happen" Roger started to plead.

"Like I said you have been working hard, had a tough time with that divorce and you need a break." Stan didn't look at him; he started to cut his banana into slices and began to eat it.

Roger sighed.

"I've booked the tickets and everything. Your passport is up to date, I'll give you some spending money. Roger, you'd be stupid not to go."

He turned around and looked at Roger.

"Very stupid"

CHAPTER EIGHTEEN

Nick stood up from his chair.

"You just went abroad the once then?"

Roger nodded.

"This bloke, did he make you do anymore."

Roger shook his head and spelt out; "No he never mentioned it again."

"So what happened to you and him? He just continued as if nothing had happened?"

Roger nodded. "He got shipped out." he tapped out on his spelling board. Roger waved to an imaginary person.

"What and you never heard from him again?"

Roger stopped waving, "My stroke. Sent me a get-well card. The deliveries too but not directly."

Nick looked at Roger. "Oh yeah, the deliveries, but shit, so he knew you had a stroke?! He knew a lot considering he was stuck in jail. This guy was a big deal then?!" he sat back down, and toyed with the handle of his empty mug, "How much did he pay you?"

Roger rubbed his thumb against two fingers.

"Right, a lot then." Nick acknowledged.

The two men looked around nervously as they heard the front door being opened. They both stood, motionless, except for Nick's shaking little finger on his right hand, waiting for whoever appeared.

"Caught ya!" Liz put her head into the living room, "Oh hello Roger," she was surprised to see him in the house.

"What are you doing home?" Nick asked, surprised to see his wife.

"Forgot my phone! Had five minutes so I thought I'd pop back. Nice to see you too love." She turned to Roger, "you ok then? Jess ok after last night?"

Roger put his thumbs down, suggesting she was not ok after last night.

"Oh dear, well she was putting them back a bit," she turned and left the room, "See you!" she called as she closed the front door. Then she re-opened the door and looked at the two of them, "you both look very guilty! What you are up to?" not waiting for a reply she left the house laughing.

"She's a whirlwind." Nick looked at the spot where she had been, his heart beating rapidly. He had no idea why he suddenly felt guilty, nervous and anxious.

"A guilty mind is always suspicious!" as his mum would say, before clipping him one over his head for something he hadn't done.

Nick went and made another cup of tea, Roger didn't want one this time. Nick came back into the room and took a tentative slurp of his hot drink, "The thing is Roger, that could have gone very badly. Your whole life could have been ruined." Nick had always been a bit cautious. Maybe a bit too cautious at times. He craved risk but when it came to the moment, he had always bottled it.

There were loads of potentially life-changing paths he could have taken when they presented themselves, but he had buried them deep in his mind. Nick was not a risk taker but had always kicked himself for not having the courage to take that risk and make a jump into the unknown.

"Why are you telling me this anyway? We've only met each other recently! I hardly know you!" Nick's face was contorted with thought and an edge of fear, "How do I know you're not setting me up? You could be an undercover copper, telling me this stuff to see what I do with it. This isn't right Roger! You're going to tell me you really have robbed banks next..." Nick was getting more agitated as he became louder, "......Is there a hidden camera somewhere?"

Roger stopped Nick's outburst by waving his arms in the air and started to grin at Nick's over-the-top reaction.

"It's not funny Roger. It's weird!"

Roger picked up his letters board and tapped, "You're ok. I can tell." He looked at Nick, "your life's difficult. Mine is too. We have stuff in common. I don't look like a copper!"

Nick looked at the dribble descending from Rogers's mouth. He agreed. The British Police Undercover Unit would be really pushing it if they employed Roger. But then again, maybe they should.

Suddenly Nick's phone rang. He pulled it out of his pocket and stopped the ringing, "medication time," he mimicked Nurse Ratchet as he popped a couple of pills into his mouth.

Roger cringed as Nick crunched his way through his tablets.

"You get used to the taste." Nick smiled.

He had calmed down, "Unfortunately when you are dehydrated, the pills in all their yellow glory, get stuck to the sides of your mouth and tongue. Once Liz pointed out to me that I looked like a rabid dog that had just eaten a yellow crayon!"

Roger pointed at his stomach and the tube.

"When I first started doing drug rounds as a junior nurse and giving patients their medication through those tubes I got into some real messes. Forget closing off that clamp and shit it's messy."

Roger grimaced as he pretended to wipe stuff off his trousers.

"Or the best one is when you start a patient's pump and forget to connect the tubes! That stuff is a bastard to clean out of someone's bed.

Not pretty!" Nick frowned, "You only make that mistake once though!"

Roger politely smiled. He didn't want to be hearing stories about a tube that he'd have forever implanted into his stomach.

"Ok, so where do we go from here?" Nick returned to Roger's criminal disclosure.

Roger leant forward and pulled an envelope from his inside pocket. He handed it to Nick:

"Heard you were unwell Roger.
Get well soon and with God's speed.
If you need anything let me know.
Regards
                Stan T."

"Blimey, this was the card he sent you. You've saved it this long, since your stroke?"

Roger took the card back from Nick and put it back in his pocket.

"Is he still inside?" Nick asked, "Surely he must be out?"

"Back in last December" Roger tapped, "broke his licence."

"What did he do?"

"Seen with wine at some posh do"

"So?"

"Not allowed alcohol. Part of license. The police wanted to get him again.

"Harsh."

"He has been in contact with me." Roger

slowly touched the letters on his word sheet.

"But you said you hadn't heard from him directly!" Nick looked surprised." Why did he get back into contact with you?"

"Job."

"What Job?"

"Rome, Italy."

"Doing what?"

"Bringing bonds back from Italy to London."

"You're mad!"

"Need someone else," Roger gingerly tapped on his letter board.

"Sorry I missed that……….Do it again!" Nick couldn't quite believe what he had just seen.

"Need another person."

"Take Jess. She'd easily walk in anywhere unnoticed!" Nick realised he had been unfair, "Well you know what I mean."

"I know!"

"Well, there you go then."

"We need three people according to Stan. Gave your name as a possible."

"Possible what?"

"Third person."

"To who? For what?"

"To Stan. When we got home from the pub the other day. Jess drunk. Sent him a text."

"You what?!"

"You could do it with us."

"Are you mucking me about? You text a major criminal to smuggle bonds into the country?"

Nick had gone very red. His dyskinesia had gone into hyperdrive as he swayed and twisted his arms around his tangled body. "Why Roger? Why?!"

"Thought you'd be ok. Jess said you would be ok." Roger's hand moved around his letter board quite quickly as he spelt out his sentence.

"Well I bloody am not ok Roger!" he shouted, "Right let's go and see Jess!" he motioned to Roger to get up.

Nick wondered what Roger's accent would be like. He knew he lived in London and spent time in Yorkshire. Was it more northern than southern? Did he have a deep Barry White voice, or a high David Beckham early Manchester United tone? Was there a bit of a stutter? Could he sing? Did he eat with his mouth open? Make a noise when chewing? Eat quickly? All these normally obvious characteristics were gone from Rogers's life. They would never return.

Nick looked at him. Roger's face looked sad. Since he'd had his stroke, he'd lost his identity, his reason for being. He had no dreams, no ambition, no "I'm going to do this or that in my retirement". He had no way of making cash legitimately, no way of improving his employment prospects, and no way of attracting a girl. He was stagnant. Stuck.

Nick suddenly had a flash of his future, sitting in a chair, unable to change the channel on the TV with the remote control on his lap, waiting for a carer to come in and feed him. Or worse still for Liz to feed him. Asking to go to the toilet. Not being able to put a cheeky bet on a horse. Never being able to go for a pint on his own. Who the hell is going to take him for a pint anyway? No one's going to want to hold and pour a beer into his mouth, while he's twitching about in his chair!

This was part of Nick's internal fight that he had going on in his mind since diagnosis. He was sure things were going to get worse; Parkinson's is a degenerative disease, so life was only going to get harder. But when? The answer was impossible to know. He often felt subtle changes with his movement as his pills wore off quicker than they used to. He also had a scary conversation with his doctor about having Deep Brain Stimulation. Full-on brain surgery as they carefully place electrodes in your head, hopefully on the parts of the brain that need stimulation. It was effective for some people, but it was a conversation he didn't want to have. Nick was not ready for electrodes in his head just yet. He'd met people who had had it and they seemed to have improved, but, no, he wasn't ready for that kind of brain-opening operation yet.

Should life be riskier while he could make that choice? Should he gamble the boredom of a shitty admin job for the possible rewards of an adventure and big money? Roger had a point. What else was there? Ok, so the odd disabled person had become famous as a sports star, actor or wealthy businessperson. But most had not. Most were kicked out of their careers and encouraged to retire or to leave their jobs, as companies and other employers hid behind their 'disability inclusive' propaganda.

But then on another day he'd think differently. How lucky he was to still be working, to have the possibility of an ill-health pension, to have pills that helped, nurses and doctors that cared, and a loving wife. There were certainly people a lot worse than himself.

That didn't help Nick though.

This was his life.

Do I, or Don't I?

What's the best thing to do?

What if?

CHAPTER NINETEEN

Jess was slumped on the couch in the living room. She had covered herself up with her bright red duvet. On the floor by her side, was a glass of water, an empty packet of crisps and the TV remote control.

Nick and Roger entered the house and immediately saw Jess sprawled out on the couch; the TV was on showing the usual antagonistic chat shows that were on daytime TV.

"Shit, are you still suffering?" Nick said, standing over her. Roger reached down and turned the TV off. He'd found over the years that Jess was addicted to trash TV. All the shows she watched involved arguing, shouting and moaning. Mainly featuring rich people or youngsters who wanted to get rich. It seemed to Roger that being rich these days involved shouting and arguing. Neither of which he could do very well. Actually, not at all.

Jess sat up and cradled herself under the duvet, "Better than I was." her hand shot up in the air. She stared, unforgivingly at the two men who had dared to ruin her daytime recovery, "What are you two doing here?"

"Well brain of Britain here," Nick put his arm around Roger's shoulders, "Has got a plan to get himself and us, locked up for a bloody long time! I suggested we came here and discussed it with you, Jess." Nick started to raise his voice, "And he tells me that you gave my name to King Don suggesting that I may help?!" he laughed sarcastically, "And to top it all, I don't know you two from Adam and Eve!"

Jess pulled the duvet over her head, "Too heavy" she bluntly said, muffled by the weight of the duvet's fabric.

"Jess, Roger wants us," he exaggeratedly circled his arm as if to indicate the three of them, "Wants us!" he repeated, "To smuggle money into the country! You have put me forward to bloody well help!"

"I know." Jess peeked from under the duvet, "talk about it another time yeah?"

Nick looked at Roger.

Roger shrugged his shoulders.

"I'd like to talk about it now," Nick asked, starting to grind his teeth.

"Not now. I'm so hung over. Stop getting on my case. You try having a discussion and following him pointing at bloody letters when you're still pissed!" Jess moaned as she peeked through a gap in the duvet, "Has Roger told you everything?"

Nick looked at Roger, "I don't know. Good question! Have you told me everything Roger?"

Roger nodded.

"Stan contacted us not long ago. We normally talk to one of his boys," Jess sighed, "I had to do the talking for him on the phone." she twitched several times under her duvet.

Nick went over to the single chair in the corner of the room. He sat on the edge of the chair, elbows on his knees, hand on the sides of his head, looking down at the ground,

"Roger did tell me he had contacted Stan whatever his name is. But you gave my name Jess?"

"Yes, don't sweat. Stan just suggested a third person may be a good idea. Obviously, it's not a good idea." Jess was becoming bored of talking when she could be sleeping. Jess was very proficient and skilled at doing hangovers.

"Ok so you are part of some criminal gang are you?" Nick leant back into the chair, "So you are smugglers then? And you want me to be one too?"

Jess pulled the duvet off her head, "Not really. Idiot, you make us sound like pirates!"

"What do you mean not really?" Nick's dyskinesia slowly started to cause him to squirm in the chair, "You either are or you're not!"

Roger left the room and returned with a larger letter board. It also had some pictures on it - a car, house, toilet, money etc. Just to make life easier. Roger pushed aside some of Jess's duvet so he could sit down on the same couch. She sighed as his body plunged down next to her feet.

"We've shipped," She was starting to wake up, "We have delivered stuff around the country on a couple of occasions"
Roger smiled at Nick.

"Like what?"

"No idea," said Jess, calmly.

"Well, drugs? People? Cats? Fruit?" Nick was becoming sarcastically annoyed, "Roger told me financial stuff."

"Yes, envelopes."

"Envelopes? Of what? What's in them?"

"In what?" Jess looked sadly at Nick.

"The bloody envelopes Jess!"

"Who knows Nick? Bondy things. I don't know. I don't understand it, do I? I was only told they might be bonds recently." Jess had no clue, no understanding and didn't want to know what bonds were or what they were used for. She didn't care either, which was becoming painfully obvious to Nick.

"Bonds you mean?" he pointed at Roger, "He told me this – I'm just checking to make sure I wasn't dreaming."

"Yeah bonds and you're not dreaming. Muppet! Muppet!"

Roger shrugged his shoulders. He held his letters board and spelt out, "We don't open them."

"So why are you telling me? I could go to the police you know!" he looked at Roger, "What would you do in my position?"

Roger shrugged his shoulders again.

"For God's sake," Nick mumbled under his breath.

"You won't go to the police Nick, you're one of us" Jess whispered sarcastically.

"What do you mean? One of you? I'm no thief or smuggler! Hell, I was a nurse!"

"People are taking the piss out of you, me, Roger, and every other idiot who can't or won't live the way they want 'em to live." Jess was waking up. "What do you mean "Hell I was a nurse"? Nurses don't steal!"

Jess pushed the duvet off her legs and onto the floor. Underneath she wore an oversized, black, rock band-printed t-shirt, and a pair of black leggings. "You've been told you can't do stuff you know you can, but because you have a stupid walk, they won't let you!"

"Yeah but..." Nick tried to give a response.

"Roger is treated like the village idiot; I get treated like a piece of scum because I shout and twitch all the time or yell Hitler or Muppet and make people uncomfortable." Jess stood up.

"We get fed up with it Nick, fed up with it all!" Jess left the room. Angry. No, she was furious.

Nick looked at Roger.

"The only thing nurses steal are pens!" Nick

suddenly paused and took a deep breath "Roger, I know your life was turned upside down, as is mine, but we can't resort to this! I'm a nurse for heaven's sake!"

"Nearly an ex-nurse" Roger tapped.

"I know and they took the piss, I know I know." Nick looked up at the ceiling, "look you must do what you have to do, but I can't be a part of it!

Jess came back in, "Nick just because we have a disability, doesn't mean we can't break rules."

"I know Jess, but it's immoral."

"Bullshit! What's immoral is being put down, buried, hidden by the shit of a society we live in!" Jess spoke quietly but sounded more deadly, "Have you seen how much they've cut my disability benefit? Who is going to employ me to make up the difference? And God knows I've tried! But still I'm being done over into a tight corner where I have to come out fighting or die!" She sat down again, nearly knocking over the glass of water that she had left on the floor.

"So sod them Nick. I'm coming out fighting! If society doesn't want us, we ain't playing by their rules."

The room went quiet.

Nick broke the silence "Yes, I understand Jess. But I do not want to be a part of it." He looked at both Jess and Roger, "Can't you try and demonstrate for disabled rights, tie yourself to railings and all that? I don't know there must be organisations that can help?"

"Forget that! People in wheelchairs have been locking themselves to Buckingham Palace for years! It doesn't work! Frankly, I don't give a shit about anyone else; I just want to improve my life! This isn't about disability rights anyway. Rights and equality are an urban myth! This is about me!" the tirade flowed from her mouth.

"But it's wrong."

"Get off that horse Nick."

"I can't do it."

"Ok, ok we hear you. We shouldn't have mentioned it."

Nick got up to leave, "I won't tell anyone about this." he looked at Roger, "Mate, I know it's tough, and I know why you're doing it, but if you get caught, you are screwed!"

Roger looked at him. His face was deadpan, he shrugged his shoulders. A long thick, wet string of spittle started to climb down from his mouth. He whipped it away with a handkerchief that had been scrunched up in his pocket.

"Look no hard feelings hey?" Jess stood up to follow Nick out of the room, "If you change your mind let me know soon. It would have been good to have you there."

Nick opened the front door, "Jess, I doubt it. I wish you both luck"

CHAPTER TWENTY

Nick took a long time to walk the short distance home from Roger and Jess's house. Occasionally his right foot would do its usual twist into a clawed mess of pain, forcing him to stop for a few minutes until it untangled itself allowing him to continue on his way. It didn't happen on the way to Roger and Jess's house, but as he was hyperstressed it was happening on the way home.

His right foot was his main issue. He knew that eventually his whole body would be affected by the disease but that damn foot spasm drove him up the wall. This added to his impatience but did not help matters, as it just prolonged the agony. Alcohol helped him to relax and seemed to help the problem, but he couldn't stay drunk for the rest of his life.

Finally getting home after his start-stop walk, he went to the kitchen and took out of the fridge a bottle of coke that had been half drunk. He downed the contents and threw the bottle in the bin.

Knowing the house was empty he let out a massive burp. There is nothing as satisfying as downing a cold bottle of fizz when you are thirsty. But Liz did not like his animalistic tendencies. If she'd been in the house during his explosive burp, a loud shout of "disgusting!" would have echoed around the house.

Nick could not stop thinking about what had happened today with Roger and Jess. He had been offered the chance of an exciting adventure and he did have to admit it intrigued him. But he knew he wouldn't do it. He was adamant that he would never see Jess and Roger again. He couldn't take the risk of being associated with them and of course, this was a shame; They'd had a few good laughs together and had a lot in common. But how could they pull him into something without even knowing him? They didn't seem to be like that, the type to break the law.

But they were smugglers.

At least they weren't smuggling drugs, or diamonds from an African mine dug out of the rock by child labour. They weren't part of a people smuggling ring or sexual slave traders. It was just money. Just money? It was still probably all linked to theft or fraud, dodging tax, or someone getting richer out of someone's loss. But he didn't have to be a part of that world. He'd always done what was "right" and "just". He did not want to be looking over his shoulder for the rest of his life waiting for a SWAT team to jump on him when he did the Friday night shop at the local supermarket.

Liz finally came home after what she felt was a long, tortuous day at work. She was knackered. She was always knackered. Walking into the house she dropped her coat off her shoulders and hung it on the hook in the hallway.

"Hiya Nick! Do me a favour darling, pour me a large glass of wine please."

Nick went to the fridge, grabbed the half-full bottle of wine and poured most of it into a large wine glass. It was unusual that there was a half-bottle of wine in the fridge, as normally any wine left would have been polished off during the previous evening by the couple.

As Liz walked into the kitchen Nick passed her the glass, spilling a little as he always did due to a shake in his outstretched hand.

"You're a bit shaky tonight? Missed a dose?"

Nick hadn't. He had been exact with his pill-taking timings all day. He shook his head.

"You look lost. What's wrong?" Liz sipped her wine looking at Nick with concerned eyes.

"Er, no nothing, I'll tell you later."

"You look a little pale. Why don't you go and sit down, I'll just get changed." Liz climbed up the stairs, wine glass in hand.

Nick went and sat down in the living room. He and Liz had been married for 20 years. They had no children as neither really wanted them. They went through the motions of trying to have kids, but Nick was to discover that he couldn't produce the goods, so it kind of took the pressure off. In the end, what was meant to be, was. They replaced the cost and time of having kids by enjoying tasty food in restaurants and drinking decent wine. Occasionally they would spend a few quid on a night away in a good hotel probably costing as much as a week in Skeggy with two kids in tow.

The sturdy foundation of Liz and Nick's relationship was that they were the best of friends. Yes, they argued and bickered, but ultimately they enjoyed each other's company. They laughed at themselves and with each other and just generally got on. Of course, they were in love, and they did all that romance stuff too, but the backbone of their marriage was friendship and spiritual kinship. He told her everything and she told him everything. Except when Liz bought new shoes. She tended to keep that quiet, seemingly smuggling them into the house. Nick often laughed and was amazed as her collection of footwear grew larger and larger. Liz's shoes multiplied like reproducing Gremlins having had water thrown over them.

"Liz I've never seen those boots before" he would say pointing at a pair of black knee-high boots in the corner of their wardrobe, "Saying that, I've never seen those blue ones either!"

"You were with me when I bought them Nick. Don't you remember? Your memory's getting worse!"

Surprisingly, Nick never did remember being 'with her' when she bought the shoes,

"Are you sure?"

"Yes, Nick! We got them in town years ago. How can you not remember!" It was at this point Liz would change the subject or just wink at Nick.

He wasn't against shoe buying. It was her money. He just couldn't understand why one person would want so many pairs of shoes! He also didn't understand why she never told him. He liked her shoes! It had become an issue without being an issue. Perhaps one day when they were rich and needed therapy the shoe shopping mania would be analysed as the result of some childhood trauma. Until that time Liz would continue to sneak shoes into her wardrobe and Nick would continue to be amazed at his wife's ever-growing shoe-hoarding collection.

The two had met on a distant, cold Christmas Eve. They were both waiting for a taxi at a rank. The queue was long and didn't seem to be moving. So they just started chatting. Nick was hammered after a heavy seasonal drinking session with his mates after a long dehydrating shift at work and Liz had been visiting a friend and was stone-cold sober. Eventually, as a taxi came, they both got in it and dropped Liz off first before getting Nick home. He'd managed to get her number though and remembered her and their conversation the next morning and the rest as they say, is history.

Liz worked as an administrative assistant for some big bank and eventually gave it up and ended up working in the care world. Nick had just qualified as a nurse but always said he wouldn't work with or for Liz in any of the nursing homes she worked in. Nick wasn't a great fan of non-clinical people telling him what to do. They tended not to know what they were talking about and the thought of Liz being his boss probably would have destroyed their marriage.

And now they were both in the midst of a new chapter as Nick's illness deteriorated and unfortunately that time had come when he was unable to do his job and Liz knew that they had passed another stage in disease progression. She was fully aware that he was going to be a pain in the arse if he didn't work and the thought of Nick being unable to work was scary. She knew she'd have to support him, direct him and guide him. He'd need motivation into doing something or he'd go mad, and she'd lose patience with his moaning. She'd get on with it and keep smiling, that's what she signed up for. She knew if it was her facing a difficult disease Nick would do the same for her.

CHAPTER TWENTY-ONE

Liz came back downstairs holding an empty wine glass. She had on a pair of tight, light blue denim jeans and a white t-shirt. Sitting down on the sofa she looked, concerned, at Nick.

"What is it?" she put her empty glass on the coffee table in front of her, "Is it something to do with Roger this morning? I knew something had happened! I could see it!" she leant forward and stared at Nick, "Your right arm is giving away your stress by going barmy! I can read you like a book! Tell me Nick! Don't play about Darling."

His right arm was going barmy, flaying and drawing unusual invisible patterns in the air.

"I don't think they are who we think they are?" he said sternly, trying to calm his movements.

"What do you mean? Who are you talking about?"

"Roger and Jess." he looked at Liz, "They are bloody smugglers!"

Liz started laughing, giggling, as she reached for the TV remote control that was on the table next to her glass.

"Don't turn it on, not yet!" he knew she was about to put on some depressing news programme.

"Why do you think they are smugglers Nick?" she turned to Nick again.

Nick told her the story. How Jess and Roger participated in delivering stuff to shady solicitor's offices, and what they proposed to do. He explained that Jess had put his name forward to join them, to perhaps one of the most dangerous men in Britain and how upset he was by it. Liz listened intently. She couldn't believe what she was hearing. But she was becoming intrigued and strangely excited about Jess and Roger.

"So are these bonds real? Fake? Stolen?" she whispered but had no idea why she was whispering.

"Don't know."

"Are they American, or English? Where do they come from?" Liz asked. This time she wasn't whispering.

"Liz, I don't know!" Nick put his head in his hands, "I don't know anything about it. Just that they smuggle bonds! And I don't want to know anything!"

"How much do they get paid?" she returned to whispering.

"Liz I didn't ask that! The fact is they are smuggling!" Nick told her what Jess had said about the discrimination that she had faced and the fact that there was no way of improving her life, so she had to take control of herself. Hence, she helped Roger with his deliveries.

"I agree with her. Nick, as soon as you're fifty you're written off in this world! Never mind if you're struck down with an incurable illness or have a life-changing accident" she looked at Nick, "No one expects it to happen to them, then Bang! Your life's upside down!" Liz was getting animated and a little scary as she spoke, "I think she's got a point. It's dog-eat-dog, and you're only going to end up as a patient where I work in the end, wetting yourself! And then there is no difference in life! You could be paying £5000 a month for private nursing or have the state pay it for you, either way, you get the same card! And I have no idea if Bill in room 4 is an axe murderer or Marion in 12 was a lawyer. Come on Nick! We all end up in the same place, staring at four walls, listening to shit music and pooing ourselves!" the hypocrisy of her job seeped into her frustrated face.

Nick tried to calm the situation down,

"Bad day?"

Liz left the room and returned with another glass of wine.

"They are going to cut our budget and make redundancies. We can't do what we do with what we've got! Never mind losing another member of staff! Greedy thieving....!"

"I thought they made a massive profit last year?" Nick asked, bemused. He was sure she had mentioned it last year.

"They did and they'll do it this year." she took a large sip of her wine, "But as ever they are pushing and pushing. I'll have to lose two full-time carers."

Nick frowned, "Jesus, the world's gone mad!"

They both sat still. Liz took another large sip of wine, "We better have another bottle somewhere Nick!" Liz was not even close to finishing the drowning of her depressing day in wine.

Nick laughed, "Yeah, I'll get it in a mo. So should I start practising walking through customs?" Nick chuckled.

Liz smiled, "Why do they think you could do it Nick? I mean I can tell when you've stolen one of my chocolates! You just can't lie!"

"They believe that no customs officer is going to stop someone who's dribbling and moving oddly!"

"Don't be daft, they're not that stupid!" Liz finished off her wine and went to leave the room to find the other bottle, "You'd look so guilty, your symptoms would go through the roof! You'd be so stressed!" she shouted from the kitchen.

Nick smiled. Got up and went into the kitchen. He slipped behind Liz and cuddled her, his arms tight around her waist, "Would you visit me in jail?"

"Oh that's nice," she liked being held tightly, "Yes I'd smuggle you a file in a cake. Where's this bottle then?"

"Somehow I don't think I'd be very good at filing my way through prison bars!" Nick bent down, opened the cereal cupboard and pulled out a new bottle of plonk.

CHAPTER TWENTY-TWO

Stan Tennant was not a happy man. He had just been moved to a different wing and was getting fed up with the upheaval. It happened now and again for security reasons but this time it was for refurbishments so he could not argue or rather dictate his wishes to stay. He'd also not long ago discovered that his latest parole hearing had been postponed again. His lawyer was doing her best, but even at the prices she charged, nothing seemed to be happening. The wheels of the British justice system turned slowly.

Stan had become used to prison life after all the years he'd spent locked up. After a change of cell, wing or even prison it never took him long to throw his weight around and get back to how he wanted to live inside. His reputation did go before him and that saved a great deal of time. His name alone would have changed the pecking order and culture of any prison he was in. He could quickly manipulate the odd screw, governor and copper. Money and violence, or the threat of violence, were particularly useful tools. After every move he was able to run his business from his cell or office as he called it. He had access to phones, and computers and there were always colleagues locked up in the prison system who worked for him. Ever since his first sentence, Stan had always been a workaholic and only stopped for two days at Christmas, and that was because no one else worked. He was proud that some of his best business deals had been conducted from his cell.

Occasionally Stan had taken young prisoners under his wing. On their release, back into the big wide world, they continued to be on his payroll. Loyalty was important. By being loyal to these kids inside the prison they were loyal to him outside. All he had to do was ring them. He could settle scores with a phone and a couple of hundred quid, and thanks to mobile phones with screens he could get involved in watching torturing and other more "hands-on" roles of the business.

Stan joined the criminal organisation pretty much straight from university. He'd just finished a three-year degree from Nottingham in economics, first class with honours, and was considering what to do next. He decided to go to London for a few days to see what the big city could offer him. Maybe a city job, marketing or accountancy. He could do it for a few years, earn a few quid whilst he decided what he really wanted to do. He had a couple of interviews lined up for his visit to the city. Nothing inspiring but all well paid.

Reading a paper with a glass of red wine in a pub in Soho on his first Sunday afternoon, he was rudely interrupted by a man who barged in shouting profanities. A sawn-off shotgun was tightly locked in the intruder's shoulder, barrels facing at two gentlemen sitting quietly with a brandy each at the back of the room. Both men continued to smoke as they looked coldly at the potential cause of the end of their lives.

Stan quietly put his paper down, took his glasses off and proceeded to beat the shit out of the guy with the gun.

"I can't concentrate if you come in and start shouting at people!" he spoke in a soft voice as the man lay on the ground. "Now please go!" the man couldn't move quickly enough and scurried out of the pub. The two men looked aghast at him, one of them accepting the gun from Stan as he passed it over. Stan calmly sat back down and continued reading his paper.

He'd been in fights before, and quickly discovered he had a talent at a very young age. His dad noticed his vicious talent and quickly put him in boxing gloves and took him to the local gym. As he got older, Stan felt boxing wasn't his sport, and so he learnt a variety of martial arts and other fighting skills. He excelled at Boxing, Judo and Jeet Kune Do. His knowledge of different fighting crafts and his controlled demeanour meant that he was able to protect himself and hurt anyone who upset him. Badly hurt them.

The two men at the bar happened to be the infamous Grimshaw brothers. A notorious surname on most police databases in Europe. Stan had never heard of them, but after a further glass of red, he'd managed to secure himself a job. The brothers, appreciating his talents, offered him the job of 'protector'. They wanted him to accompany them everywhere and move in to 'neutralise any threat'. This very rarely happened as you had to be stupid to try it on with the Grimshaw brothers but there were stupid people out there. One of which had just entered a pub and tried to kill them.

The Grimshaws were big players in an international crime organisation that made colossal amounts of money from drugs, robberies, extortion and any other crime you'd care to mention that enabled them to make lots and lots of money. Stan was now on the bottom rung of the crime ladder in his new career. Within three years he ran London. Then the UK and now Europe. He sat on the top table of the crime syndicate after his meteoric rise of violently bringing in a great deal of money for the organisation.

He hadn't had a proper fight for five-odd years now and still kept in touch with the last remaining Grimshaw brother, who unfortunately had to be taken into a nursing home due to dementia. The other died of bladder cancer years before he should have done. Shame.

The routine in prison was the same every day. Wake up, get breakfast, have association, lunch, association, dinner, association, bed. Association could be going to work involving gardening, making stuff in the factory on-site, education and other therapy classes. When the prison was short of staff, or something happened, a fight, suicide or drug search, then you were banged up in your cell as the whole place went into lockdown. This could happen over several days or weeks. Meals would be brought round, which was very civilised, though you were stuck between four walls.

Over the years as staffing levels of prison officers dwindled, lockdowns became more frequent. Prisoners became more agitated, especially in the heat of summer when they were stuck sweltering in their cells. This resulted in the odd riot. Riots had become a useful cover for Stan's business ventures. It was strange how someone always died tied to a chair during a summer riot.

Having a slightly raised blood pressure Stan had a daily appointment in the healthcare block to pick up his pills. He had had it for several years now, and even though he was toned and slim, fit and agile he still had high blood pressure.

His wife put it down to stress, but he never felt stressed. Ever. Every morning he'd wander through the gates, get to the healthcare block, a screw would let him in and then see the nurse on duty that morning. He had half the nurses on his payroll. They were easy to recruit. Money talks and the nurses were paid sod all since some private company had taken them over. So, his daily nurse visits were an ideal place to pick up mobile phones or anything else he'd requested.

Stan never touched drugs. It wasn't the fact he didn't approve, he earned most of his money from drugs, he just didn't get involved. Mug's game. He was far too high up the ladder to worry about the need to put powder up his nose. It was something to be sold to the customers, or idiots as he liked to call them. Most of the time he had someone else get his phones or deal drugs, but he liked to get stuff from the nurses himself. He enjoyed the conversation. It was real and he liked to hear what was happening on the other side of the wall. Several of the nurses would put the kettle on and he'd listen to them moaning about this and that and talk about their families and what they did at the weekends. He'd always clock the information, knowing that he might use it at a later date, but he also liked a bit of a social natter.

The nurse manager was his biggest pawn. A total chatterbox. Stan knew everything about him. Everything. Senior staff nurse Michael did a lot for Stan. He'd learnt very quickly that working for Stan was a pretty sensible thing to do. Ok, so senior staff nurse Michael's beloved dog had to mysteriously die, but it pushed Michael through the correct door and so Stan was happy, which made Michael happy. More relieved.

Michael often made sure Stan left the prison for hospital appointments that he 'urgently' had to attend. Of course, these were a cover for business meetings in person. He'd be chained to two screws, who would take him to the hospital canteen, put a long chain on him, and sit at a table behind Stan, who would have his associates queue up to sit down with him and have five minutes with each. Of course, the screws with him turned a blind eye enabling him to have in person meetings on an almost monthly basis.

The obvious obstruction to getting out of prison for a hospital visit was of course security. The prisoner shouldn't know the time of the appointment, let alone the day, as then it would be easy to get some mates to meet at the hospital, Whack the officers with a cosh and you're off into the sunset. Stan had to know though, so he cut a deal with prison security, a lot of cash and a promise he wouldn't escape. Stan didn't want to escape - he needed a life without looking over his shoulder. He wanted to be out on fair terms and the idea of plastic surgery was not welcome.

Stan's wife Sue had stuck by her man for over

twenty years. She met him at a party put on by the Grimshaw brothers. It was some celebration for the opening of a new business, a car sales room. Sue didn't look like the type who would fall in love with a gangster. She was quite prim and proper, had a very posh accent, and looked a bit like a librarian. She had small glasses, and her hair was always tightly pulled into a bun. The librarian look was finished off with her love of brown and autumn colour clothing, ensuring that she never stuck out in a room.

Sue and Stan got on, fell in love and soon they were married. Sue knew what Stan's business was, but never spoke about it. Even when he was sent to prison the first time it was never discussed. Sue just got on with it. She'd try and visit Stan at least once a month, sometimes even three or four times. The officers would fall over themselves to make sure Sue had what she wanted, a cup of tea, a biscuit and a pen (she always asked for a pen for some reason), and that Stan was aware of what they were doing for his wife. She wasn't too happy the time he was moved to the Isle of Wight. Sue wasn't a fan of boats and made the Southampton ferry trip over to the Island with gritted teeth. But she got her head down, faced her fears and got on with it. She was relieved though when he was moved back to the mainland due to an 'accident' on the yard.

Sue and Stan never had children. They both

wanted them, but it didn't happen. Sue pushed Stan into the idea of fostering, but an hour with the social worker broke his spirit and they never took it further. Far too much paperwork and questions he didn't want to answer. Sue regretted it for some years, but she started breeding dogs, Golden Retrievers, and that became her passion. They had the land for it. She had won competitions with her dogs, but most were sold as puppies. Stan used to love getting up early in the morning and taking the odd dog for a long walk around their fields. A simple life for a not so simple crook.

But to get the simple life he needed to get out of prison. He had more than enough money to live an extremely comfortable life and when the next international job had been completed then he would be thrust into a different league. The only problem was that he was still banged up in a not-so-cosy cell. Even all his wealth would not and could not turn the Home Secretary to release him. Even Stan Tennant had to follow the bureaucratic rules that had miffed and stifled numerous releases: The Krays, Ronnie Biggs, Charlie Bronson and now Stan Tennant.

Stan would have to wait and play the game. A game he needed to win.

CHAPTER TWENTY-THREE

Stan wanted to make a phone call to his most trusted employee Jason Morrison. Jason had worked for Stan since he was a teenager and along with his partner Sam Wyatt had forged a reputation for being able to encourage others to do what they were told. He had a few minutes before six, when the telephones were accessible to prisoners. There was one phone on the landing, and two or three inmates started to queue up eager to talk to their loved ones. Due to the case that there was only one phone for the landing of 80 inmates, the calls were limited to eight minutes. Stan always made longer calls on a mobile phone, but sometimes he would make a quick call on the landing phone as he didn't want to go through the rigmarole and risk of using a mobile. He also knew that all prison calls were recorded, so sometimes he would like to act like a regular prisoner and use the landing phone to stop any awkward suspicion. Although he had the run of the prison it could get complicated and bad for business if his manipulation was blatantly rubbed in the authorities faces. It's much better to be under the radar.

As he left his cell and reached the end of the corridor, the queue of prisoners stood back, allowing Stan to go straight to the phone.

"Thank you Gentlemen, that's kind," he thanked the other prisoners as he walked past, "I shall be quick."

No one replied. They knew the score.

Stan put his payment phone card in the slot, and then tapped the phone number on the phone.

"Hello Mr. Tennant," the voice said as soon as the call was picked up.

"Evening Mr. Morrison," Stan coughed, clearing his throat, "Any news?"

"I think it's going to be just the two parties for the trip. Unfortunately, the third does not wish to go. Our two friends spoke to him last week and haven't heard from him yet."

"Mr. Morrison that is a shame, three would have been more suitable. Will you try and organise the third yourself, maybe you can sell the benefits with greater savoir faire than our friends can?"

"Of course Mr. Tennant. I shall let you know how I get on."

"Thank you," with that Stan hung the phone up and walked back to his cell.

Stan entered his cell, sat on his chair and

poured himself a glass of lemonade. His mouth was dry, he had a lot on his plate, and he needed the next job to go well. His contacts were ready, he just needed his team to go. But he wanted three people. Three people to spread the risk and to make it look more natural. It had to happen in one month's time, or he'd miss the window of opportunity that had been created by his Italian associates.

Stan had been looking at the demographics of the organisation and realised that maybe they didn't have the best people in certain posts. Yes, they needed the meat heads to crack skulls, but the business also needed variety and he felt there wasn't a wide enough diversity of staff. He had been looking at skills that would optimise profit. Profit was the name of the game, nothing more, nothing less. Therefore, he was becoming passionate about getting the best candidate for each role.

The smuggling job he was organising needed staff that had something different. They had to be invisible but also able to prey on people's fears. There was a fantastic amount of money at stake, and it had to be right. It had to be perfect. Using Roger and his friend Jess seemed perfect to him. It would be difficult for any customs officer to read their body language as their body language was not straightforward. Their own disabilities had made them difficult to read, and to understand what they were thinking. The addition of the third person was believed by Stan to add a bit more credence to the operation. Jess and Roger would just look like an odd couple whereas three people would look like they really wanted to go to the conference on neurological disorders that was to be their cover for the trip.

He just needed that third person to agree, and it was very disappointing that the third person hadn't so far. He knew they would though.

They always did.

CHAPTER TWENTY-FOUR

Jess opened the cupboards in the kitchen. She peered into each cupboard then discovering there was nothing nice to eat she slammed the doors shut.

"I'm starving Roger!" she moaned, "I'm going to ring for a Chinese to be delivered, I can't be arsed to cook and I'm not walking to get it!"

Roger was still sitting in the living room; he had the TV on and was watching the news. He tried to ignore her somewhat selfish statement.

Jess picked up her mobile from the kitchen sideboard and rang her order through.

"I don't think we should have involved him," she walked into the living room having ordered a meal. Roger was glued to the television, "I mean he is right, we have only just met him! I don't know Nick or Liz from Adam, Rog. They could be cops or tell the cops anyway!"

Roger stayed looking at the TV and nodded his head.

"I guess I'm just being paranoid," Jess twitched

her head, "I'll leave him a couple of days more and then contact him, just to see he's ok. Would be sad if we lost them as mates."

Jess didn't have many friends. She was exceedingly difficult to get to know because she put up such an aggressive protective shield. All she was trying to do was not get hurt. She knew that people tended not to understand her Tourette's. She craved company, friends, even a boyfriend would be nice, but she didn't make it easy for strangers to get close.

She had tried being nice, but eventually, her tics would become more evident, her language more embarrassing and the whole relationship would fall apart. As soon as she and a potential friend were to leave a noisy bar where the conversation had previously been difficult, her true Tourette's would kick in as it was no longer hidden by loud music. This would result in the newly acquired friend starting to back off. Then ultimately disappear for good.

Ok, so she knew that she was taking risks and was being used by doing the 'deliveries' for Stan, but who wasn't being manipulated in their life? Someone's always creaming the top layer off any job, wherever people work.

Jess felt it sad that all three of them couldn't be supported in meaningful employment due to their disabilities. The overseas job that she had been offered, the crime of smuggling, organised by Stan Tennant, would financially reward her because of her disability! She was wanted because of her tics and offensive language! The money was fantastic, and the upcoming adventure would definitely not be boring.

It was just a shame that Nick didn't want to get involved.

CHAPTER TWENTY-FIVE

Detective Inspector Craig Bullen had an untroubled home life. His wife of 20 years, Mandy, was still as beautiful as when he'd first met her on a lad's holiday in Malaga, dancing to some Euro crap music in a ropy club, sangria flowing. Their drunken eyes met over a sticky dance floor in "Bar New York" and the night ended with Mandy throwing up all over Craig's shared hotel room. Luckily the two guys he was rooming with were still out, and waking the next day, remembering nothing, his two friends blamed each other for the dry vomit splattered on beds and the floor.

Craig and Mandy had two almost grown-up kids, Matt and Sophie. He doted on his family, and he always loved doing things with them. Holidays to Spain, Greece, Lake District and Cornwall had been their destinations of choice over the past 20 years. Craig had taken Matt to football practice when he was younger, they also did a bit of rock climbing and as Matt got older, they had become more like mates than father and son. Sophie, being the apple of his eye, was experiencing the protectiveness of her father as every one of her male friends were vetted and grilled if they were brave enough to venture into the family home. The rows Sophie had with her father concerning her social media accounts were legendary on their street. If he saw one bit of flesh in her selfies or photos of nights out, he became overbearingly, irrationally protective using his 'police presence' to gently lean on any boy he saw in her photos. Unprofessional maybe, but she was his little girl.

Sophie gave up in the end with that particular social media site and changed to another social platform. One that her dad didn't know about yet. If her dad had seen her recently posted photos? Well, his Taser would have thrown off more electricity than the National Grid if England achieved penalties in the World Cup final.

His family were so important to him that he would have taken a bullet for them. He loved and adored them, and they loved and adored him. Life was perfect. Of course, they had their ups and downs, but they always got through them and always stuck together.

Unfortunately, and out of character for the loving father, Craig was keeping a secret from his family. He couldn't talk to Mandy about it; he couldn't talk to anyone about it. His secret was starting to worry him, eating and gnawing at his thoughts. He didn't like it, but he did not want to worry his family.

"Craig, what's going on?" Mandy had said as they were getting ready for bed. She sat down on the bed and slipped her cream nightie over her head, tidying her blonde hair once the nightie was on. It was obvious that Mandy went to a gym regularly, the muscles on her arms were very defined especially as she had a dark tan from their last holiday. Craig always thought she was a bit thin for her height, but he was very proud to have her on his arm at various police events, knowing that his colleagues would always compliment her.

Craig put his head out of the en-suite bathroom.

"What do you mean?" he had a mouth full of toothpaste and as he spoke he sprayed some of it onto the top of his bare chest. Disappearing back into the en-suite Mandy could hear him rinsing his mouth out.

"You're not right darling. What going on? Is it me?"

Craig gave out a large sigh.

"Nothing is going on Mand. Everything is fine."

"But you're not yourself I can feel it."

"Probably work. It's stressful. Can't tell you details as it's all a bit hush-hush."

"No, it's not a work thing Craig," she stood

up from the bed and pulled her nightie over her legs and straightened it, as it snugly clung to her body.

"Oh right." Craig sounded bored.

"You're not having an affair are you?" Mandy asked getting into bed.

"For fucks sake. Course I'm not! When do I ever have time for an affair," Craig walked into the bedroom, wearing a black pair of tight-fitting boxer shorts.

"You would tell me wouldn't you?"

"Mandy I am not having an affair. It's just work!" he hoped that she would listen to what he was saying.

"It's not that woman you work with?"

"What?"

"The one who works in your office. You know what's her name?"

"Jane?"

"That's it."

"No Mandy I am not having an affair with Jane." Craig was getting angry and agitated. He so wanted to tell her about what was going on with his health but knew she would worry even more.

"Somethings going on Craig. I know it." Mandy sat bolt upright and looked at her husband, "I know you. I know when something's not right!" her voice became louder.

"Ok, ok" Craig got out of bed and pulling a dressing gown on went to leave the room.

"Where are you going?"

"Downstairs to get a drink." Craig lied. He knew he had to leave the room. He'd go downstairs and see what was on the television. He just needed to avoid any kind of argument.

As he left the room he called back, "Mandy I am not having an affair. I Love you!"

Mandy didn't answer.

❖ ❖ ❖

His neurology appointment day finally arrived. He went on his own and was in the consultant's office for about half an hour. During that time she moved, bent, and assessed every limb of his body. The neurologist also looked into his eyes and asked about his work, life and family diseases. She listened to his speech, prodded him with a sharp needle and softer cotton wool whilst his eyes were closed, watched him walk and pushed and pulled him to see if he'd fall over.

Craig had no idea what she was doing but was happy to have someone have a thorough look at him. The consultant neurologist said that she had requested some tests and scans and would see him again when they had been completed.

Craig didn't want to ask her what she thought it was and she didn't offer her thoughts. She just said that she may have a clearer picture after all the test results come back.

Her blasé manner put Craig at ease. He'd

talked himself into the fact that her nonchalant conclusion was probably a good sign.

The next few months seemed to last forever. Craig had to undergo various tests from the torment of spending 20 minutes in an MRI scanner to explore the depths of his brain, to the delights of a lumbar puncture and nerve tests. Each time he had a new diagnostic procedure his mind wandered to the scariest thoughts he had had. If he had a disease that made him mute like the witness at the post office robbery, how would he cope? Would his kids still love him, and would Mandy stick around?

After the barrage of modern medicine's testing, all he had to do now was to wait for the neurologist to give him an appointment, tell him it was nothing and then he could get on with his life. His symptoms seemed to have disappeared over the last few weeks, but he did have a strange time when he momentarily stumbled, causing great hysterics from his colleagues in the police station's car park. He didn't hit the deck but rescued his fall with a kind of complex dance move that kept him on his feet at the same time entertaining half the police station staff.

Mandy still believed something wasn't quite right with her husband. He wouldn't tell her anything. Claiming all was fine, that he was just tired. She even went as far as to ring his best mate from work, who told her he hadn't noticed anything out of the ordinary. So maybe she was just imagining things? She knew her husband though but couldn't put her finger on what was bothering her about him. He was just "cagey and more pensive" than normal. She discounted an affair. She knew he'd never have an affair, but there was definitely something. Something was troubling his soul.

CHAPTER TWENTY-SIX

Over the next week, Nick thought about the opportunity he had been offered. He thought about little else. He wanted to have a bit of excitement in his life but the more he thought about it, the more he thought it may not be such a good idea. Nick had always had lofty ideas and never take them to the next level. He'd always bottled things at the last moment. Deep down he was scared. Scared of doing the wrong thing, scared of looking like an idiot and scared of being judged. He had boasted that he never worried about what people thought of him. But he did. Over the years he had discussed projects and business ventures over some beers with friends. Told them they could make millions and be free of their bullshit lives. But when the cold light of day hit and with a sober head the excitement evaporated.

"You still thinking about it?" Liz asked Nick as they both sat in the living room. Liz had a glass of dry white and Nick had a bottle of lager. On the table in front of them was a plate full of dry roasted nuts and crisps. Alcohol and nibbles had become an unfortunate normal evening habit.

"I think you should go for it! What's the worst that can happen?"

Nick finished munching his mouthful of peanuts, "I don't know. Ten years locked up in a shitty cell somewhere?"

"They wouldn't lock you up! You'd be a nightmare in prison. For a start they'd have to give you your pills every four hours! You'd cost them a fortune!"

"Thanks. I love you too!"

"No seriously what is the worst that can happen? I don't know. Would you get ten years?"

"I looked on the net and the average time for money smuggling is 27 months," Nick took a swig of his beer, "that's over two years. Good behaviour I guess you're talking a year and a half. But then I've lost my job and any hope of a pension. You'd bugger off with the plumber and I'll come out of prison homeless."

"Window cleaner!" Liz said abruptly correcting her husband.

"What?"

"I would not run off with our plumber, it would be the window cleaner. He's gorgeous! That bloke who fixed our boiler stunk of stale cabbage!"

Nick didn't answer, briefly trying to imagine what stale cabbage smelt like.

"You know I'd support you in anything you want to do Nick."

"I know. But that? I couldn't do it Liz. I know the money would be good, and if I didn't have this stupid disease I may be up for it, but I don't know." Nick made his normal excuses.

"The point is you do it because you have Parkinson's Nick. You wouldn't do it if you didn't have it!"

"I know. I know. It just isn't right though, I've only met Jess and Roger, what half a dozen times? And they ask me to do this crazy smuggling thing with them? Come on that ain't right."

Liz nodded, "Yes I do agree, it's a bit weird."

"So I'd be an idiot to do it?"

"Maybe? You'll never...."

The knock on the door was very strong and forthright. Liz and Nick looked at each other startled by the force of the knock.

"That's a copper's knock!" Nick joked. He knew it would be the little old lady selling the "Watchtower" magazine. She had the heaviest knock but was just a small elderly smiling lady selling her magazines.

"Don't be so stupid, go and see who it is," she ushered Nick with her hand towards the front door.

"I know who it is, it's that woman who flogs that magazine."

Nick stood up and went to the door. Through

the glass he could see two figures. That wasn't the usual little old lady. He cautiously opened the door.

"Er, hello?" he asked.

Standing in front of him were two smartly dressed men looking directly at him. The taller of the two was wearing a grey suit, and had a clean-shaven face, with greying short hair. The second, younger by about ten years, wore a black suit and sported a full head of blonde hair.

Nick automatically thought they were selling something, could even be Jehovah's Witnesses taking over from the elderly lady whilst she gave her knuckles a rest. He relaxed at this thought of two blokes wanting to sell him the word of God and was just about to say "no thanks" as he pushed the door to.

"Mr. Goldsmith?" the older man asked, "Mr. Nicholas Goldsmith?"

"Er Yes."

"My name is Sam Wyatt, and this is my colleague Mr. Jason Morrison."

"Er, ok, how can I help you?"

"Can we come in?" the tall man asked.

"Er, excuse me but who are you?" Nick was feeling a little aggrieved about the slowness and awkwardness of this sudden evening social interaction taking place at his front door.

"Mr. Goldsmith, my name as my colleague has said is Jason Morrison, and we would like to discuss a business opportunity with you on behalf of our business associate."

"Ok, that's good, and who is that? God? Jesus? Mr. Hoover and Mrs. Dyson?" Nick a bit pissed off and a little nervous, started to stutter and his arm started to snake out by the side of him as his Parkinson's symptoms kicked in.

"Mr. Tennant." the smaller man answered.

"Who?" Nick was baffled.

"Mr. Stan Tennant. He is our business associate."

Nick thought for a second. He knew the name but couldn't place it.

"Stan Tennant." as soon as he said it to himself he knew. His mind quickly flashed back to the card that had been sent to Roger by Stan Tennant. Nick intuitively knew that standing in front of him were two extremely dangerous men. His arm and trunk began to sway as the stress ramped up his movement.

"Well yes, um, you better come in." he nervously said and turned and shuffled down the hall with the men following behind.

"Er shut the door please," he called to the last man coming through the door.

Liz was still sitting on the sofa, glass in hand, her feet comfortably tucked underneath her.

"Who was that Nick?"

Nick entered the room, the two men behind him,

"This is Mr. Morrison and a Mr. Wyatt." he looked at Liz, trying to indicate to her to make room. Liz sat upright on the sofa, and Nick ushered the two men to sit down on two single armchairs whilst he sat next to Liz.

"So who are you two? I can tell you now, I probably won't buy anything" Liz smiled. "Unless you're from Ernie? Nick, they're not from Ernie are they? How much have we won?!" Liz suddenly felt excited at the thought of a premium bond win. A big win was possibly about to be revealed to herself and Nick. She'd read that if you won the monthly draw, a man in a suit would arrive and break the fantastic news. Maybe they travelled in pairs now? She couldn't think why, but didn't care then, she just wanted the cheque!

Nick laughed, uncomfortably, "They're not here to sell anything darling, and they are not from the premium bonds people. They are here to talk 'business'."

Mr. Wyatt leant forward in his chair, "Is there anywhere quieter we can go Mr. Goldsmith?"

"Hey whatever you say to my husband, you say to me!" Liz informed the two men, "Who are you anyway?"

"Yes, yes, here is fine, we can talk here." Nick confirmed, "They're friends of Jess and Roger darling."

Liz suddenly stared at Nick, "You're joking?"

"No no, they are, I'm sure"

"Well they work for us yes," said the blonde man.

"Liz, these two gentlemen work with that chap I told you about who Roger and Jess work for."

"What the one in prison? I thought that sort of stuff didn't interest you?"

"It doesn't, er didn't." Nick stood up, "Would you like a drink?" he asked the two men.

"No thank you," Mr. Morrison calmly said, "we won't be here long."

"Ok, sure."

"We are here to offer you the opportunity to go to Italy Nick. Rome to be precise."

"Well that seems good!" Liz smiled, "I think..."

"We would like you Nick, and just you, with our two other colleagues to go to Rome next month." Liz slipped her feet under her bottom again, and took a gulp of wine, sheepishly realising it was not her who had been invited to Rome, "There is a neurological conference happening there and it would be useful for you to attend."

Nick looked bemused, "You want me to go to a conference? I thought there was more to this job than just a conference?"

"All you have to do is go with our two colleagues to Rome, attend the conference, and then all three of you come back to England."

"Sorry I don't understand. I thought they smuggled stuff for you?"

"I wouldn't think of it as traditional smuggling Mr. Goldsmith."

"But why am I going then? If I agree to go? Are you going to slip something in my suitcase?"

"No, everything you take and bring back you will be aware of."

"So why can't your colleagues go without me?" he couldn't understand the proposal.

"We need three of you. It looks more natural and more chaotic shall we say."

"Chaotic?"

"All three of you have an element of unique attributes due to your unfortunate disabilities. We have found on other similar operations around the world that you are 75% less likely to get stopped by any border guards or customs."

"Really?" asked Liz, "I love the way you think my husband's problem with not being able to stay still is a skill!"

"Really Mrs. Goldsmith. Our experience shows that there is a great deal of discrimination in this sector and well, we are taking advantage of it. We are exploiting the naivety and lack of equality to our advantage. We are not trying to make fun of you, we want to hire you. You are the best people for the job." he looked at Liz, then back to Nick, "We know what we are doing."

"So I'm not carrying anything illegal in my suitcase?"

"I would say that you will meet our Italian partners and they would discuss the job with the three of you." the man smiled, his teeth were perfect as he grinned, "I think they may ask you to bring one or two packages back to the UK. But only small and nothing to be worried about."

"Small packages?" Nick looked at Liz. Liz shrugged her shoulders.

Nick had to ask, "So what's in the packages? Drugs? I'm not taking drugs through customs!"

"I agree Sir! No drugs!" Mr. Morrison said wholeheartedly.

"Well, what would it be?"

"Bonds Nick, old bonds"

"I guess it's illegal?" Nick asked, obviously knowing the answer.

"Only if you get caught." answered Mr. Morrison, "And I am sure the Italians will help and advise you."

Liz was looking nonplussed about the whole affair and asked: "What happens if Nick doesn't want to do it? We did speak to Roger and Jess, so they know Nick's feelings on the subject."

"I know and that's why we thought we'd visit personally, come and discuss it with you. Put your mind at rest. We wanted you to know what the situation was so that you make an informed decision."

Nick looked at Liz, "I'm still not sure...."

Mr. Morrison reached into the inside pocket of his Saville Row suit and pulled out an old-fashioned leather chequebook holder and handed it to Nick.

Nick opened it and saw his name on a cheque. He looked back at Mr. Morrison and then at Liz.

"We'll pay you the same when you get back."

Nick handed the wallet over to Liz.

"Jesus H Christ!" she whispered, "Just for carrying back a package?"

"And not getting caught."

"And not getting caught...." Liz repeated the words, "Of course he'll go! Won't you Nick, you'll go!"

No one said a word.

Nick's alarm went off on his phone breaking the silence. He turned it off and picked up two torn-off strips of medication that were on the table and took two of the yellow pills. One large and one small. He reached over to Liz, took her wine glass and washed the pills down.

"Ok I'll think about it," he said once he'd finished the tablets and mouthful of wine.

The two men stood up.

"Ok, Mr. and Mrs. Goldsmith. Thank you for your time, we will see ourselves out." the two men went to leave the room, "Nick, I will ring you in two days. I'm sure you'll make the right decision. Unfortunately, I feel we may have told you too much, so if you don't do it, we will have to discuss our non-disclosure policy." Mr. Morrison turned to Nick and smiled, "goodbye."

"Oh don't worry I won't tell anyone" Nick promised.

"I know. Our non-disclosure policy would also cover your wife. Nick, our policy would ensure you both are unable to say anything or tell anybody. It involves a couple of bullets. Do you understand?" The atmosphere had suddenly gone cold, violent and unpredictable.

Nick slowly nodded his head. He couldn't believe he'd been openly threatened.

Nick ensured the front door was well and truly locked once the two men had left and returned to the living room. Liz was still holding the wallet open staring at the cheque.

"That's a lot of money Nick."

"I know." He said sitting down "I know." he looked at Liz, "Will you pour me a glass of wine, I'm seizing up here!"

Liz got up and left the room. She returned a minute later with a three-quarter full bottle of white wine and a glass. She poured a full glass of wine and handed it to Nick,

"You going to do it then?"

"I don't think I have much choice." he took a large sip of the wine.

"Course you have…"

Nick cut in, "Liz these are major criminals, they are not going to let us just go. We know far too much, didn't you hear what that bloke said."

Liz looked at him, "Lot of money, isn't it?"

Nick finished his wine and put it on the table,

"For Pete's sake! Trust me to be married to a shopaholic with a shoe habit, who's just been given the chance to buy the entire Imelda Marcos' collection of shoes supplied to her by her mug, twat of a shaky husband!"

"Good boy." Liz smiled, gently slapping his cheek several times.

CHAPTER TWENTY-SEVEN

Nick had agreed to meet Jess at the park on one of the benches. The grass still had the tyre markings left by the bike after the post office robbery. The weather was a little cooler than it had been and hence Nick wore an old, brown coat that he had had for years. Every autumn he'd promise Liz he'd get a new one in the summer when they were cheaper for the following year. By the time summer came, he had forgotten about the coat and hence the cycle would continue.

Sitting on the bench Nick looked across the grass in the direction that he presumed Jess would come from.

"Boo!" a voice startled Nick from behind. Turning around he saw Jess appear from a bush.

"What on Earth?" he stood up, "How long have you been there?"

Jess joined Nick and they both sat on the bench.

"I've only just got here. I wasn't hiding or

anything! You can cut through from the road. It's quicker!"

"Well let's not do that again. You nearly gave me a bloody heart attack!"

"Oh, come on precious, you'll be ok!" she said sarcastically.

The two sat in silence for a few minutes looking over the broad stretch of grass in front of them.

Jess broke the silence, "Sorry about everything Nick."

Nick didn't answer.

"I didn't want to drop you in it. I just thought that you'd be ok with it."

"You hardly know me Jess." Nick looked down at the ground.

"I know, I know." she paused for a second, "I was being impulsive" her arm suddenly twitched, "See I can't help it!" she laughed.

Nick chuckled, looking at Jess.

"How the hell did I get myself into this shit?!"

Jess smiled, "It'll be fine."

"Oh, you think I'll thank you one day?" Nick interrupted.

"Yes, that's it. You'll thank me one day!" Jess clutched Nick's arm, "Stick with me kid. I'll take you far!" she sounded like an old boxing coach who had just found the next Mohamed Ali.

She didn't let go of his arm.

Nick smiled, a little uncomfortable about Jess holding his arm. It felt quite protective, without being too personal as it would if she had held his hand. She squeezed his arm and then let go.

"I feel a little trapped Jess. Two scary blokes come into my house and let's face it they didn't give me a choice on whether to be involved or not!"

Jess listened whilst looking out over the park. She knew that she and now Nick had become involved in a world that was alien to them both. Yes, she had dropped off some envelopes to various solicitors' offices before, but that just seemed like a bit of a courier job. Nothing dangerous or illegal.

Smuggling stuff into the country was a whole different ball game.

"Did they tell you how much you are going to get paid?"

Nick nodded.

"It's a lot hey?"

Nick nodded again.

"Game over isn't it if we do this?"

Again, Nick nodded.

"You stopped talking?"

"I'm bloody scared Jess. We're taking all the risk!"

"But we get a crackin' reward for doing it!"

Jess's mobile phone rang. She reached into her inside pocket and pulled out one of the oldest phones Nick had ever seen. He chuckled at the fact Jess tugged up the small aerial to answer it.

Jess started to speak into the phone, then

stopped and offered it to Nick.

"What? Who is it?" Nick had no idea that he was going to speak to someone. Who would ring him on Jess's phone?

He put the phone to his ear and nervously said hello.

"Ah, Nick. How are you?"

"Fine. Fine. Who is this?"

"Nick. My name is Stan Tennant. I thought I'd call to make sure you are happy with things?"

Nick didn't speak. He was shocked. On the other end of the phone line was one of the most notorious gangsters in UK history. This man, this killer was talking to him in the middle of a park!

"Nick, I've chosen you three for a reason. You are perfect for this role. All I want you to do is go and have an educational experience at the conference, have a beautiful meal, a beer or two and then come home. Rome is a beautiful city with beautiful people! I know it well."

"Ok," Nick whispered.

"Don't worry about anything else. You will be safe, I shall be watching and in control of everything. It won't fail and you three will be top of my list of protection." the line went quiet, "Nick I've done this before, there is no one better to work for. Any questions?"

"Er. Nope. I think I understand everything."

"Good. Put me back onto Jess."

Jess spoke to Stan for a few minutes then hung

up.

She looked at Nick. His world had suddenly become smaller than it was five minutes ago.

"We are being looked after Nick."

Nick looked pale as the weight of what was going on suddenly became a great deal heavier.

"He looks after his staff Nick. No bullshit. Well paid. No politics. No 'you can't do that' or bloody pointless sickness interviews if you're ill, no crappy appraisals or bullshit HR! He doesn't care who or how we are. He just wants the job done. End of!" Jess's arm flew up in the air.

"Jess, I've been bullied into a situation that could ruin my whole life just because I have a funny walk and can be a bit slow sometimes. Oh yes and occasionally look like I'm inebriated!"

"Good. You are getting work for who you are and what you can do. Not to tick a box or meet a quota! You've been bullied out of a career you loved and now you are being bullied into a new career! Happy days!"

Nick looked at Jess. She was right. His eyes had been opened to the bullshit the world spouted off about how the disabled should be involved but weren't. Protected by legislation but if you wanted to use it you had to pay a fortune to a leeching lawyer and then you'd probably lose! It was not easy to prove disabled discrimination. He had been castigated out of his career because of his Parkinson's and now he was being employed because of his Parkinson's and was

about to be paid a massive amount of money.
"Yes, you're right Jess. Let's do it!"

CHAPTER TWENTY-EIGHT

At work and awaiting his test results, Craig put on a brave face and continued to try and do his job. He'd try and block out all his fears, but every now and then a little seed of doubt would creep back into his head, throwing his concentration.

Craig had been asked by his senior commander to go to London, to New Scotland Yard. He had to attend a meeting regarding a possible crime that may be committed in the UK in the following six months.

He had endured this type of meeting before. He never knew why he and some of his less urban colleagues had to attend such boring and very irrelevant, intelligence-led meetings. They always had nothing to do with anyone outside of London, Manchester or Liverpool, and maybe at a push Birmingham. But on orders from high up he and thirty or so fellow regional representatives made their way up to the big smoke to drink coffee and listen to the latest crime intelligence.

Sometimes the meetings were led by Interpol, MI6 or the FBI. They'd either been following some drug dealer or terrorist and were warning the local national police that something could potentially happen in their region. Thankfully Craig had never been involved in a terrorist attack and knew how difficult and complicated they were to police against. He would much prefer reconnaissance on a couple of guys doing a drug deal in the local Premier Inn.

Grabbing a chair at the back of the meeting room, he took his jacket off, sat down and took the lid off his coffee to cool it down. He didn't want to speak to anyone as he'd come across as being rude and off due, to his anxiety regarding his imminent medical news.

The meeting began with talk of US Treasury bonds that were smuggled 13 odd years ago into Switzerland, involving the Japanese, Italian mafia, blah blah blah.

Craig broke off his concentration almost as soon as the presenter had started to talk. The fact that this related to something that happened 13 years ago was a definite indication of where this was going.

Nowhere.

He did his best to cover up a deep yawn and took a sip of his black coffee. He could feel his leg starting to twitch. Crossing his legs didn't help, so he tried to sit as still as he could to endure the jumping of the skin on his thighs.

"..............and we believe Stan Tennant is masterminding the UK side of the operation........."

Craig looked up suddenly, that name had triggered his interest. "Stan Tennant" was a name he'd not heard for a very long time. Stan Tennant was a major crime boss in charge of a very large international crime family. Craig thought he was still in prison. He must be. There's no way he was out at the moment.

Craig leant into the woman sitting next to him and asked her if Stan was still in prison. He'd recognised her as his equivalent in Cornwall. She confirmed that as far as she knew Sam Tennant was still in prison.

Craig concluded that he must be conducting his business from inside the prison walls. Well, he was more than powerful enough to do so. An extremely dangerous and evil man.

Although Craig had nothing to do with Stan Tennant, he had dealt with some of his victims who were placed in his area under the witness protection scheme. A pleasant middle-aged couple had witnessed Tennant and some of his heavies kidnap a man from the house opposite theirs in a leafy North London suburb. The couple was happy to testify but the consequences of their evidence hadn't been explained to them. During the trial, they had been threatened by Tennant's henchmen and hence the couple were rapidly moved under witness protection to Craig's patch. A year later they disappeared. Gone. Never to be seen again.

That's how dangerous Stan Tennant was. He had managed to find the innocent couple in hiding and probably got his revenge.

Focusing back on the meeting he heard that the airport and ports had been put on alert as it was expected that a massive smuggling operation was potentially going to happen in the next six months. The UK police were to work with Interpol, the Americans and European police including border forces to gather more intelligence on where and when this was likely to occur.

Eventually, the meeting ended as tediously as it had started. It only took about an hour and as it ended Craig and the other representatives stood up and exchanged a few pleasantries before leaving the meeting room.

"Craig! Beer?" a couple of his colleagues called after Craig.

"Another time guys. I have to go!"

"Just a quick one Craig?"

Craig stopped walking and shaking his head replied, "No thanks, another time! I have to go!" he quickly made for the stairs and out of the building. Craig would have loved to have stayed for a couple of drinks, it always ended up being a full-on night. But his thoughts were elsewhere, and he just wanted to get home to his family.

Back on the train returning home, Craig

couldn't help but wonder if he actually needed to be at today's meeting. Surely a memo would have sufficed. It wasn't guaranteed to happen in the UK either! Never mind Craig's sleepy small town. In reality, there wasn't anything Craig could do about it until he knew more about what could possibly happen and Scotland Yard were none the wiser at the moment.

"A total waste of my time." he muttered as he tried to get comfortable in his seat, "A total waste."

CHAPTER TWENTY-NINE

"What time are you going out Nick?" Liz called up.

"Jess said about seven. You not coming?" Nick was brushing his teeth in the upstairs bathroom. He needed a shave but really couldn't be bothered.

"No, I don't fancy it. It was bad enough going clubbing when I was a kid. Plus you are the ones going to Rome. Not me."

Nick had to agree. He hated clubs and "discos." The queuing up to get in, handing over your coat for a ticket that could never be found at the end of an evening after seven pints, fighting for half an hour at the bar just to get a beer, followed by a night of horrendous teenage pop music, watching and dodging drunk blokes and underage youths making complete idiots of themselves.

He put on a black pair of trousers, black shoes, and a shirt he'd worn once last summer. It was a conservative blue in colour and didn't get worn as it had migrated to the back of the wardrobe and was too much hassle to try and get it for day-to-day use. That's how he decided on his fashion wear for an evening. If it was to hand and convenient, pop it on! If it was going to be the slightest bit of hassle to get it - don't wear it. Hence, he often wore the same shirts repeatedly. Liz had tried on many occasions to tidy him up, and get him to dress smarter, but failed miserably.

Nick wasn't a scruff. He would get suited and booted when required: Posh restaurant, wedding, or funeral. He looked quite good in a suit. But when it didn't matter, he tended to have the middle-aged male, fashionable look of 'at home'.

He descended the stairs and walked into the living room where Liz was sitting, a book in her hand.

"Tuck your shirt in Nick" she ordered, as she stood to do up the few buttons that were too fiddly for Nick to do up.

"Do you think? I've no idea now what people do with shirts on a night out now. To tuck or not to tuck that is the question?"

"It would look more stylish." Liz pointed out, "You're not eighteen anymore."

Strange how Liz was slowly beginning to sound like his mother. Admittedly, she was becoming 'her' mother, which was even weirder and slightly disconcerting.

Nick tucked his shirt in, "It looks bad no matter how you cut it."

"You look lovely darling." Liz sat down, her eyes returning to her book.

Nick sat down. He had about twenty minutes until the taxi was due to pick him up.

"So what sort of work has Roger and Jess done for this guy before?" Liz placed the book down on her lap.

"Well other than the job Roger did when he was younger, I think they've just done delivery jobs in the UK. Picking up stuff here and dropping it off there."

"All seems a bit odd when it's just bits of paper. A lot of mucking about"

"Liz, I've no idea what they do." Nick smiled, "Be interesting to see how invisible the three of us are tonight though. Will we blend in the dark streets and seedy bars? We are going to stick out badly! I mean, I don't look great with my arms all over the shop! Jess, you can hear effing and Jeffing a mile away! And Roger? Well enough said I think!" Nick chuckled. He did not have the motivation to go but knew if he didn't Jess would be extremely annoyed.

"Who's got the practice-run drugs then?"

"Jess. Well, she's got a bag of sugar!"

"Can't you get in trouble for impersonating drugs?"

"No idea," Nick laughed, "I don't think the law cares about nicking someone with sugar – but trying to sell it as cocaine may not go down too well with the buying public! But I don't know Liz."

"You don't seem to know much Nick," Liz stated.

"No, I don't. They just want to prove to me that they can smuggle stuff in anywhere because no one's going to go near and search Roger if he's drooling or Jess if she's having to tic all over the shop!"

"I know why you're doing it Nick. Well, no one's going to search you either! Not with your arms flouncing all over the place!"

"Oi! You wait. I'll be dribbling like Rog one day!" Nick smiled.

"You already do dear!"

"Well, we shall see if the 'disabled don't get searched' theory works!"

"If you make it home, please don't be too drunk. I may need to do some interrogation of you myself!"

The banging at the door broke the banter,

"I'm presuming that's Jess?" he went over and kissed Liz before walking towards the front door, "Keep the door on its hinges Jess!" he laughed as he went to open the front door.

The taxi was waiting on the road and Nick could see Roger in the front seat and Jess walking to get in the back.

Before Nick ducked to get in the taxi, he patted his pockets, "phone, yep. Wallet yep, pills no!" he quickly turned around and stumbled back into the house to get his pills.

"Where you going?" shouted Jess after him.

"Forgot pills" she heard him say as he went through his front door.

Jess opening the back door of the taxi shouted, "Muppet! Muppet! Bill Clinton! Come on Nick!"

CHAPTER THIRTY

The taxi ride took about twenty minutes to get to the centre of town. Roger was not looking forward to this. He feared they'd stick out like sore thumbs amongst the throng of Friday night revellers. Not necessarily because of their disabilities but because they were all too old for clubbing and weekend partying.

Who wants to go to a club with three old gits leaning on the bar frustratingly waiting to get served? They looked like the parents of the kids who went out into town to party. Roger had on a pair of black trousers that probably had 'HMP' on the label, with a dark patterned shirt and his normal coat and shoes. Jess wore a grey trouser suit that she probably borrowed from her mum. It fitted her comfortably, but she looked as though she just come out of court for breaking an ASBO. Nick appeared to look uncannily like someone who worked in a TV rental shop.

They arrived in town and paid for the taxi. Jess stopped the two from men walking any further.

She appeared to have a plan that she wanted to share,

"Ok, gentleman. The Pig and Whistle first."

The three walked up together to the pub at the top of the High Street. Outside stood a bouncer not much taller than Nick, in a dark suit with a yellow band on his arm, he ushered them straight into the pub. Inside a few people were sitting at the bar, but it was pretty empty.

They found a table, which was not hard. Jess went to the bar for a couple of bottles of beer and gave one to Nick.

"We didn't get searched!" smiled Jess, "Easy!"

"It's early Jess. I don't think they're that bothered at the moment. I mean there's no one here really to sell drugs to!"

"Yes, I guess you're right. Well after these drinks we'll go where they search everyone."

"Where?"

"The Black Orchid"

Nick looked at Roger. "What the hell is and where is the Black Orchid?"

Roger shrugged his shoulders.

"It's a meet-up for a lot of people before moving on to clubs. Very loud!"

"I don't know how people come to these places?" Nick asked rhetorically.

"Come on Nick you were young once! Just get into the spirit of it all. We might as well try and enjoy ourselves."

"I hated it when I was a kid. Anyway, at

least you don't have to shout in here, there's no music ..."

At that moment, a loud burst of music filled the bar as the DJ on the opposite side of the pub started to do his stuff.

Nick put his hands out "Typical" he shouted over the uninvited racket.

Roger shrugged.

"It's not that bad," Jess leant forward shouting in Nick's ear.

Nick took a large gulp of his beer. The pain of the music was evident in his scowling face.

After five minutes of looking at each other, pretending to enjoy the music, Jess started to get her bag and phone together, "Come on then you old farts, let's go."

"Where?"

"Where I said! The Black Orchid!"

The three stood up but hadn't noticed how busy the pub had become. Roger couldn't put his stick freely on the ground, so he hung on to Nick as they both shuffled through the crowd.

This was hell, thought Nick, trying to get past people without knocking their drinks or banging into someone's girlfriend, starting World War three. When your balance is poor anyway, one of your legs is stiff, and you have uncontrollable movement, it's really difficult to guide a bloke who has had a stroke. Nick prayed for a Moses moment whereby the partying drinkers would part in the middle enabling safe passage to the exit.

At the front door, Jess smiled at the guy in the suit with the yellow armband and said, "Goodbye." she then did a twitch and yelled "Muppet! This doorman sells drugs!" into the outside air.

"You are joking?" the bouncer suddenly grabbed her arm. Jess spun around clearly shocked at being held.

"What did you call me?" the bouncer stared at her threateningly.

Some of the people waiting to get into the pub were also confused as to why she had suddenly called the bouncer a Muppet and accused him of selling drugs.

Jess broke free and managed to move clear of the inquisitive crowd of young clubbers who had gone from muttering to each other to waiting for Jess to reply to the bouncer.

"What the hell is going on?" screeched a girl with thick jet-black eyebrows last seen on Ming the Merciless, evil foe of Flash Gordon.

As soon as she could, she started to run from the pub. Nick and Roger got to the door and saw her disappearing up the road,

"Jess! Hold on," Nick called out to her, oblivious as to what had just happened.

"Hey mate what happened there?" he asked the bouncer.

"She just called me a Muppet! I've never even seen her before!"

"And she said you had a small dick" a girl shouted, laughing from the queue.

"Oh No! She didn't mean it mate, she's got Tourette's."

The bouncer started to let the eager drinkers enter the pub, "Well I didn't know that pal. She needs to get it sorted, probably wise not to come back here."

Nick was just about to retort when Roger pulled him away. It just wasn't the time or place to explain to the bouncer the concept and consequences of excluding groups of people. It also probably wasn't worth it.

Nick composed himself and then walked after Jess. Roger hobbled on behind him. Eventually, they found her sitting on a bench in the empty marketplace. Nick sat down next to her, she was staring into nothingness,

"You all right?"

"Yep."

"I don't think that bouncer realised Jess."

"Oh, it's not him. He probably is a Muppet. It's just that, well you know."

Nick followed her gaze into nothingness,

"Not really" he smiled.

"Well, I can't go anywhere, or do anything, because people just can't handle it. They get embarrassed or take offence like that tosser did!" she sighed deeply, "All I wanted to do was see if we could get fake drugs past a bouncer, to show you that people don't notice people like you and me."

"We passed on the drugs part, but failed terribly on the getting noticed bit!" he laughed.

"Yes I know, but for the wrong bloody reason!"

"So maybe we need to show people that we are disabled in some way, like those badges or lanyards that some people who are deaf wear? I mean it's not obvious that you are not just shouting out to people, or that Roger and me are not drunk."

"Oh great, I might as well have a sticker on my forehead!"

"Bit extreme."

"Is it? I guess there's a place for such labelling Nick, but not in town on a Friday night! I sometimes think I'll get one of those cards that explain Tourette's from their website."

"Yeah, perhaps not in town!"

"Why can't people just be nice to each other? Why do you have to be wearing a badge with 'I've got a hidden disability' on it before people are polite and civil to you? Just be bloody nice! Simple."

"Yeah, and I guess it's like, why do we have a diversity director job being advertised at my hospital?"

"Yes, why? Just everyone be nice. Just get on with it!"

"Great T-shirt slogan. 'Just be nice!' I'll get some printed!" Jess smiled.

Roger eventually caught them up. He was

breathing quite heavily and sweating. He motioned for the two to let him sit down. Nick stood up to give him his seat. As he sat down, Roger accidentally broke wind, diminishing the seriousness of the situation.

Jess burst out laughing.

"Let's have a beer in The Oak House." Nick suggested smiling, "It's only up the road and I'm sure it will be quiet."

Roger nodded and stood up, pulling Jess with him. Gaining his balance with his stick the three walked, shuffled, and limped towards The Oak House.

CHAPTER THIRTY-ONE

Nick hadn't been in The Oak House pub since he was about eighteen. It used to be a complete dive and had a certain clientele who would frequent the place. This was often bikers, leather jackets smelling of petunia oil, and a general rag-tag of alternative people. His group of friends often ended up in the pub on a Friday night as there was no dress code, the music wasn't stupidly loud and generally there was no trouble. Everyone thought it was a rough pub and had a bad reputation, but any problems often got sorted quickly and everyone would just carry on drinking.

The pub used to have a strange morality policy too. Nick can remember being told to stop swearing in front of an older guy's girlfriend whilst people were doing coke, heroin, or smoking a joint in the toilets. He always thought that a pub that turned a blind eye to such heavy drug use probably would ignore the unsavoury language of a snake bite fuelled teenager.

Anyway, the policy of The Oak House taught him that swearing in public places was frowned upon, so maybe it was a worthwhile telling-off. He learnt a lot in pubs as a teenager and did a lot of growing up. Put him off drugs too. Why the toilets? You wouldn't eat in a cubicle, but you'd sniff a bit of Cocaine off a loo cistern?!

Roger was the first to enter the pub. He opened the large wooden door and the three walked into a very poorly lit traditional pub. A dozen or so tables and an old high wooden bar with gold chrome footrests and severely tall ancient tailored, but tattered, stools trapped in time met their gaze. The pub was not busy. There were just a group of men, four or five drinking and talking, and on another table a couple who looked like they'd never met as they weren't talking or looking at each other. Ironically, they'd probably been married for thirty years. Sitting on the stools at the bar sat a couple of guys cradling a beer each.

"What you having Jess?"

"Dry cider."

"Yes sounds like a plan, you guys go and sit over there and I'll bring them over."

Nick went to the bar, whilst Jess took Roger by the arm to find a seat. Nick followed after ordering drinks, concentrating hard to carry one of the ciders to their table. He then went back to pay and collect the other glass.

"I used to come here as a kid, about thirty-odd

years ago," he said to the barman as he gave him a note.

"Nothing's changed, mate. Still get the same people in." he dropped the change into Nick's hand, "I took over about fifteen years ago. Tried to clean it up a bit, but well, we tick along."

"It looks exactly the same in here too,"

"I know. Crap isn't it?" the barman frowned.

"Nostalgic" Nick smiled.

"Yep something like that." the barman sounded bitter and beaten by his difficult years at the rough end of the pub trade.

Nick made his escape from the obvious lack of happy banter from the bartender. He took the glass of cider over to the table.

"He's a cheerful bloke," he whispered to Roger and Jess.

"Not surprised. This place is a dump, Nick." Jess whispered back.

"I agree. But no queuing, no bouncers, can wear trainers and straight to the bar, with grumpy service thrown in. That's all you need on a night out!"

"I need a new pair of shoes, this carpet is disgusting," she followed with a cry of "Bush for president!"

No one in the pub blinked or looked around at her.

After chatting and a few laughs about their encounter with the bouncer, the door of the pub burst open. Within seconds about ten police officers had stormed into the pub. Jess looked at Nick,

"What the hell is going on?" Jess was noticeably shocked at the sudden change in ambience.

"Who knows?" Nick went to stand up, but Roger put his hand on his knee to keep him sitting.

A couple of police officers quickly ran to the toilets to check if anyone was in there whilst the drinkers in the bar were herded up and lined up against the wall. Everyone was very passive and compliant as though they had experienced regular police raids.

Jess had by now relaxed and feeling a bit cocky whispered to Nick as they were standing up against the wall, "Are they going to shoot us?" she started twitching, "This

isn't how I imagined the end!"

Nick's dyskinesia started to do its thing. His arms started jumping around and his upper body twisted and turned. At the same time, Jess's shoulder began to twitch and her right arm shot up into the air,

"Hitler!" she shouted.

A police officer walked over to Nick and Jess and standing between them asked sternly if they were ok.

"I've got Parkinson's and she has Tourette's."

The police officer looked at them both and quickly realised that they didn't appear to be making it up,

"Ok, you two go and sit down over there." she pointed to an empty table, "We'll keep an eye on you and search you both in a minute."

This left about nine people in the lineup including the bartender and Roger. Roger smiled at the officers facing the line of potential villains and began to dribble. He wiped the string of saliva away with the handkerchief he had from his pocket.

One of the officers came up to him and looked shocked at the state of the saliva-ridden handkerchief. The officer made a mental note that he was not going to check it for illegal substances.

"Name and address?" he asked abruptly.

Roger put his hand in his jacket pocket to pull out his spelling card.

"Sir, take your hands out of your pocket and tell me your name and address."

Watching what was happening Nick got up to help Roger. He was stopped in his tracks by the arm of a policeman.

"Where are you going?" the young officer asked him.

"That guy can't talk, he's had a stroke."

"Sarge, he's mute," the young officer said loudly across the pub, pointing at Roger.

After the initial shock of being outed as a 'mute', Roger was shown over to the table where Jess and Nick were. They suddenly felt as if they were being segregated. All three sat on their own 'special table' – a mute, a shaker, and an expert in profanity.

"Well hello boys, fancy meeting you two here!" laughed Jess, "The disabled table!" she twitched.

"I don't think they are going to search us you know," said Nick quietly. "This whole thing could bloody work".

As each customer was dealt with, they were thanked politely and told they could go and sit back down again. Within what seemed like a lifetime, the customers were back at their original tables and the barman was talking to the officer who appeared to be in charge.

Nick stood up and started to walk to the bar, he felt another drink was needed. It wasn't every day that he was in a pub when the police decided to do a drug raid. In fact, it had never happened. He was once in a pub when a fight broke out and the owner locked the front door, to keep everyone in until the police arrived. Big mistake. The whole pub got trashed whilst people tried to break out. Cowering under a table, Nick managed to get through the broken front door and thus wasn't there when the cops arrived. Note to bar owners - never lock the front door. It's better to let those inside walk out easily to avoid the police thus keeping your business intact.

"Sir! excuse me where are you going now?" asked one of the plain-clothed policemen. In hindsight, the officer was obviously watching the three more than they realised.

"To get a beer?" Nick was surprised at the question.

"We haven't searched you three yet."

Nick's arm started to flail. "But I have Parkinson's disease?"

"Ok. You are still getting searched though Sir."

Nick sheepishly returned to his seat. He looked at Roger and Jess with a 'well that didn't work, did it?' look.

Roger suddenly recognised the officer who had stopped Nick. It was the one from the post office robbery who cut things short because he couldn't understand him. He rolled his eyes and smiled to himself remembering the lost crime-busting opportunity.

The police officer asked the three to stand up and searched Nick and Roger. A female officer began to do the same with Jess.

Roger and Nick were clear, though Nick did have to explain his medication as it wasn't in a packet. The officer searching Jess pulled out the clear bag of sugar from Jess's left trouser pocket causing Jess to twitch suddenly, causing the officer to jump,

"Sorry! Drugs!" Jess shouted.

The officer opened the packet and put her finger in the bag and tasted the white powder.

"Sweet tooth hey?"

"Yes." she flinched, "Cocaine!"

The police officer handed her back the sugar and smiled at her, "Why have you got a small packet of sugar on you madam?"

"I like a lot of sugar in my coffee." Jess lied, "Escobar! Escobar!" she shouted, trying desperately to stop her arms from jumping. It didn't work.

Whilst Jess was justifying carrying a bag of sugar into the pub with the worst reputation for drug use. One of the police officers pulled Nick to one side,

"My name's Detective Inspector Bullen, can I ask you a personal question?"

"Er, yes?" Nick automatically felt uncomfortable.

"What were your first signs of Parkinson's?"

Nick looked at him strangely. "Why? Why do you want to know?" this wasn't the sort of question he expected during a drugs raid.

"It's a mate of mine. Been having weird feelings in his legs" DI Bullen lied. "Thought he might have what you've got?"

"Oh right ok, foot cramp. I'd walk about twenty minutes then my right foot would cramp, dystonia, it's like a twisting of the muscle." Nick acted out the twisting of his foot, "after a few minutes of rest it would settle, go back to normal, and off I'd walk again."

"I don't think he has that, he gets jumpy

muscles in his legs."

"No, not had that."

"What about a stroke?" DI Bullen asked, "Could he have had that?"

"I don't know mate, I think your mate needs to see someone."

"He has. He's just waiting for results."

Nick clocked that the policeman was actually talking about himself. The concern and worry were obvious in his frowning, scared face.

Nick put his professional head on and tuned into nurse mode explaining it may be a muscle or a brain problem. "I'm not sure it is Parkinson's, but if it is tell your mate to give me a bell. I've had it for so long that I may be able to help or point him in the right direction."

DI Bullen took out his notebook and wrote down Nick's mobile number.

"Thanks, I'll pass it on."

DI Bullen broke a small smile.

"Ok, you can all go. Enjoy your night." his colleague told the three.

"Cheers," said Jess, "What's all this about anyway?"

"Routine check," said the officer in charge as the police started to leave.

DI Bullen started to walk away. "Cheers. Thanks for this" he put his notebook back in his pocket and left with the other police officers.

As they left Nick ordered two beers and quizzed the bartender, "What was that all about?"

The barman pulled on the pump, "Reputation of this place. We get raided once a year. They haven't found anything for two years now, so hopefully that'll be it." he started to laugh, "It has scared off some of our best customers. Unfortunately, that's why we get raided. Bit of a cycle, I guess! They'll come back and the police will think, mmm let's raid them again, and then the druggies will leave, and on it goes!"

Nick returned to the table after two trips to get the drinks from the bar.

"Well, that's us done then! Our theory of 'they won't search us' has failed!" Jess whispered.

Roger shook his head. He didn't agree.

"Yep seems to have done." Nick shrugged, quite pleased as it probably meant the whole smuggling thing to Italy was off.

Roger shook his head again. He got out his letters board and pointed at the letters,

"Targeted search, not random. Different."

Jess smiled, "Good point Rog. They had to search everyone here! On the other hand, customs officers search and question the odd person who they believe to be suspicious and could be carrying illegal goods! They don't search a whole plane full of people."

Nick sighed and took a large swig of beer.

He had to agree. Rome was going to happen. He would become that smuggler.

Bollocks!

CHAPTER THIRTY-TWO

Liz kissed Nick on his cheek and did up his top three shirt buttons,

"Now are you really sure about this?"

"I don't think I can get out of it, Liz,"

"We all have choices. Have you got your pills, passport, and tickets?"

"Yes. I just need to get some water at the airport."

"Don't drink anything alcoholic Nick, you don't want to get plastered before you get there."

"I'm just going to have one glass of wine on the flight."

"Buy me some perfume darling"

"Oh come on! My mind is not going to be able to remember that. I just want to get there and get home."

"Well if you can…." Liz was putting a brave face on the situation. Underneath her manicured polished exterior she was scared, very scared that she may not see her husband again.

Although he felt that the experimental, 'they

won't search the disabled' trial they attempted in town was a failure, Nick still decided to risk his future and freedom and go to Rome. If two blokes suited and booted turned up on any doorstep on behalf of a notorious criminal gang, then maybe it would be impolite not to do what they politely suggested you should do.

Roger and Jess had finalised the final details with Stan Tennant's men, and as far as Nick was concerned, he was just going to look at the beautiful city of Rome and bring some papers back. The three were booked to go to a Neurology Conference as a cover for their trip to Rome. The conference would not only benefit the three, as they may get something personal out of attending (Stan was thoughtful like that), it was also believable that a short trip to attend a conference would be very plausible for such passengers. Stan had not only booked the conference passes and booked a lovely hotel he had also supplied cash for all expenses. As an employer, he excelled in providing staff benefits – expenses, and equal opportunities, and he didn't have a disciplinary policy. Just a permanent termination policy. This didn't involve lengthy wishy-washy meetings with unions and verbal warnings. His dismissive process just involved a quick, human resource-free bullet in the back of the head.

Nick had researched the conference. It was quite a large meeting of neurological experts and allowed patients to attend which was unusual for medical events. The conference went to a different city in Europe every two years and the last time it was in Madrid. Reading the description and looking at the pictures he thought he'd find it interesting to learn more about his own condition. He'd been to a conference before in London which he found to be encouraging regarding Parkinson's disease. He had been invited to the opening reception the night before the heavy stuff started and had a wonderful time with Liz. Endless supplies of red and white wine flowed for the delegates, no doubt backed by a big drug company. But after a couple of glasses, all moral values seemed to be not that important. As the evening drew to a close, so much wine had been consumed that those with Parkinson's stopped shaking and the neurologists started to shake.

Although this conference in Rome covered a lot of neurological diseases including Parkinson's disease and stroke, it appeared to lean heavily towards information and lectures on MS and MND. He wondered if there would be something for Jess on Tourette's this year. Unfortunately, after looking, there hadn't been in previous years.

So, he and his accomplices were set for a trip to Rome, visit a conference, see the colosseum, and smuggle back a billion pounds worth of financial bonds. The perfectly packed mini break!

Nick had managed to get his sick certificate extended for another fortnight from his doctor but knew he would have to sort out what to do with work on his return. He had an appointment with his neurologist in a couple of weeks, so he would discuss his future with him. That is if he wasn't banged up in some dark, dank cell contemplating a long couple of years in prison. If the smuggling job went wrong, he'd be seen in a cell by the prison doctor. He imagined it to be an old man, hunched back, just escaped from being banned from his last general practice for years of medical incompetence. The prison was the only place he could get a job and the complexities of a prisoner with advanced Parkinson's was about to be his newest patient.

Nick shook at the thought.

◆ ◆ ◆

Nick hated flying. It wasn't necessarily the height the plane flew at, it was the lack of control and not being able to escape if the plane were to crash. For comfort and supposed divine support, Nick always flew with Rosary beads and had a glass of wine or two on the plane. No matter what time of day the flight, he'd have a drink to steady his worn-out nerves. The Rosary wasn't because Nick was a Catholic, but because he was stressed and scared, therefore he always became very religious at 30,000 feet doing 500mph in a tube of metal. Never mind the science of flight, praying and holding a Rosary was a major part of his comforting belief that he was keeping the plane in the air.

His prayers seemed to work so far. God's side of the deal was to keep the aeroplane at 30,000 feet, and He hadn't let Nick down yet. Though Nick and Liz did endure a rather ropey landing in Alicante two years ago. This certainly didn't help his fear.

Sitting on either side of him on the plane were Jess and Roger. Roger had the window seat. Nick didn't want to see anything through the window - clouds, mountains, small houses, or the sea. He just wanted to imagine he was in a tunnel and would come out of it soon. In about two hours, and step out of the plane into glorious sunshine. Nick never ate on the plane, he just literally wanted to sit and be left alone. He needed to keep his eyes shut, pray and hopefully land at the other end. Many had tried to talk to him during flights, but he always dismissed them. Rudely waving them away with his hand.

"Nick please put that Rosary away – you're making me nervous!" Jess whispered to Nick.

Jess had been quite content during most of the flight. She had had a couple of twitches and shouted a few expletives, especially as the plane taxied along the runway just before takeoff. No one seemed to take any notice, and this put Jess at ease. The baby crying at the front of the plane probably deflected all the attention away from her.

Roger was in a world of his own. He loved sitting next to a window while flying. He was mesmerised by the view and stared at the expanse of clouds below; now and again a break in the clouds would reveal the land far below. It had been clear skies over the channel and Paris but as the plane flew nearer to the Alps it became noticeably cloudier. The sight of mountains squeezing through the clouds was strangely a comforting sight for Roger. The spiritual experience of looking down upon the planet, the sun engulfing the plane and the gentle hum of the engines permitted Roger to think of better times to come.

Nick leant his head back onto his seat, closed his eyes shut, and wondered how he managed to get himself into this situation. One minute he was an ex-nurse with Parkinson's disease working in hospital administration, stuck between whether he could retire with disability benefits or carry on working for another year, and now he was to become an international money smuggler. He still really wasn't quite sure what these bonds were and what they did for that matter, but he knew they were very, very valuable.

Why couldn't the bonds be posted? Why couldn't they be couriered? He answered his own question, realising that he was the bloody courier!

He knew he had to get on with it and there was no turning back. Payment for the job was a crazy amount of money. It was a life-changing amount for him and Liz. If he did this without getting caught, his stress levels regarding his finances and his future would vanish into thin air. On the other side of the coin though, if he was stopped, searched, and arrested his stress levels would go into orbit!

While the pilot informed the passengers that they were on their descent into Rome airport, Nick leant forward and looked either side at Jess and Roger. They both smiled at him. He smiled back. They were going to do this! This was happening.

CHAPTER THIRTY-THREE

Getting through Italian customs was simple. All three of them were herded along with the crowds as they meandered through passport control and out of the airport. Nick was pushing a trolley with all the baggage on, while the other two just carried a rucksack each. They were only there for two nights, and he couldn't understand the need for all the cases. Roger had pointed out that one of his bags was full of his liquid food and spare bits of kit for his tube feeding. Jess had no such excuse.

"Il Duce!" Jess barked as the three politely eased their way through a mass of people waiting eagerly for passengers coming through arrivals. Jess's sudden fascist outburst triggered Nick's dyskinesia, he could feel his arms beginning to move. He concentrated hard on just pushing the trolley and getting out of the airport quickly. He didn't know how the Italians were going to react to three British travellers shouting and staggering, appearing the worse for wear, drunkenly through their airport.

"Cornetto!"

"Oh hell," Nick winced.

"Oi! Do I embarrass you?" Jess smiled.

"No no," Nick grinned, "Just glad we're not in Israel or North Korea!"

"Hail Caesar!" Jess shouted.

"That wasn't your Tourette's was it?"

Jess laughed, "Correct! Just my little joke!"

"Well let's just get out of here! I don't know the Italian for Tourette's or Parkinson's!"

As Nick pushed a little faster away from Jess she shouted after him, "I'm guessing the Italian is Parkinson's and Tourette's! Just a wild guess though,"

Nick heard her laughing as he finally and thankfully saw the exit.

Outside the large glass-fronted Leonardo da Vinci International Airport in the blistering hot sun, they eventually managed to get one of the white city taxis to take them on the hour-long journey to the centre of Rome. Driving along the motorway all three of them started to get excited as they neared the city's outskirts. Nick began to relax as he gazed through the car window, enjoying the new sights and listening to Italian chatter on the radio.

Entering the city, the traffic became considerably denser and busier. Horns would start to sound off and small bikes and scooters would suddenly appear from nowhere, zipping and zapping in no particular direction.

"They are crazy!" Roger mimed, looking over his shoulder at the two in the back seat. If you didn't know Roger his mime could have been misinterpreted as, "Don't forget ...."

"Forget what Roger? Oh, he's crazy?! It's the way you tapped your head Rog!"

As they went deeper into the centre of the city the streets were thronged with tourists milling around the crowded restaurants and expensive boutique shops. It was easy to spot the holidaymaker's as they shuffled slowly along the busy pavements taking in all the smells, sights, and noises that were on offer. The tourists seemed to lack the finesse and demure that the locals had as they suavely navigated the busy streets. Even the street beggars seemed to have a little something extra about them.

The hotel where they were staying was close to the Spanish Steps, very much at the heart of the packed tourist trail. The taxi driver wasn't able to park outside the hotel due to the congestion so he stopped on a parallel road to the hotel and indicated to the three travellers that the hotel was just up the next alleyway. Thanking him and paying him, the three made their way to the hotel.

It was hot. Too hot. Nick looked at Roger as he struggled with his bags in the heat, his head dripping with sweat. Nick was also sweating profusely. He always sweated. Apparently, it was a symptom of his Parkinson's disease, but with the addition of a blazing hot sun, his shirt looked like he had swum to Rome. He was drenched. His forehead was dripping and his salty sweat seeped into his eyes.

Roger smiled at him, as he caught Nick looking at him.

"Rog, I can't stand this heat; I need to get some shorts on!" Nick was wearing blue jeans, brogues, a shirt, and a light summer suit jacket.

Roger smiled in agreement. Neither of them were expecting the extreme heat after they stepped out of the cool air that they had enjoyed in the air-conditioned taxi.

Jess suddenly stopped walking. Her suitcase on wheels abruptly halted behind her like an obedient dog.

"Where the chuff is this hotel?" she looked around at the various tall wooden doors, looking for clues.

Roger then strangely disappeared through an open glass door.

"Where the hell is he going?" Nick asked Jess.

Jess peeked through the doorway that Roger appeared to enter,

"It's the hotel!" she gasped relieved, pointing at the sign hidden behind a tall plant next to the door.

"Hotel Roma."

"Thank heavens!" Nick sighed, entering the hotel. Instantly he felt the glorious relief of air conditioning rescuing him from the torturous heat.

Jess and Nick caught up with Roger. At the end of the corridor was a smartly dressed man in a black suit, sitting behind a desk. Roger stopped, allowing Nick to go in front of him. He'd learnt that due to lack of speech, it was best to hold back at various times! His days of checking in to hotels and ordering restaurant food were far behind him. Like most English tourists abroad he had become adept at pointing at things in shops and bars but was unable to do the British shouty bit.

"Welcome to The Hotel Roma." the man said in English with a hint of a cockney accent. Although it was nice to hear an English voice, it was a bit of a disappointment being welcomed to Rome by someone who would have sounded at home at Billingsgate Market or on a city trading floor selling stocks and shares.

"Hello, we have three rooms booked." Nick eventually replied, quite pleased that he didn't have to attempt to use the little Italian he knew.

"Excellent! Can I have your passports and names please and we'll get you checked in." the man took the passports, and checked them into the computer, "Yes, we have been expecting you. If you need anything you must ask and enjoy your stay." he looked at the three on the other side of the desk, "Rome is a safe city. We will make sure all is well."

Nick thanked him, taking back the passports

and handing them to their respective owners.

"Mafia!" jumped Jess, "Thanks"

The receptionist didn't raise an eyebrow at Jess's outburst, "Enjoy Jess." he said as he typed into the computer on the table in front of him.

Jess looked at Nick, surprised he knew her name. Nick smiled, opening his hands as though opening a book to indicate that he had read her name from her passport.

Jess giggled slightly embarrassed at her paranoia.

Once they were checked in, one of the hotel staff carried their bags on a trolley to the building next door. The lift, taking them up a couple of floors was an old iron open lift, mechanical and slow. It would have been quicker to use the stairs even with all the luggage. but when in Rome....

The three rooms were next to each other on the same floor. They were the same size, and had a double bed, TV, and en-suite bathroom. The windows all looked over a courtyard, which was immersed in shade darkening the rooms. The air conditioning system was fantastic and as each entered their own room the change to a cooler temperature was welcoming and refreshing. They agreed to freshen up and meet in the bar in thirty minutes.

Jess, hot and sweaty, decided to have a quick shower. After getting dry she slipped on a yellow summer dress and some sandals, looked at the time, and excitedly left her room for the bar on the terrace. On opening her hotel room door, she saw Roger leaving his room at the same time. She called after him and he stopped waiting for her before they walked together, "Roger I need a big drink! Have you had some water? You'll need to up it in this heat."

Roger looked at her up and down. He had never seen her in a summer dress before.

"What?" Jess snapped.

Roger smiled and pretended to whistle.

"I've worn this before!"

Roger smiled and shrugged his shoulders.

"Now have you given yourself extra water Roger?"

Roger nodded. Tapping his thumb with his index finger to illustrate a nagging duck's beak.

"Well if I don't nag you no one else will!" Jess smiled, playfully slapping Roger's cheek.

The bar of the hotel was on a terrace overlooking the streets below. Looking out from the terrace the tiled roofs of Rome could be seen. Spotting a table with a large red umbrella protecting them from the sun, Jess and Roger sat down, relaxed, and enjoyed the subtle breeze. The waiter came over and Jess ordered a couple of beers for herself and Nick. Roger closed his eyes and enjoyed the heat of the sun on his face.

Nick came out onto the terrace wearing blue shorts and a plain light blue T-shirt, and brown sandals. He sat down between the two and drank half of his beer in one gulp.

"Blimey! I needed that." he wiped his lips, "That was gorgeous. Well worth the wait!" the beer was cold and refreshing, enabling Nick to forgive the heat he had just endured.

As there were now three people sitting at the table, the waiter came over to take another order.

Nick indicated to the waiter that only two of them wanted to drink, Roger stood up and pulled out his feeding tube to show the waiter. The waiter looked confused before realising what it was and apologising, walked away.

Roger shrugged his shoulders.

"So I guess the plan is to have an easy night tonight, go to the conference tomorrow, get the stuff the following day and go home," Nick said.

Jess pulled some sunglasses from her bag put them on and smiled, "let's chill first, may as well enjoy ourselves," she finished her glass of beer, "we're getting the goods tomorrow night by the way, we won't have time the following day. Our flight home is early."

"I'm up for that," Nick looked at Jess, "Hey by the way you look really good!"

Roger nodded in agreement.

Jess smiled, she didn't know how to deal with these types of compliments,

"Threesome! Perverts!" her head suddenly turned, "oh sorry,"

Roger and Nick stared out blankly over the streets below, hiding their embarrassment.

CHAPTER THIRTY-FOUR

After a late afternoon snooze, a requirement and necessity due to a few beers in the hot sun, the three met in the bar again and decided to go and find somewhere to eat. Roger and Nick still had their shorts on, and both were wearing short-sleeved white shirts. Jess had changed into her jeans and a simple light green top. The streets were still very warm, not as stiflingly oppressive as it had been, but they clearly weren't in soggy Britain anymore.

At the top of one of the small roads leading up to the Spanish steps square, was a little restaurant with tables outside. They decided to sit at one of the outside tables that littered the side street. Opposite the restaurant, still open with evening shoppers was a sparsely stocked Gucci shop. It was obviously a posh shop with expensive clobber as there was only one handbag in a brightly lit-up window display.

Jess, gazing into the shop window from the table, whispered, "When we get back home I'm going to buy a bloody expensive handbag!"

Nick laughed, "I didn't think you were into that sort of thing, Jess!"

"Hey, a girl's got to dream hasn't she? Just because I drink a beer doesn't mean I'm not partial to a drop of Champagne!" Jess started to twitch, her arm jumping into the air and then back down again. "You up to date on your pills Nick, not heard that alarm go off for a while, don't want you flouncing around as well,"

"Yes I am up to date. It's the bloody pills that cause my stupid movement. It's a side effect. I do take tablets that try and lessen some of my movement, but they can be hit or miss!"

"Pills!" Jess retorted, "You have to take pills to stop the side effects of the pills you're already on? Typical drug company thieves!"

Roger pulled out his spelling board and laid it on the table, "Just money!"

Jess agreed, "Yep, no cures just keeping things ticking over and if they are lucky the pills will get side effects and they'll sell you another pill to deal with the side effect!"

Nick glanced at people walking up and down the street, "I'd be lost without my pills. I wouldn't be able to move."

"I guess so. You ever stopped taking them, to see?"

"Only once. Not a good move. I walked like Frankenstein for a week. Had to pull a sickie as there was no way I could've worked!"

The three or rather two enjoyed their meal and drinks in the warm evening air watching Rome saunter by. Jess and Nick ate and drank whilst Roger tried to ignore the smells and munching noise of the food being eaten. Although he had become used to sitting in a restaurant or a pub watching everyone eat and drink, thoughts of resentment and jealousy would occasionally find their way into his head. He had learnt to try and repel thoughts of 'if only' otherwise his life would have been a living nightmare. He just struggled sometimes because food and drink were in every aspect of everyone's social life. Even watching football or going to the cinema or church involved a cup of tea, a pie, or popcorn. He couldn't escape it, so he had to mentally be able to take the fact that he couldn't eat or drink again.

After the meal, Roger decided to return to the hotel so that he could administer his food and fluid and then he wanted to sleep. Tiredness and fatigue had become a big problem after his stroke. It crept up on him quite slowly. Then bang! He had to get horizontal. It felt like a ton of bricks had been dropped on his shoulders and all his energy had been sucked out at the same time.

Having wished Roger a good night, and checking he was ok, Jess decided to order some ice cream. Tucking into the luxurious fresh Italian ice cream, she was rudely disturbed by the alarm going off on Nick's phone.

"Medication time" she grimly mimicked nurse Ratchet from the film "One Flew over the Cuckoo's Nest." "Ding dong, medication time!" she repeated. She'd never heard of Nurse Ratchet until after Nick had a habit of saying the same phrase when his alarm went off. He knew how to bore people and Jess decided to utter the phrase first to take away the chance of Nick repeating his tedious joke.

"Ok ok, I get it, no need to go on!" Nick took the spoon out of Jess's hand and scooped some of her ice cream into his mouth, then took a couple of pills.

"Oi, that's mine!" she laughed, a bit tipsy. "Get your own!"

Nick gave her the spoon back and indicated to the waiter for a couple more beers and another spoon.

"Nick I'll be hammered!" Jess weakly protested.

"Yep, but we are on holiday!" he smiled watching the waiter glide into the restaurant.

"To being Different!" Nick toasted once they received their cold beers. He raised his glass towards Jess.

"Exactly." she clinked her glass of beer with Nick's.

The two were getting nicely drunk in the heat of the Roman night. It had been a lovely evening. The food had been fantastic, the beer had flowed, and they had both had a giggle.

"Have you noticed something Nick?" Jess asked.

"What's that then?"

"Your crazy movement is causing your arms to drag the tablecloth off the table. My tics are working in the opposite direction and pulling the tablecloth back onto the table. So, I think we work very well together!"

Nick laughed. He looked at how rucked up the tablecloth had become.

Jess continued to giggle at what she had noticed.

"We'd have a big fight over a duvet" Nick chuckled.

Jess didn't answer. She took an uncomfortable sip of her beer.

Nick stopped laughing sensing a wave of embarrassment and changed the subject, "Jess. This thing we're doing. Do you think we are being taken for mugs?"

Jess looked at Nick, "I have thought about this Nick, and I can tell you I am not going to be mucked about with and do stuff I don't want to."

"Yes but the three of us? Is this right? I mean none of us are an advert for health. We're a bit special!"

"Special? What are you twelve? Bit offensive Nick!"

"Of course not, sorry. But we all have our problems, we are all a little, well, neurologically challenged!"

"Yeah, I know."

"So are we being used?" Nick asked again.

"I don't think so. I think these people just want to make money." she smiled, "and we are going to make a shit load out of this!"

"I know, just feels a bit like lambs to the slaughter. Plus, I feel I have been somewhat bullied into this."

"I know, but that's life. No, I believe that we are being er 'employed' by people who have common sense. They want to make money and we have the tools to help. Like a bank employing a banker, a building site a bricky."

"I agree, but they are not often disabled. If they are disabled and able to work, they still have those skills. They're not employed because they are in a wheelchair. We are being hired specifically because of our disability, not the fact that we are skilled smugglers!" Nick quaffed down his beer, "It's no different from using people with dwarfism to play in Snow White!"

"Exactly. We are being hired for our disability! Able-bodied ain't good for this job! And how often do you go into your bank and see someone disabled working there? Never, I'll bet," Jess flinched, "We are not doing this for anyone's entertainment, we are doing this to get one over on the man. We are using our problems to get a solution!"

"It doesn't feel right when I think deeply about it" Nick leant back in his chair. The air was still warm and there seemed to be more people meandering by than a few hours ago.

"You just don't see people like us as criminals – saying that you don't often see many disabled people working."

"Exactly. Disabled people are working out there, but there's more like you and me who've been shunned by the world and left to rot on the scrap heap!" she grabbed Nick's hand, "so screw 'em!"

Nick smiled at Jess. She was an attractive strong woman. Feeling mildly drunk he looked into her captivating dark eyes. If he hadn't have been so in love with Liz, in a different life he could have fallen for Jess. He was pissed.

She let go of his hand.

"Nick, since I've had Tourette's, no one has employed me properly other than Roger, because they see it as a big problem, an embarrassment. Now someone wants me because of it. Great!"

Nick, drunk, sunk into his chair, "I get it. I investigate stuff too much,"

Jess, herself a little tipsy, continued her rousing claim, "Listen, Nick just because we are different, disabled, not able-bodied, or whatever else, does not mean that we can't do anything. We can just do what we want, but maybe in a different way. My goal is to make money. I can't do it working in a shop, so I'll find another way, and I've found it!" She took a deep breath, "They wouldn't let me work in a shop anyway!"

"Someone once told me that it's not the person that's disabled it's the environment that's wrong 'cause it can't accommodate them,"

"Er Yeah, something like that! Nick you've been a nurse for however long, you telling me the health service can only use you inputting data? Can't they use you properly? Can't they use your skills and experience? Bullshit! Instead, you're wasting your time doing what you're doing. Sod them, Nick, forget them. They can't see it. They can't see the potential in you and how you'd benefit them!" The passion in her speech was extraordinarily strong, sounding like a warrior about to lead her people into battle.

"I agree! Forget 'em!" Nick was delighted that someone understood him and his situation.

The two clanked glasses.

"Fuck 'em" he grinned.

CHAPTER THIRTY-FIVE

It took the taxi carrying the three apprentice smugglers just over half an hour to get to the hotel that was hosting the Neurology conference. Nick paid the taxi driver and they walked into the hotel. All three were dressed in cooling, summer clothing. Jess wearing a white blouse and black tailor cut wide-legged trousers. Both Nick and Roger had on light-coloured trousers but Roger wore a black short-sleeved shirt and Nick a cream linen shirt, Nick also wore a matching cream linen jacket. After picking up their conference ID badges and itinerary, they wandered into a large auditorium full of a variety of displays showing what different organisations did within the neurological world, research projects, and health companies promoting their wares.

Although slightly hung over, Nick was in good spirits. He had thought long and hard about his conversation with Jess last night. He started to re-engage with his rebellious teenage years with a "don't care", liberating, no-fear attitude. He was in Rome to do a job and that's what he had to do.

Jess was a little quiet and looked slightly delicate after the previous night's eating and drinking. After a strong espresso coffee at the venue, she started to perk up and began to look forward to what was to come. She had never been to a conference before, never mind a neurology conference. She was excited to see if she could learn anything new about her Tourette's and what was being done in the science world to cure it. An opportunity, for her, that had never arisen before.

The three decided to wander around and see what was what. There were more people than expected in the auditorium, some were dressed smartly in suits which amazed Roger as the weather was scorching outside. Apparently, there was a mixture of patients and health professionals, but other than the obvious limp, or jerk, or wheelchair, it was difficult to tell who was who - patient, doctor, or anything else. But then again as Nick proudly observed, there was no reason why someone with a neurological disease couldn't be a doctor or scientist.

Jess suddenly stopped as they meandered around the displays. In front of her was a table and stand with a backdrop that read "Tourette Roma".

"Roger, come with me to see what's happening here."

She turned round to Roger, but he had drifted away from Jess and Nick. "Roger!" she whispered loudly.

Roger waved and continued with what he was doing, reading information on another stand.

"Come on Jess I'll come," Nick said, "I'm guessing it's about Tourette's in er, well, Rome!"

Jess gave him a playful dig in his stomach, giggling, "Even I can figure that out!"

Reaching the display Jess stood in front of the table and started to gaze at the leaflets on the table. A casually dressed man sat on the other side of the table, reading a book. He looked up and smiled as Jess picked up a leaflet. She couldn't understand it as it was written in Italian.

"Do you have anything in English? Sorry, I don't speak Italian," she asked the man who slowly stood up. He was tall and dark with black curly hair and wore a pair of smart jeans with a styled mauve-coloured shirt. Jess, now she was nearer, realised how handsome the man was, now that he had stood up from behind the stand. She embarrassingly spluttered "I have Tourette's," followed by an arm raised in the air, "Shit! Italiano!"

"I'm sorry to hear that." he spoke English with an American accent, "I have Tourette's too."

"Do you?" Jess seemed surprised.

"Yeah, very mild thankfully. Inherited from my mother. Didn't inherit her brains though, she became a surgeon and I'm, well, here!"

"Your mum's a surgeon? Cool"

"Yeah, it kind of is," he replied proudly.

"Is any of this stuff in English?" she asked holding up the leaflet.

"No, all our information is in Italian. There's not a great deal about Tourette's at this conference, other than the lecture this afternoon. He handed her a flyer with times and room numbers of the proposed heavy, academic presentations. Jess looked down the list, stopping at "The Future of Tourette's."

He smiled, "……and it's in English. A French neurologist. Dr. Sanguere is the presenter."

"Oh thanks," she smiled, taking the leaflet.

"I'm Paolo."

"Jess," she shook his outstretched hand.

"Hi I'm Nick," Nick, in turn, shook Paolo's hand.

"Oh, Nick didn't you want to go and find that Parkinson's thing?" Jess nudged Nick away. She didn't want Nick spoiling her conversation with this handsome man who had just entered her life.

"Er yes, yes, we'll catch up later" Nick got the hint and gingerly turned and wandered off.

"So you've come from the UK?" Paolo asked.

"Yes, I go back tomorrow. I mean well I'm here with two friends and we leave tomorrow." she looked at him, at his hands, she couldn't see a ring, "So are you an American?"

"Yes. But we moved here when I was a kid. My mother and father are from Rome. It's home to them, well and me I guess. Well, my spiritual home anyway."

"And this is your job?"

"No, I work at the US embassy. This is just some voluntary work I do."

"How long have you had Tourette's?" he asked.

"Too long," Jess could not take her eyes off him. "Are you working here alone today?"

"No, I've got the morning shift, then someone takes over. Which is great because I want to attend that lecture I told you about."

"Oh, I need to go don't I?"

"Hey, it's up to you Jess. I get a great deal of knowledge from them. He's a good speaker, you'll learn a lot and they can be very motivating for the future. You know, see what research is being done, what the scientists know……..and don't know of course."

"Yes I will go, I need to be inspired!" she was slowly melting inside, "and it will be good to hear someone French speak about Tourette's" she quipped.

"Er yes, it will." Paolo had no idea what the joke was, "It'll inspire you and give you some hope. We all need a little hope."

Meanwhile, Roger stood enthralled by a stroke research poster that was displayed on a wall. He had never seen anything like it. The posters had short descriptions of the research that had been done by various universities around the world. What they wanted to achieve, how they did their study, whether it was worth it and a lot of statistics that Roger did not understand at all. After reading a few of the posters Roger disappointedly noticed a pattern in the conclusions of the studies as they all ended with the same statement,

'Further research is needed in this area.'

"Great, lots of words but more needed," he thought, "Why bother doing all this work if it wasn't working?"

Doctors had told Roger he would never speak or be able to eat or drink again. They were right. Just after his stroke, with a tube inserted in his nose to get food and water into his system, he remembered sneaking a sip of water from a plastic glass that had been inadvertently left on his hospital bedside table. The liquid went straight to his lungs, and he suddenly could not breathe, he tried to cough but just couldn't, he felt like he was drowning, slowly suffocating. After a few minutes he was back to normal, but he vowed never to drink or eat again.

The next poster drew his attention straight away:

'Improving sex for patients following a stroke.'
'Conclusion: more research is needed in this important area.'

"No shit!" Roger thought. "It's not the fact that I can't have sex it's the problem that I can't get anyone to have sex with!" he laughed to himself. "But well done for your years of studying that subject and coming to a nothing conclusion." Roger was becoming a little sceptical about the world of research. "Just find a damn cure, stop playing about, and then we can all get on with our lives."

The last poster on the display was entitled:

'Stem cells and improvements in the stroke patients' speech - a study on rats.'
A study by Dr. Marcus Repo

That was more like it. Roger read the poster. Apparently, they put stem cells from a lab into the part of the brain that helps with speech. Simple.

'Conclusion: more research is required in this field.'

"Yep figures." he thought. Roger turned round to walk off. He was rapidly becoming bored with the whole subject.

"What are your thoughts then?" a young man, mid-20s, in a pair of trousers and a scruffy blue jumper, asked Roger in a very posh English accent.

Roger shrugged his shoulders.

"I wasn't sure at first, but having worked in

this field and studied stem cells for about seven years this paper to me, well it excites me. It was part of my PhD."

Roger nodded, he was having problems hearing him, as he spoke quite softly, Roger needed to lean in a little.

The young man continued talking, "the hardest part of this study is causing a dysphasia-focused stroke in a rat. And of course, you're not sure if you fully restore speech, rats don't talk as we understand it. But it showed that we had improved the damage done to that part of the brain." he put out his hand for Roger to shake, "I'm Dr. Marcus Repo, I'm with the Newcastle team. "

Roger shook his hand, Dr. Marcus Repo pulled his hand away, looked at it, and realised it was slightly damp. Roger habitually used the same hand to pull his hanky out of his pocket and proceeded to wipe the pool of saliva building up in his mouth. Then he pulled out his folded-up speech board from his pocket and pointed to the letters. Dr. Repo's eyes followed Roger's fingers to spell his name.

"Oh I see, can I ask you have you had a stroke?"

Roger nodded and pointed to the "Yes" on his board.

"And it affected your speech I see." Marcus subtly wiped his hand on the top of his trousers, "well I'd like to say that one day stem cells will be the future, and I thoroughly believe it. We need to do more on humans though but that comes down to money. But there is potential."

'Further research is needed' Roger pointed to the words at the end of the poster. Then Roger walked to the next-door poster and pointed at the bottom, 'further research is needed.'

Marcus smiled, "Yes, we don't know much about anything, to be honest with you. The more we do the more questions we have. But we are doing our best to try and improve things. To make lives better."

Roger made the sign of a 'T', he knew he couldn't have one, but he'd be able to sit down and chat.

Marcus looked at his watch, "yes why not. I think coffee might be better as we are in Italy!"

Roger nodded.

◆ ◆ ◆

Nick had been to a few conferences as a nurse. He enjoyed them but after a while he tended to walk around in circles or drink too much coffee waiting for the next presentation or lecture.

Today though he was starting to feel increasingly nervous about what was to come. He just wanted to get it over and done with and was hoping that the conference would have taken his mind off it all, if only for a short time.

There didn't seem to be much on Parkinson's disease at the conference and he didn't really want to know too much about other conditions. What there was on Parkinson's disease didn't interest Nick. Just studies of new drugs that would help this symptom or that symptom. Of course he would be grateful for any help in improving his life, and he had done his fair share of raising money for research. But it all became a bit disheartening cycling or running to raise a few quid from 'here we go again!' friends and family sponsoring each of his escapades.

But he wasn't in Italy to learn more about Parkinson's disease. He knew the conference was a cover, a camouflage of their task to smuggle a massive amount of money to the United Kingdom. Although he was becoming bored, he still had to immerse himself into the whole charade.

CHAPTER THIRTY-SIX

After wandering around the conference several times and finding nothing really of interest but putting on the façade of an interested visitor, Nick decided to pop outside and get some air. The moment he stepped into the fresh air he felt the heat of the sun hit him. This city was so hot. Spying a café selling ice creams across the road from the conference, he smiled to himself and decided to see what was on offer.

Having bought a vanilla ice cream, after dithering about what to have from the multitude of flavours, he sat down on a bench in the shade near the hotel entrance. A few minutes later, a lady came and sat next to him on the bench. She looked as though she was in her early 60s, wearing a white blouse and a yellow flowing flowery skirt. She reached into her bag and pulled out a book. Nick carried on licking his rapidly melting ice cream.

The noise of his alarm on his phone going off made him jump. He tried to slip his hand into his trouser pocket to pull out his phone to stop the alarm but was unable to do it sitting down. After standing up he managed to get his phone and muted the alarm. Sitting back down he continued with his ice cream. A few minutes later the annoying alarm sounded again. Luckily this time with the phone on his lap he was able to stop it straight away. Taking the hint from his alarm he slipped his hand deep into the same pocket and bought out a strip of pills. Getting them out of the packet though was going to be difficult due to the fact the rapidly melting ice cream was being held by his good hand.

Did he finish the ice cream first or attempt to break into the medication?

If he decided on finishing to eat his ice cream, he knew he'd forget to take his medication and then suddenly realise 30 minutes later. This would be too late, and his Parkinson's symptoms would get worse, his walking would decline, and his right arm would become heavy and stiffer. This was always the case when he was distracted from taking his time-sensitive and critical pills. Forget your pills then try and rush to an appointment or meeting. No chance. The disabling, twisting of the foot would put a stop to that.

Or did he drop the ice cream? Balance the cone between his legs? Or stuff it in his mouth resulting in him looking like that photo we all have when we were three years old with ice cream all over our chops?

"Sod it!" he thought.

He went for the balance. The cone gripped between his thighs, he used both hands to take a couple of the pills out of the badly designed packet and swallowed them. The irony of a pharmaceutical company making medication to ease the symptoms of Parkinson's for a patient, but the patient had to not have Parkinson's to be able to physically manipulate the pills from the packet didn't quite make sense. Having solved a crazy dilemma, Nick returned to eating his ice cream. The stress of the ice cream/pill saga had triggered his dyskinesia, and so eating the ice cream became even more horrendous as his arm and hand holding the ice cream bounced around in the air. He resembled someone made from jelly holding the Olympic torch.

He could feel the woman next to him getting uncomfortable, this in turn made him more uncomfortable which in turn increased his movement.

He stood up, still flouncing around, holding the ice cream, looking like a drunk trying desperately hard not to let go of a pint of beer.

Forget it, he thought to himself. Staggering away from the seat he threw the cone into a bin.

He'd had it with ice cream.

Nick decided he'd better return to the conference centre but first he needed to rearrange his pockets. Taking from his inside pocket he put his wallet and passport on the bench, replacing them with his phone and medication. Picking his wallet and passport up to put them in another pocket he felt himself being unceremoniously pushed over onto the ground. He felt his right hand being pulled as his passport and wallet were snatched from it.

The woman who had sat so calmly on the bench next to him not five minutes ago let out a huge scream, followed by shouting in a near hysterical manner, "Scippatori! Scippatori!"

Nick used the bin to support himself getting off the ground and stood up.

"Wanker!" he shouted, watching a moped speeding into the distance and suddenly realizing whoever was riding it had nicked his belongings.

Luckily, they had dropped his wallet, relieved he picked it up.

"Shit!" he angrily muttered through gritted teeth as it registered they still had his passport.

Nick automatically started to run but felt his leg stiffen. Standing next to the cafe he saw a bicycle. He grabbed the bike and jumped on it, getting his balance he slowly began to pedal towards the disappearing moped. Getting used to being on a bicycle again he dug into the pedals and began to get a bit of speed up, following the moped down a long, narrow side street.

He could still see the moped, but it was a long way in front of him.

His legs pumped faster and faster, his backside off the bike saddle as he pushed down harder and harder with his thighs! The moped had turned up an even narrower street, and alarmed pedestrians jumped quickly out of its way. Nick was not getting any nearer. On the contrary, he was losing it.

Getting to the top of the road a large, grand, open square rose up in front of him. Cars were quickly zooming around a statue of a man on a rearing horse proudly displayed in the centre of the square. The moped was nowhere to be seen. He stopped and scanned the square, searching the cafes, pedestrians, streams of tourists, and coaches looking for the slightest glimpse of the offending muggers.

He'd lost them, but worse, he'd lost his stupid passport.

He slowly turned the bike around and gently peddled the cycle back to the conference centre. It took about ten minutes to get back, and his legs were aching as the adrenaline wore off. He realised he'd gone further than he thought.

Outside the main entrance to the conference hotel, he saw Roger, Jess, and a man, Marcus, waiting patiently for Nick.

"Bloody hell Nick – I've never seen you move so fast!" Jess blurted out, amazed at the sudden athleticism Nick had just shown.

Roger smiled at Nick.

"We saw what happened, did you get your

things back?" Marcus, who was standing next to Roger, asked.

"What did they get?" Jess asked.

"My passport," Nick replied, breathing hard, "How the hell am I going to get home?!"

"You didn't get him then?"

Nick shook his head.

"Ok Roger, I have to go, so when we start our new stem cell research in humans you will be the first patient!" Marcus smiled at Roger. "Unlucky my friend. But you went off like a rocket. I'd be inclined to ring the embassy for advice and of course the police." he told Nick.

Roger shook Marcus' hand and watched him go back to the conference.

"Bugger it!" Nick whispered angrily under his breath. His hands dropped lower on the handlebars as he dropped his head through exhaustion and disappointment.

Roger pointed at Nick's face.

"What?" Nick asked, wiping his mouth of the ice cream residue.

Roger did the thumbs-up sign.

"I need a beer" Nick sighed, "A big beer!"

"Anyway boys, I just wanted to say, I'm off to a lecture then being taken to dinner." a broad grin flashed across her face, "So don't wait up, and make sure you ring the embassy Nick" Jess began to walk back into the hotel.

"But what about tonight's....?" Nick called after her. As far as Nick was concerned, they were meant to pick up the bonds from their Italian contact tonight.

She turned round walking backwards, "You don't need me for that. After watching you ride that bike I think your Parkinson's has gone anyway!"

"Oh right then, just you and me then Rog. What time are we picking up this stuff, eight?" Nick was becoming agitated due to the heat and lack of fluids, "I hope you know what the plan is Rog!"

Roger nodded as Nick started to walk to the cafe to return the bicycle. The lady who was on the bench had disappeared and obviously didn't want to get involved in identifying any moped-riding muggers. He couldn't see the point in ringing the police. What were they going to do about it? He knew the muggers were off somewhere else, probably about to pounce on another unsuspecting victim.

Nick started to limp as he could feel his foot clawing in his shoe, getting tighter and tighter, twisting each time he took a step.

"Oh great - the day just gets better."

CHAPTER THIRTY-SEVEN

Returning to the hotel, Nick sat with a much-needed beer in the hotel bar, whilst Roger sat looking at the busy, hustling street below. It had been a long day and Roger was thinking about Jess. He knew she'd be safe, she wasn't stupid, but she was alone in a strange city in a strange country.

"Don't worry Roger, I haven't known her very long but she ain't stupid! She'll be fine."

Roger knew she could look after herself, but there was still something not right for him. His fatherly instincts kicked in as a wave of worry rolled over him.

Nick downed his beer and stood up abruptly,

"Right Rog, I'm off to search the net to find out what to do with my passport – get some advice. See you outside the hotel at half seven?"

Roger gave him the thumbs up.

After finding out where the British Embassy was situated and reading that he could apply for an emergency travel document online, Nick decided he'd leave it until later to sort it out. He was absolutely knackered and needed a snooze.

"You sound exhausted," Liz stated as she spoke to Nick on his mobile.

"You woke me up!" Nick yawned, "Been a bad day, had my passport nicked."

"You are joking!"

"It's ok, I'll sort it later. Too tired right now."

"You should do it now Nick! How are you going to get home?!"

"Liz I'll sort it later. I apply online apparently."

"You need to sort it now Nick," Liz was getting angry, "It probably takes a couple of days! Where will you stay? You'll have all that money on you too!"

"I know, I know" the grim reality was starting to hit home. He'd have to pay for a few more nights and potentially have a fortune of bonds in his case! Jess would go mad and hit the wall, and Stan! Shit! what would Stan do?!

"I don't think you'll get an emergency passport and fly the same day Nick!" Liz tried to calm herself down.

"Do you remember that bloke Mark you knew? He lost his in Spain and got back the same day."

"Nick that was blooming twenty years ago! We're out of Europe now!"

"Yes, I suppose it was. I can't do anything now Liz. I'll have to sort it out later. I've got no choice."

Liz sighed.

"So you're getting the bonds tonight then?" Liz

tried to calm the situation down.

"Yes, apparently Roger knows where to go. It's so hot here though Liz, I can't stand it!"

"Oh, my heart bleeds for you! I bet you are in a lovely hotel room with air-conditioning."

"Well yes but…"

"Stop complaining then! It's been pouring down here!" Liz paused, "How are you getting back from the airport? That is presuming you come home!"

"A car's being sent apparently."

"And what time will you be home?"

"Hopefully early afternoon passport permitting." Nick paused, "I think we should go for a beer in the afternoon if we make it."

"Yes. Agreed. You could go straight from the airport. I could meet you there."

"Of course."

"It'll be ok Nick, remember you've got sod all to lose. You can do this. Just relax, take your pills on time, and be normal."

"Liz, will you stick by me if I get caught?"

"I'm not going anywhere, Nick. No matter what happens."

"I love you."

"Just get that damn passport sorted! Please do it soon Nick."

◆ ◆ ◆

After a perfectly cool, refreshing shower and

getting dressed, Nick glanced at himself in the mirror. He was wearing a pair of brown sandals, a cream pair of cotton trousers, and a light cotton shirt. Nick had always tried to gel with what the locals looked like, so it wasn't obvious he was a tourist. But he didn't have a chance with the Italian finesse and couldn't have looked more English if he tried. All that was missing was a severe sunburn and a large, coloured football tattoo on the back of one of his calves.

As agreed Nick met Roger at seven thirty outside the front of the hotel. Nick had put his missing passport to the back of his mind. He couldn't face it right now, preferring to plant his head deep in the sand. It was another beautiful evening, and the sun was slowly going down. Roger had tapped out that it was a ten-minute walk to where they were going to be picked up and taken to the meeting spot to collect the bonds. Walking along the pavement, dodging the evening shoppers, Nick couldn't quite understand why the bonds hadn't been dropped off at the hotel. Surely it was easier than trying to find out where they were going in a city they didn't know and spoke a language that was alien to them. But this was the plan Roger had been told.

Reaching the square in front of the Spanish Steps Nick asked Roger if he knew where he was going. Roger pointed towards the steps and the two men crossed the busy Square, filled with tourists in the early evening sun, milling about and chatting. Nick noticed the two Carabinieri vans at the side of the square as they walked up the steps to the road at the top. They didn't seem interested in anything, they were just enjoying having their photos taken with a large group of kids.

At the top of the steps, Nick could feel his legs starting to ache. The earlier frantic cycle ride had tested muscles he hadn't used for years. Roger stopped as they reached the road and pulled out a piece of paper from his pocket, handed it to Nick and indicated that he send the message to the phone number written on the paper. Nick complied but had no idea what he had just sent as it was in Italian.

Within minutes of sending the text a large black dusty car, that looked like a Mercedes, stopped where the two men were standing.

The driver lowered his window instructing the two men to get in the back of the car. Roger shuffled to the other side of the car and nodded at Nick as they both hesitantly climbed into the car. Inside the car, sitting on the black leather seats, Nick started coughing and began to wave his hands in the air to clear the smoke that puffed from the driver's cigar, which was engulfing the interior. The driver ignored the hint and continued to enjoy his cigar.

As the car erratically pushed its way through the evening traffic the car radio blasted out what sounded like a man commentating on a football game, getting very excited and speaking very quickly in Italian. The crowd roared and the commentator got louder and quicker, elated at the potential of a goal. The driver encouragingly gestured to the radio, ash flicking in all directions from the end of his cigar.

Nick, a little anxious, wished the driver would look where he was going instead of getting engrossed in the football blaring from the radio.

Ten minutes later the car came to an abrupt halt, parking outside a picturesque restaurant. There was a scattering of tables outside, with tall fans giving the welcome relief of cooler air to the diners. Most of the tables were full, and two waiters hurried between tables and back and forth to the restaurant carrying trays of food and drink. The driver indicated that Roger and Nick needed to go into the restaurant. Nick looked at Roger. Nervously he followed Roger into the restaurant and slowed his pace right down as it took a few seconds for his eyes to get accustomed to the darker room. Inside were a few people sitting at the bar, and one chap sitting at the table in the window. The barman behind the bar saw them and motioned for them to walk further through the restaurant.

They came to a dead end, a wall adorned with old black and white photographs of old footballers. A closed door was situated to the right of the wall. The Barman ushered them to open the door and go through. Once inside the adjoining room, they saw about five or six people playing cards at a large card table. The card players seemed engrossed in the game, concentrating on what to do next. On the dimly lit table were large bundles of notes proudly piled in front of each player. A show of wealth and risk. On the wall opposite Nick and Roger was a massive, overbearing mural of the Italian Footballer Roberto Baggio. Nick knew his football and remembered the player from a World Cup when he was younger.

One of the card players, a plump, olive-skinned man, probably aged about 60, slightly older than the other players, laid his cards down on the table. He Spoke Italian to the other card players and they responded by also placing their cards face down on the table. He stood up and gestured for Nick and Roger to sit at some chairs next to a small round table that was in the corner of the room. A carafe of red wine was waiting for them on the table along with two glasses. Ringing a small bell he summoned a waiter who entered the room. Words of Italian were exchanged, and it appeared that the plump man seemed to chastise the waiter. Looking confused the waiter walked over to where Nick and Roger had sat and removed one of the wine glasses.

The man walked slowly from the card table and poured a glass from the carafe and placed it in front of Nick.

"I apologise, Roger, the waiter forgot you do not drink." Sucking hard on his half-smoked cigar he introduced himself, "My name is Matteo."

Roger smiled and nodded.

"What do you think of the picture of 'Il Divin Codino,' Nick, do you like it?" Matteo proudly pointed to the excessively large painting as though it had just been finished.

"Impressive. I remember him in a world cup scoring loads of goals for you guys,"

"1994 USA Nick. You English didn't qualify. Shame. He would have liked to have scored against your team," the man smiled, "I think he did in 1990?"

"3rd place playoffs – yes I'm sure he did" Nick agreed, "hand of God and all that."

Matteo laughed, "but he!" he pointed at the large painting, "he had the feet of God!"

Matteo picked up his glass of brandy from the card table and toasted the footballer. Nick sheepishly did the same with his glass of wine.

"Do you know why you are here?" he asked in pretty good English.

Nick nodded.

"Why are you here?"

All the men sitting at the card table were staring at Nick,

"Apparently to take some packages back to England,"

"Do you know what's in these packages?"

Roger nodded.

"What's in them Nick?" Matteo smiled.

"Bonds I think." Nick felt a bit uncomfortable being asked all the questions and started to squirm in his seat.

Matteo smiled, "Where did the bonds come from?"

"I don't know if I want to know."

"You should Nick. It's history. They will change your life. They will change my life!"

"I've no idea where they came from." Nick took a sip of the wine, "Do you think I should know where they come from?" he was desperately trying not to sound sarcastic.

"Of course Nick. There is history in what you are handling."

"Ok, if you feel we should." he looked at Roger for agreement. Roger nodded.

"They are American bonds. They are American bonds, and they are worth an incredible amount of money. It has been reported in the past that they were fake, but I can assure you they are not." he looked sternly at Nick and Roger, "it has taken us a long time to get them back, and you are the final leg of the journey. A journey that should have ended a lot of years ago."

As the man was talking, he walked slowly around the room,

"A great number of people will become wealthy beyond the imagination of the man on the street. Your task is so important, and you cannot fail,"

Matteo shuffled back to his seat at the card table.

"No pressure then?" Nick said. He could feel his dyskinesia starting to do its thing as his arms started flailing about.

"You are the best people for the job. We know what we are doing. We just must be sure you know what you are doing?"

Roger smiled. He was starting to enjoy the conversation. He felt as if he was in a film and in a minute Al Pacino would smash his way into the room. Scary as it was, it was quite refreshing to be wanted and a part of something. Something with meaning and also he was an important part of the team.

"We know what we are doing," Nick replied.

"You need more confidence in who you are Nick. I can sense insecurities in you. Don't let the world put you down. You put the world down. Take control."

At that moment, another man came into the room. He had three slim leather cases.

"Here are the three cases. One each. The bonds are in two of them." all three cases were given to Roger. "To repeat, two of the cases have the bonds and one does not. One has brochures from the conference in it, so the weights are the same."

"Why not split between all three?" Nick asked.

"So you all feel there is a one in three chance

that you do not have the bonds."

"That won't make a difference to me walking through customs!" Roger nodded and grinned at Nick's statement.

"You'll be surprised by the games our minds can play."

"Bit like the World War One execution squads, one blank bullet?"

"If you think so." Matteo agreed. "Make sure Jess understands this when you next see her. She is ok by the way. We have been watching you since you arrived and will continue to do so until you are on the plane."

"You have been watching us? Do you know where Jess is? I'm not sure if I feel safer!" Nick quipped.

"I can guarantee you are safe. You are doing an especially important thing for us. Of course, we will watch you."

"So you know where Jess is then?"

"Of course. She is out with a young American from the conference."

"Blimey, you are watching us."

"Except he is FBI."

"He's what?"

"He is an FBI agent."

"What is Jess doing with an FBI agent?"

Roger stood up and it was obvious he was genuinely concerned with who Jess was with.

"I presume he is trying to find out why Jess is in Rome?" Matteo suggested, "Roger, sit down, she is safe. I promise you."

"What? They know?"

"Of course. They are not stupid. The value of the bonds could wipe out an economy."

"Is she safe?.......Roger, we have to warn her!...............I'll ring her!"

"Don't worry. It's in hand."

"How? What do you mean? What about Jess?"

Roger held Nick's arm, trying to stop him from getting agitated.

"Nick. We have men watching...............she will be fine...........you are in Rome. My city."

Nick calmed down, "Yeah, I guess."

"No concerns Nick. As I told you we know what we are doing."

"So how much are these bonds worth?" Nick had to know. Especially if the FBI were involved.

"We acquired the bonds a long, long time ago. You can read all the lies on the internet. Look at what they say happened to them in Chiasso!" He looked at the other men around the table, some of whom nodded, "There is a lot of myth and nonsense about them."

Nick just wanted to know what they were worth.

"In June 2009, we lost them. We believe someone had informed, snitched as you say, to the authorities about what we were doing. But anyway, two of our colleagues were found smuggling bonds into Switzerland and apprehended in Chiasso on the Swiss border with Italia."

"Hell! The police got them. Got the bonds?" Nick started to feel nervous.

Roger pulled out his spell board, "how much?"

"They were caught smuggling $134.5 billion worth of Bonds!" Matteo whispered dramatically.

Nick suddenly felt ridiculously hot and sweaty. He gulped down the rest of his glass of wine, and immediately poured another.

Roger went cold. Shit, this was becoming a little bigger than the previous jobs he had done for Stan.

"And these are the bonds we have here?" Nick asked, hoping that they were not worth that much money.

"There was a rumour that the North Koreans or Chinese produced them to mess up the American economy. But this was not true," the man smiled. "As I have said they are not fake. They are, I think you would say, 'The real McCoy'!"

"So how did you get them back?"

"Time, money, and conversations" he sipped his drink, "There is always a way."

"So, hold on a minute, are we taking $135 odd billion tomorrow back to the UK?"

"Yes, when you think about it that is their market value. At least."

"And if we get caught? What if someone has grassed again?"

The room became very silent and still.

"I assure you no one will 'grass again'."

"Ok, so what happens when we get the bonds to England?"

"You don't need to worry about that. You just need to get them to the airport in London. It will all become clear. You've been told a car will meet you."

Matteo stood up, "Ok nice to meet you," he put out his hand to Roger who shook it, and then Nick, "Francesco will take you back." He pointed to a young man dressed in a very sharp, black, single-breasted suit. He couldn't look any more like a member of the mafia.

"Can I just...." Nick had a few more questions he wanted to ask.

"Gentlemen, There is nothing more to say." a large, square mountain of a man wearing a very tight pink shirt stood up, "Francesco will get you back to the hotel. Be nice to Francesco, he is not nicknamed 'Mr. Discipline' for no reason!"

Matteo reached into his side pocket and pulled out a small envelope, "Nick before you go this is for you."

Nick took the envelope and apprehensively opened it.

His passport.

"As I said we have been watching you. Two men have been punished. We do not tolerate this type of crime in Rome!"

Before they knew it, Francesco had ushered them back through the restaurant and into another black car. Francesco sat in the front, gave instructions to the driver, and leant down to put the radio on. The football game from earlier was still going on though the commentary was a little calmer than before. Sitting quietly and looking out of their respective windows, Roger and Nick were reflecting on what had just happened. Roger held two of the cases to his chest, and Nick had the other one gripped tightly between his thighs.

What the hell had they managed to get themselves into?

Francesco walked the two men to their hotel and then left them at the entrance to the lift. The hotel lobby was cool and inviting. Both men kept quiet as they went up in the lift to their floor. They knew what effect the gravity of their day tomorrow will have on them.

❖ ❖ ❖

Just as they reached their room doors, Jess opened hers.

"Thought I could hear you two coming up in the lift. How goes?" she had one of the hotel's white towelling dressing gowns on and her hair was wet, "All good then? You both look a bit pale."

"Did you have a good night?"

"It was going well 'til he bailed."

"What do you mean, bailed?"

"We had a few drinks after the lecture, then went for a meal. After our starters, he went to the loo and never came back. It's happened before. Bit pissed off it happened in Rome though. Bet he was married!"

"Oh."

"Good lecture though." she smiled. "You'd have thought someone who had Tourette's would be able to put up with me!"

"I'm glad the lecture was good." Nick smiled, "Shall we have a quick drink in my room and discuss a few things?"

Before leaving her room Jess wrapped a towel around her wet hair. Inside Nick's room, he opened two miniature bottles of wine from the mini bar and handed one to Jess. Neither bothered with glasses. Roger gave one of the cases he had been given by Matteo to Jess.

"I'd sleep with that tonight if I were you," Nick advised sternly.

"Worth a lot are they?"

"You may not have any in yours."

"What? Why not. I didn't come all this way for nothing!" she started to get agitated.

"Keep your hair on. They've only been put in two cases. So, if you get stopped you may not have the bonds in your case. The third has conference brochures in it."

Jess looked confused.

"Don't ask."

"Did you feel you were being watched at

dinner?"

"Well this strange old guy was sitting in the corner of the restaurant, but I don't think he was watching me! He knew the waiters very well but was staggering around every time he stood up. He looked as though he was walking on a ship in a storm."

Roger looked at Nick.

"When he left I felt guilty, I thought he was pissed, but he walked out with two sticks."

"Yep I think we can safely say he was watching you." he took a swig of wine from the small bottle, "we've been watched since we arrived."

Roger nodded.

"I don't think you were ditched either Jess."

"Well, he didn't come back!"

"He was FBI!"

"Oh shit what the hell?!"

"Yep,"

"Why the....I thought he was asking some pretty personal stuff."

"Please tell me you didn't tell him about our job?"

"Course I bloody didn't! He knew we are here for the conference." Jess looked at Nick, squinting her eyes, frowning at his stupid question. "So why is the FBI looking into us? Shit. Do you think we should do this job tomorrow?" Jess started to nervously pace the room.

Roger had his spelling board out, "Stan won't let anything happen to us!" he tapped.

"Roger the FB bloody I!"

Nick sat on the end of his bed, "I don't think we've got a choice. That Matteo sort of made that clear."

Roger nodded.

"Yes, we are going to have to do it. I've also got my passport back! Thank God!"

"Really? Where the hell was it?" Jess stopped pacing the room.

"The Mafia, or whoever they are, had it. It seems nothing can happen here without them knowing about it."

Jess opened the hotel door, "Right I'm off to bed then. If we are going to do the stupidest thing ever, I need to sleep."

"Sorry you got ditched, Jess." Nick stood up and smiled, "Don't think it was you though. I think he got what info he needed and left. Job done."

Jess's arm jumped, "I guess so. But why me?"

"Not sure. But what we do know is everyone is watching us!"

She wiped a tear from her cheek and left for her room. It wasn't the fact that Paolo was probably FBI or that he used her. But just once she wanted to date a nice guy, who understood her, who wanted to be with her. A man she could fall in love with and grow alongside her. Someone who could see past her Tourette's and not reject her as soon as the first tic left her mouth as had happened so often before.

THE UNREASONABLE ADJUSTMENT

Jess just wanted to be loved.

CHAPTER THIRTY-EIGHT

Nick opened his eyes but could not see anything in the pitch dark of his hotel room. He was wide awake. He had eventually drifted off to sleep, but as far as he was concerned it felt like it was only twenty minutes ago. Deep in his mind conflicting thoughts had been whirling between the return trip home, getting caught and thrown into jail and what to spend the money on if they pulled it off.

He always fancied a hot tub in the garden. It would be therapeutic. Plus, he fancied the idea of lounging in it during summer evenings, a glass of wine in hand, losing himself in the relaxing extravagance of the moment. Liz was adamantly against it. She said that if you went to any housing estate at 9 p.m. on a Friday all you could hear was the bubbling in back gardens from inflatable hot tubs. To Liz they were filthy, germ-filled, adult paddling pools because people probably just had sex in them. Nick didn't quite see her argument and told her that he would like to have sex in one. This did not go down well with Liz.

Waking up early was not uncommon for Nick. He'd often wake at three in the morning. It was a Parkinson's symptom that he never knew about before it started to happen. Something to do with REM sleep so he'd been told. When he wasn't working it wasn't a problem, but if he had to work it was a nightmare as he would be shot through with fatigue the whole of the next day. It caused a real struggle to get through the working day.

Thankfully there had been improvements in technology that had been a godsend to the modern insomniac. He could watch literally anything on the TV now at three in the morning or speak to people who were also awake at such a dreadfully early hour via social media. His mum used to suffer from insomnia, the television in those days was terrible at night, with three channels of nothing at four in the morning. She used to iron instead. His school shirts were perfect every day of his school life, and on particularly wakeful nights he'd awake to the smell of baking cakes wafting from the oven. All Liz woke up to was Nick, feet up on the sofa, watching some documentary on crime or the French news channel.

Nick turned the main light on in the hotel room and limped over to turn the kettle on. He flicked on the TV and began watching the news.

The news at three in the morning is exactly the same as the news at ten. It had become a strange phenomenon that anything else that happened in the world between the headline slots was considered to be "breaking news". He remembered as a kid when there used to be news flashes for proper breaking news - President Reagan had been shot, the shuttle exploded or a football crowd disaster. Now it would be breaking news if a soldier fainted outside Buckingham Palace, or a train had broken down causing delays in Carlisle.

Nick began to think about the day ahead. They'd have to be at the airport early. Being the anxious person he was, Nick had to be at the airport hours before a flight just in case there was an accident, the taxi broke down or a meteor hit the planet. This of course meant that he and whoever he was travelling with would have to endure hours of boredom wandering through the host of duty-free shops that skirted the departure lounge.

The reality of his day was playing on his paranoid mind. By tonight he could be in a cell charged with major international money smuggling. The amount of money the three of them had between them was fantastically breathtaking. He'd be 'breaking news' then, and on the front cover of every newspaper in the world. Social media would go mad with memes and comments and his life would be scrutinised with a microscope, never mind the press camping on his doorstep. Liz for all her promises would eventually get fed up and leave him, he'd lose his house and have nowhere to go when he was finally released from a probable long prison sentence. The day in front of him was getting scarier and scarier the more he thought about it!

Nick inquisitively peered at the case that with high odds contained the bonds, which was lying on the bedside table. He really wanted to open the case just to see if he had the bonds inside or not. But opening them would mean he'd be touching them, and as far as he was concerned, fingerprints inside the case would implicate him further. He'd also agreed with the other two not to have a look inside the case and peep at the papers inside. He lay back down on the bed and stared at the ceiling.

What the hell had he got himself into?

His mobile phone alarm went off at five. He must have fallen back to sleep as the TV was still on and there was a half-finished cold cup of coffee on the bedside table next to the case of bonds. He took his pills with a slurp of cold coffee and then slowly tried to sit up. It's not that he couldn't, it was just that he had no real motivational connection between brain and body and frankly wanted to stay in bed. He had to dig deep to make it happen. At three in the morning he could get up relatively easily but at seven in the morning his meds from the evening before had totally worn off and his recently swallowed morning pills would take half an hour to kick in.

He took six pills in the morning just so he could get moving properly. Nick could do very short steps around a hotel room without them, but he wouldn't be able to walk along a corridor without being forced to stop by his stiff limbs. His medication had increased over the years as his Parkinson's marched on, destroying brain cells that controlled his movement. His symptoms had become worse but as far as Nick was concerned he was on the right dose of pills at the moment and didn't want them changed or increased. The side effects of an increased dose or a potential new pill could outweigh any benefit.

Picking up the telephone that was next to the bed he rang reception and booked a taxi for 07.30 to take them to the airport. He was a bit miffed that a car hadn't been organised by the Italians but presumed it was to keep things low-key. Then he rang the other two rooms to make sure the occupants were up. Roger picked the phone up and tapped the telephone receiver on his bedside table twice to confirm that he had heard and understood what Nick had said. Jess, being woken by the call and on hearing what Nick had to say moaned "yes. Piss off!" then hung up the phone.

After asking the receptionist to let them know when their taxi arrived, Nick met Jess and Roger for an early breakfast on the terrace. It was going to be a scorcher of a day, the heat in the morning sun was already becoming oppressive. The mood of the three over breakfast was a little solemn and no one said much. Nick couldn't eat so he just had a coffee and Jess had some pastries and fruit. Roger looked out at the blue sky over the rooftops; he'd done his normal feeding ritual in his room before coming out to meet the others.

Nick broke the silence,

"I'd like to come back and see the sights," he said sipping his black coffee.

Jess nodded.

"I mean the conference was ok, but we just did it for the sake of it. I'd like to go and see the colosseum and the Vatican."

"I'd like to go to southern Italy"

Roger waved his hand to indicate a fan.

"I know it would be hot Rog, but just lying on the beach would be lovely. Maybe next year?"

"What you going to do with the money then Jess?"

"Don't know. Maybe start a business or something."

"I'm going to pay off my mortgage and quit. I can't do that job anymore."

Roger pretended to steer a car.

"Oh Yeah, here we go, Roger and his Porsche!" Jess teased.

"Have you still got a licence Roger?" asked Nick, thinking there was no way Roger could drive.

He shook his head.

"He needs to do some sort of assessment. But I think he would be ok now. Christ! There are some seriously old people who shouldn't be driving! So, I don't know why he can't."

"Well, you still have to be safe."

"Just put your foot down and go for it!" encouraged Jess.

"No chance." he changed the subject, "So what happened last night then Jess?"

"Well, we went to the lecture in the afternoon, then had a walk around the city, getting all romantic and stuff. Then we went for a meal, but he buggered off after the starter. It was lovely food. Oh, and I paid. If I'd have known he was FBI I would have bailed first!"

Roger suddenly remembered something. He pulled out his phone, pressed a button and showed the screen displaying an email he had received in the middle of the night.

"What? You want me to read the email?" Nick asked.

Roger nodded.

Nick read the email Roger had received. He then looked up at Roger and smiled.

"Well, what does it say then?" Jess was eager to know.

"I Know about FBI. Not a concern. They had heard noise about Jess and you doing work for me so

wanted to know what was going on in Rome. Trust me I know what I'm doing. Stan"

"So, you were right, the FBI man was on a date with me?" Jess asked, confused.

"Yep. But Stan's obviously being watched, and they know about you two working for him, so they just wanted to check out why you were in Rome." Nick re-read the email, "I think the FBI mucked up. They should have followed me and Roger, we'd have taken them right to the top people!"

"No, no. They haven't mucked up! I did a wonderful job of making him think we were here for a valid reason!"

Nick laughed, "Yes you did. Now let's do this thing."

"Where are you putting the cases we're taking?" Jess asked.

Roger indicated his hand luggage and Nick said he'd carry his. Jess agreed and decided to carry it with her rucksack.

Nick stood upright and stretched his arms out wide taking a deep breath.

"Hey, whatever happens, I wouldn't have missed this for the world. We'll always be friends hey?"

Jess and Roger stood up. The three hugged.

CHAPTER THIRTY-NINE

The taxi arrived on time. A big black people carrier with smoked glass windows stopped directly outside the front of the hotel. Anyone wanting to drive past would have to be incredibly careful to manoeuvre past the taxi as it was far too large for the very narrow street. A queue of cars began to build, waiting for the taxi to depart.

The receptionist who checked them in on their first day informed them of the taxi's arrival and wished them luck. Nick looked at Jess and silently mouthed "Luck?" to her. Jess ignored him and carried her bags out to the awaiting car.

The taxi driver was already out of his seat and had opened the boot ready for their baggage. He took both of Jess's bags and hoisted them into the boot.

"I think I'd like that case with me in the taxi!" Jess pointed at the case containing the bonds.

"They'll be fine Jess. They're not going anywhere."

"I'm not sure Nick, we should have them in

our view all the time."

"Yep, I guess you're right." Nick reached into the boot and took out the slim leather case and gave it to her.

"Nice day again," Nick tried to make small talk with the driver. The driver tried to take both of Nick's cases, but Nick held onto the case that held the bonds. Noticing Roger was struggling with a suitcase, the bond's case, a rucksack and a stick, Nick tried to assist Roger. Belligerently Roger refused to let go of the cases and shuffling past the driver hoisted the suitcase and rucksack into the boot of the taxi. The driver closed the boot door.

"In!" the driver pointed to the back door.

Jess looked at the door perplexed.

"How the hell do you open this?" she whispered under her breath. It didn't look like a pull-open door. The driver, observing her hesitation, grabbed the handle of the door and gently slid it open.

"Easy," Jess could see his gold teeth glinting as he gave her a slight smile.

The three climbed into the taxi and donned their seat belts instinctively. All three held their cases containing $134 billion of bonds tightly to their chests as if their lives depended upon them. The driver took his seat and reached down to the radio and started to play some classical music. The sound wafted around the cab as they pulled away from the hotel. Jess gave out a large sigh as she relaxed into the very posh, cool, leather seats. She was soon asleep.

Nick looked at Roger and gave half a smile. Roger knew what he was thinking. Something was not quite right. He couldn't put his finger on it but there was something amiss with the driver. It just didn't feel right.

As the taxi wound its way through the busy roads of Rome Nick was beginning to get nervous. The route the taxi had taken seemed unfamiliar. The streets, apartments and people looked vastly different to when they first arrived in Rome. They were definitely following a new route to the airport.

"How long until we get to the airport?" he asked the driver, trying to get some normality into a slowly unnerving situation.

The taxi driver didn't answer.

"Excuse me, how long until we get to the airport?" Nick resorted to his very upper-class English accent. He had this ingrained belief that going posh English had some kind of influence in the world.

It didn't.

The taxi driver still failed to reply. Nick looked at Roger who shrugged his shoulders.

"Airport one hour." the taxi driver suddenly retorted.

Nick felt a bit more comfortable and eased himself back into his seat. Roger though was having other suspicious thoughts.

Roger peered out of the window. They were in the suburbs and Roger presumed not far from the motorway that would take them to the airport. He looked at Nick who seemed to be happy watching through the front windscreen, and then at Jess who was sound asleep. Roger's grip tightened around his walking stick. He had a bad feeling about this journey.

After about fifteen minutes the taxi pulled into a side road and stopped outside a relatively small sand-coloured apartment block about four stories high. On the side of the building was an elaborate mural of Michael Angelo's two hands touching, but with a modern addition of a glass of red wine on a table on the corner of the giant painting.

Nick, realising they had unexpectedly stopped, became a little anxious again, "Driver why have we stopped? What's going on?"

The driver opened his door to get out of the car, then closed it and locked all the doors in the vehicle with one press of his key button. Then he proceeded to enter the apartment block without giving any explanations to his confused passengers.

"What the fuck is going on?" Nick started to sweat.

Roger shook Jess to wake her up, "Are we there?" she yawned as she woke.

"No, we are not there!"

Jess looked out of her window, "Where the hell

are we?"

Roger re-adjusted his hold on his stick in preparation to use it as a weapon. He knew something wasn't right.

"Maybe he's just gone in to get something? Could be his home? Stop panicking you Muppet!" Jess leant back into her seat, her arm twitching up to the roof of the car.

"Jess we are carrying $134 billion, about to smuggle it out of Italy into the UK, a strange taxi has picked us up and stopped in the middle of I don't know where and you think he's forgotten his bloody lunch box!"

Nick looked at Roger who shrugged at him in an "I don't know" way.

"Look he's coming back and he has a bag with him. Told you."

The driver got back into the taxi and placed the bag on the seat next to him. Then reaching into it he pulled out a gun that looked as though it had just come from an old Dirty Harry Movie. It looked very shiny and heavy with a long Clint Eastwood style barrel.

No one in the back said a word. The three just stared at the gun that was now pointing at them. Nick gingerly placed the case containing the bonds slowly on the car floor.

"Ok, I now have your attention. Do not worry. But make sure you do what I tell you,"

The driver motioned with the gun that they should get out of the taxi.

"Are you going to kill us? Nick asked, his voice quiet yet clear.

"Do what I tell you. Go into the apartment building." the taxi driver motioned with his head. "There's someone to see you."

"No one knows we are here!" Jess was confused. She only knew that Stan and Nick's wife Liz knew where they were.

CHAPTER FORTY

Stan ended the telephone call and threw it menacingly at the cell wall. The phone shattered into several pieces rendering it useless.

"Bastard." he whispered under his breath, "Bastard!" taking a seat at his table he put his head in his hands. This was not good. He had to sort the unpleasant situation out quickly. His reputation depended upon it.

Stan had just been told that his three smugglers had been taken by some of the Italian Mafia. A group of Rome's mafia had broken away from their family and decided that they wanted the bonds. The value was far too much for them to ignore. Stan hadn't expected this.

He had to make sure the bonds didn't leave his team's sight. He needed to make sure they were going to get to the airport. Feeling under his mattress for one of his spare phones he dialled his Italian contact number.

"Hey, Xavier. That problem you told me about a few minutes ago. I've thought about it. We need to get my people on the plane today."

"As I said Mr. Tennant, I think it would be wise

to let the bonds go and recover them overnight. Less attention. My people are watching the building. No one can come or go without us knowing."

Stan paused. He wasn't used to problems being thrown into conversations and knew the Italians liked to be a bit more stealth-like in their operations. Silent but deadly. Stan's approach was a bit more direct. Get the job done and get out.

"No Xavier. I want them on the plane today. I don't care how, but they must be on that plane!"

"Ok, if that's what you want."

"Yes, that's what I want."

CHAPTER FORTY-ONE

Inside the apartment building lobby, the taxi driver told them to go through the first door and into one of the downstairs apartments. Walking in they noticed that the apartment was completely void of furniture. There were no light fittings, carpets or curtains. The walls were painted a neutral white and as they went into what felt like the living room, they were greeted with bright sunshine pouring into the room. The room's double windows were open wide, and they were able to see the taxi outside the building.

The three stood with their backs to the wide-open window. Nick's dyskinesia had started to show its true colours as he squirmed from side to side. Jess's twitch in her arm revealed itself a couple of times and her head uncontrollably jumped up and down, her chin seemingly leading the movement. Roger stood, his walking stick still firmly in his hand. His knuckles clenched around the handle.

Stepping back towards the door the taxi driver lowered his gun and shouted something in Italian. From another room Matteo, dressed in a very stylish dark blue suit, marched into the room. A smoking cigar was nestled in his right hand.

"What on Earth? Matteo, what is going on?" Nick was surprised to see Matteo again.

"Who is this bloke?" Jess looked at Roger and then Nick.

"He gave us the bonds at that restaurant," Nick stated, still looking at Matteo.

Roger tapped his stick on the ground angrily.

"Ok Roger. You will be on your way soon." Matteo looked at Roger. The taxi driver had his gun pointed at Roger's head. Matteo gently reached across and lowered the gun arm of the taxi driver and spoke in Italian.

"We don't need that do we?" he said turning back to the three.

"What's going on?" Nick repeated.

Matteo took several puffs of his cigar sending several plumes of smoke into the air. Jess coughed. She hated the smell of cigars.

"My apologies Jess." Matteo nodded his head towards Jess, "You are carrying $134 billion worth of bonds in your cases."

"Yes. You know we are!" Nick gabbled. "So why are we here? We should be at the airport."

Roger tapped his stick on the floor several times again.

"I think you know Roger." he smiled at Roger, "I am taking the bonds back."

Jess laughed, "But you gave us the bonds!"

"Yes on behalf of my colleagues. Now I take them back on behalf of my family."

Nick was confused.

"So, you're robbing us!" Jess spluttered.

Matteo walked to the centre of the room; he was about three meters away from the three.

"Yes."

"Well not us." corrected Nick, "Stan Tennant."

"Stan yes. The whole outfit too." Matteo's smile disappeared from his face, "I am taking an elevated risk. But $134 billion? Surely it is a risk worth taking."

"Well as far as I'm concerned you can take 'em" Nick nodded, "I don't care. I just want to get home." he placed his case on the floor.

"Of course, Nick. But that is too high a risk. Just to take them. You will know and we can't have that!"

Nick looked at Jess and Roger, "You're going to kill us?!"

"I cannot have you alive Nick. For obvious reasons. If you disappear it will look like you have taken the bonds!"

"But we won't tell anybody will we?"

Jess chipped in, "Not a soul."

"We'll tell everyone that we got robbed by a masked gang or something!"

Roger stared aggressively at Matteo.

"Matteo, I'm begging you. We won't tell,"

"No, you are right, you won't." Matteo started to walk to the open door, "I shall leave you with my friend here. Che Dio sia con te" He left the room and a few seconds later the apartment.

"Che Dio what?" Said Jess.

"God be with you." The taxi driver said, raising the gun at Roger's head.

The gun was quieter than Nick thought it would be. He had closed his eyes and was mumbling under his breath. On hearing the thud of Roger hitting the floor he cried out, the pure stress and tension ripped its way through his body. His dyskinesia went into overdrive and rolling up into a ball on the ground he waited for the next shot.

The next shot didn't happen.

Nick stayed tightly in a ball, his arms tightening his hold on his legs, bracing himself with what was going to happen. He didn't want to die. He wanted to live. He knew his disease was degenerative, but he had a list of stuff to do in his life. He still wanted to be with Liz and be happy and grow old disgracefully. He hadn't finished with life yet. But how could he fight a man with a gun pointed at his head? This was it. This was how it would end for him. Shot in the backstreets of Rome.

He cried out in absolute terror, "Please don't kill me!"

Jess had her eyes closed as Roger was shot. Her

automatic response was to turn and look at her dead friend, her dear friend, lying on the floor. This was going to be a horrible sight and she knew she was next.

She looked at Roger.

He wasn't on the floor. He was standing, frozen it seemed, in the same position as he had been a few seconds ago.

Jess looked at the gunman. He was lying on his back, a deep claret of blood pooled at the back of his head. A tiny red hole bled slightly in the middle of his forehead.

She looked back at Roger who had escaped from his frozen self. He smiled at her. A comforting smile then shrugged his shoulders.

"What the hell is going on?"

Nick let out another cry.

"Nick get up!" Jess instructed.

He didn't move. He was too scared to move.

Jess kicked him gently with her foot, "Nick get up!" she whispered sternly.

Nick opened his eyes to see his two colleagues standing staring at a man on the floor.

"Is that the taxi driver?" he whimpered, confused and still frightened about what was going to happen.

Jess acknowledged Nick.

"He's got a hole in his head!" Nick observed as he climbed to his feet, "He's been shot!"

"What? He shot himself?"

Roger shook his head and pointed out of the

window.

"What, from outside?" Jess asked.

Roger nodded. He went to the open windows and looked out. There wasn't another building opposite for some way and he certainly couldn't see anyone in a window, never mind a gun.

He held his arms up and pretended to shoot a long riffle.

"Yes, I think you're right Roger. It can only have been a sniper."

Jess walked to the window and looked out, "Are we at risk?"

Roger shook his head.

"I hope you're right Rog."

"Where's Matteo?" Nick looked into the hallway of the corridor. It was empty. He walked to the front door and peered cautiously into the lobby. Nothing.

Walking back into the room Nick asked if the taxi was still outside.

Roger gave the thumbs up.

"I think we should get out of here fast and get on that plane!" Nick suggested, still looking sheepishly around the room, slightly crouching as if the ceiling were too low, anticipating another gunshot.

"Agreed. How do we get there?" Jess asked.

Roger pointed at the taxi.

"Agreed" Nick bent down next to the dead body and put his hand into the corpse's trouser pocket. He pulled out a set of keys.

"Come on, let's go!" he started to leave, "Hold on, who's driving?"

"I never passed my test!" Jess admitted.

"I can't drive! Bloody hell we'll never get to the end of the road! Looking at Roger I can't see how he can drive either!" stuttered Nick, still scared of what could happen.

"He'll have to!" proclaimed Jess.

"Have you had lessons Jess?"

"Yes, years ago! Wouldn't have a clue now!"

"Roger can't drive Jess. His right leg is buggered and if you ask me his perception is pretty poor too!"

Roger took the keys off Nick and made his way out of the apartment.

Nick sighed and raised his eyebrows, "Christ, we are all going to die!"

Jess stared at Nick, "Bloody nearly did! Now let's go!"

Nick followed the two out of the building. All three were carrying their cases.

"Where's Matteo?" Nick looked around the street as they exited the apartment.

"Who cares?! Let's get out of here!" Jess called back.

Jess sat in the front with Roger, and Nick climbed into the back.

"Oh No! it's automatic Roger!" she looked at the car's controls, "You ok with that?"

Roger started up the engine, put the car in drive and pulled away. He hadn't driven since he had his stroke but was very pleased and relieved that the car was automatic!

"You know where to go Roger?!"

Roger shook his head.

"Great." she looked at Roger sternly, "I've got total faith in you."

Roger winked at Jess.

Jess turned round and looked at Nick, "Don't judge a book hey?!"

Nick gave no reply. He knew she was right, but the thought of Roger killing them in a car when they had just escaped being shot was not something he wanted to happen.

Jess turned back and started laughing. Her laugh was quite infectious, and Roger began to smile, a wide grin! Nick looked bemused. He couldn't believe what had just happened. He nearly died. They all nearly died and here they were in a car, a stolen car, laughing!

"What's so funny?"

"You Nick!"

"What do you mean?"

"The foetal position didn't make you look good!" she sniggered

"We were about to die Jess! What the hell?!"

"Come on Nick! I'm just teasing you" she twitched and broke down into a fit of giggles. She wasn't necessarily laughing at Nick, she was laughing at the relief of getting out of a very frightening situation. She had had her stress levels pulled up to the highest level and suddenly like a shaken bottle of pop had been opened resulting in a gush of demented laughter, "I cannot believe we got out of that!"

Nick started chuckling to himself. He could touch the relief in Jess' voice, "Think I may have wet myself too!"

The two of them erupted into a breakdown of tears and howling laughter as Roger drove them onto the motorway signposted "Fiumicino Leonardo da Vinci International Airport." Roger had a big grin on his face.

◆ ◆ ◆

Waking up, Matteo's head was thumping. He tried to stretch his legs, but he couldn't. It was as though he was inside a box. Then the reality hit him. He was in the boot of a car, hog-tied with a hood over his head. He could hear voices and concentrating hard he thought he recognised one of them. It sounded like Francesco.

It was at that point that Matteo realised he had made a massive mistake.

CHAPTER FORTY-TWO

The check-in was packed with the hustle and bustle of chattering travellers. After finding the correct desk, they off-loaded their main bags and walked to passport control so that they could relax and wait for their plane in the departure lounge. The queue was long, snaking its way into the main hall. The three joined the back of the queue and waited. As they edged nearer Nick became more nervous. His arm started to move as his dyskinesia forced his arms to sway and twist. He knew he could never hide his emotions with this disease. He tried to stop the movement and by concentrating hard he could slow it down. But the second his mind stopped focusing on trying to stay still he would start to move again.

Jess suddenly jerked having just remembered something. She opened her handbag and pulled out two square badges and gave one to Nick and the other she kept herself, pinning it on the lapel of her shirt. Nick looked at his badge,

'I have Parkinson's disease. Please be understanding.'

"I'm not wearing that!"

"Don't be daft Nick, put it on. We've had this conversation before."

He looked at Jess's badge,

'I have Tourette's syndrome. Please be understanding.'

Nick relented and put his on. They were quite small badges and discreet, but Nick felt uncomfortable telling the world about his condition.

Roger put his hand out, waiting to be given a badge.

"They didn't have any stroke ones Roger." she looked at Roger, "to be honest Roger you don't need a badge, it's pretty obvious you're not quite right!" she laughed, winking at Roger.

Roger smiled, playfully slapping Jess's shoulder.

The queue staggered slowly forward. Roger was the first to reach the security desk and conveyer belt. He emptied his pockets into the plastic tray and put his small case containing the bonds in it too. He shuffled his way through the metal detecting gate and picked his stuff up at the other end. Nick followed closely behind doing the same. The security officer asked him to take off his shoes and belt and put them on the conveyer belt before walking through the detector.

Nick's hands were not playing the game. He couldn't get the buckle undone; his left arm was moving about, and his right arm was getting stiffer and stiffer. Jess, thankfully, stopped the pain of embarrassment. She looked at him straight in his eyes at the same time unbuckling and pulling his belt off.

"There we go lover!" she laughed.

Relieved to have the belt removed, Nick pulled his shoes off, put them in the tray and walked through the detector.

The detector sounded.

Jess twitched, "Hitler!" she shouted.

Nick, trying to thread his belt back onto his trousers, stopped and stared at her. Did she just say that at Security at Rome International airport, Italy?

None of the security staff flinched. She was told in Italian to empty her pockets. Jess pulled out her mobile phone and put it in the tray, kicking herself that she had not put it in the tray with her other bits including the leather case.

She was then instructed to move through the gate again. This time it didn't go off. Nick could feel his shoulders lighten as she walked towards him and Roger.

Jess smiled,

"Get a grip" she whispered as she walked past

him, "and I'm not doing your belt up!"

The last hour of waiting for the flight dragged on. They set up base on some seats and took turns wandering around the shops. Nick went to the loo about five times which is what he normally did before flying. Jess bought some perfume and Roger just mooched around and bought nothing.

Nick suddenly felt his phone vibrate. It wasn't time for his pills and the only person to ever text him was Liz. He looked at the phone. The number was withheld.

Nick opened the text,

"Hi, it's Craig, the policeman from The Oak House pub. The neurology appointment is today. Will let you know."

As Nick was trying to make sense of the text a call came for their flight prompting people to stand and walk towards the gate. Nick suddenly realised who the text was from, DI Bullen, the copper from the pub raid. The irony of it all! A copper was messaging him as he was about to smuggle the largest amount ever into the UK. He slipped his phone back into his pocket. He'd text him back when they arrived in the UK.

This was it. All they had to do was get on the plane and then get off at the other end. Simple. All three had their cases, no one knew who had the bonds but all three believed they probably had them. Deep down they were all nervous. Within the next couple of hours, after the flight, they would either be locked up or walking out of the airport with big, relieved smiles into whatever delights the London weather had for them.

Their flight was called again. As they left their seats Nick saw a man out of the corner of his eye. Nick stopped and looked at him. He was obviously watching the three and for a split second their eyes locked onto each other before the mystery man turned and left through a glass door.

Nick stood still. A massive wave of fear suddenly engulfed him. He remembered reading on the web last night, as suggested by Matteo, that the bonds they were smuggling were originally carried by two Japanese men. They were caught on a train in Chiasso.

How the hell did the police know where they were and what they were carrying? You don't just board a train and suddenly decide to arrest a couple of Japanese guys out of a hunch. Who would have set them up to fail? Who told the authorities?

Were they told to take the cases knowing what was in them? Were they recruited because they were Japanese? Was that relevant? Or a double bluff? Why hadn't the Italian Mafia used Italians?

"Hold on a minute," Nick whispered to himself. Had he and his co-smugglers been recruited because they would stick out?! Like the Japanese travellers on that fateful day.

Nick knew that he, Jess and Roger had been employed because they acted and looked out of the ordinary through society's normal, blinkered perception, that was the point. It was so obvious they were disabled in their own way and would be noticed by everyone. But it was believed that their disability would take away suspicion. It was hoped that the Customs officers would be too uncomfortable to search them. Customs officers are not that stupid? Surely not? The Japanese men stood out! The three of them stood out! Was this clever business from Stan and his organisation or were they all being used and stitched up?

"Nick! I've been shouting to you!" Jess broke his thoughts, "Roger's on the plane – we have to go now!"

CHAPTER FORTY-THREE

All three sat on the same row of the plane as it ascended into the air taking off from Rome airport. Thankfully, the seats were extremely comfortable, and it had the feel and smell of being a relatively new plane. As soon as the plane reached cruising height Jess bought two small bottles of wine and gave one to Nick. Nick unscrewed the bottle and poured it into the plastic glass that came with it. It didn't take him long to finish it. Although a nervous flyer, he had other things at the forefront of his mind.

The strange man who was looking at him in the airport had spooked him. Who the hell was he? Maybe he worked for Stan and was just making sure they got on the plane safely? Or maybe he was Interpol checking on the three of them, contacting customs in England who would be waiting for them when they landed?

He managed to buy another bottle of wine, unscrewed it and took a swig straight from the small bottle.

"Jesus Nick, slow down. You'll be hammered by the time we land."

Nick poured the rest of the bottle into the plastic glass, "Yeah, I know. It's flying. I hate it."

"It'll all be fine Nick" she twitched her head, "tosser!"

"Thanks." smiled Nick.

"You're welcome"

Nick finished his wine, leant back in the seat, and closed his eyes. He tried to let his thoughts disappear to somewhere relaxing, a beach, boating on a lake and sitting in a flower-filled meadow. No matter how hard he tried he couldn't stop thinking about his case that was in the compartment above his head. Did he have the bonds in his case? Could they trust Stan? They obviously should not have trusted Matteo. Why had the FBI taken so much effort to get closer to Jess? They pretended to be part of the Italian Tourette's organisation! Were they being set up? Who was that man at the airport?

Roger and Jess both looked out of their window. Roger was next to the window, so Jess had to lean across him to see out. She pointed out the snow-covered mountains as they flew over the Alps, captivated by the perfect view due to the lack of clouds. Nick opened an eye, delicately leant forward, and peered at them. He quickly returned to his original position, closed his eyes, and did his best to imagine he wasn't flying at thirty thousand feet. He was envious of Roger and Jess. They looked so relaxed peering out of the plane window.

Should he tell them about the man at the airport? He decided against it. It was too late. He'd have to get on with it and see what fate had in store.

But why would they want him to get caught? A gangster turf war? Eye for an eye type of thing? Maybe Stan had stitched the two Japanese smugglers up to challenge the mafia and now it was payback time. Made more sense to stitch your enemy up than leave a horse's head in their bed. Nick's thoughts and paranoia ran wild through his head and there was nothing he could do. He was stuck. Stuck in a steel tube at thirty thousand feet.

About an hour into the flight they were over Paris and looking down onto the city. Roger could just make out a dot which he believed could have been the Eiffel Tower just before the plane slowly began its descent. The flight had been smooth and very quick. A bit too quick for three people who were about to enter a country with stolen bonds worth an eye-watering, ridiculous amount of money.

As they flew lower and lower Nick felt his alarm go off. It was time to take his pills. Cancelling the alarm, he knew he'd get another alarm call in ten minutes to remind him again. Hopefully, they'd be on the ground, and he could get at his pills easily by standing up as they were currently inaccessible in his trouser pocket.

CHAPTER FORTY-FOUR

Craig entered the Chief Inspectors office. Around a table sat the Chief Inspector and a man and a woman both clothed in civvies.

"Come in Craig and take a seat." he gestured towards an empty chair, "I know you've met Jimmy Hillier and Karen Thomas."

Craig leant across the table and shook both their hands, "Yes, yes of course. This has got to be important to have both of you guys here."

The Chief Inspector smiled and acknowledged that it was. It was rare for MI6 and the special operations team to be together in the same room as your everyday detective.

"Karen, can you fill Craig in with the details."

Karen smiled, and turned to Craig, "It's quite simple Craig, you remember that meeting at Scotland Yard regarding extremely high-value bonds that were smuggled into Switzerland in 2009?"

How could Craig forget one of the most tedious meetings ever, "Yes of course." he replied.

"Well, we have intelligence suggesting that the bonds are to be brought into the United Kingdom by someone in your patch."

"Who? When?" Craig sat upright, straightening his back. This was going to be exciting for a change.

"We don't know who yet. We know it's today, but we haven't found out which airport they are coming into yet."

"Today?!"

"Yes. We know it's an airport and not a port."

"How do you know the smugglers are from our patch?"

"That's highly confidential" Jimmy interrupted.

Karen smiled at Jimmy, a sort of curt exaggerated smile.

"Thank you, Jimmy. It is confidential."

"So, what do you want my team to do?"

"Be ready on standby today. We are not sure how this is going to unfold." She stood up, "We are awaiting more information."

"Ok, I'll get my guys ready."

"All we will require is a team to raid the smuggler's house or houses when we've lifted them. If they have partners, lodgers or family living with them then we want them taken into custody. It needs to be shut down quickly so that we can trace it all back to Stan Tennant."

"You know it's him?"

"As sure as we can be."

"And if you don't find out who the smuggler is?"

"We know he or she is from this area, and we are currently going through databases for those with a history to find out if they are abroad at the moment." Jimmy intervened again, "We will take care of them."

"Ok, makes sense." Craig agreed.

"We are not going to find anything else until it's the last minute I'm afraid, so the theme of today is speed and being ready."

"I've got an important appointment later, but I'm only out of the picture for an hour tops."

"Sorry, Craig you won't be out of the picture. I need you to have your phone on and be contactable if required."

"Yes, yes of course." Craig had to be at his neurology appointment, but he knew he wouldn't be long, and in any case, it didn't matter where he was as long as he was contactable.

"I'll go and let the troops know in this morning's meeting then."

"Oh, and Craig." Karen stopped him, "This is big."

CHAPTER FORTY–FIVE

The plane touched down and started to ease up as it bumped along the smooth runway. Seat belts could be heard unlocking around the plane, but Nick kept his on until the plane stopped and the seat belt sign went off. He knew he couldn't go anywhere so why bother?

As soon as the seatbelt sign went off after the aeroplane had taxied to the relevant disembarking area, the doors were opened, and everyone stood up to get off the plane. Nick's phone started to buzz with a reminder again, and he quickly turned it off. He'd have to take a pill as soon as they arrived at the airport building. He couldn't do it in the aisle as he'd just stop everyone getting off while he mucked about trying to take his pills. Jess and Roger were standing up, with Roger bent over as he couldn't fully stand due to the luggage compartments over his head. Nick opened up the luggage compartment and handed them their relevant bags, including the cases containing the contraband.

It looked like a lovely day outside. Nothing like Rome, but sunny with a cool breeze. Nick was definitely in no rush to get off the plane. This was very unusual for him. normally he'd get out as quickly as he could and breathe in the welcome air, glad he survived the plane journey. Free from its claustrophobic shell.

Jess on the other hand was very keen to get off. It was as though she had forgotten the magnitude of what she was about to do. She was very blasé as she moved down the plane, even thanking the air steward excitedly as she exited the door. She was keen to get home even though she had only been away for a couple of nights. Walking down the disembarking steps following the other passengers she started to twitch, shouting the odd profanity as she started to walk on the tarmac. No one seemed to take any notice. Instead, the passengers looked away from her, trying to avoid eye contact with the supposed mad girl swearing.

Roger just wanted to leave his seat which he'd sat down on again due to the slow movement of the queue. He gazed through the window at the luggage being unloaded from another plane and wiped his mouth free from any dribble.

"They'd better not be treating my bag like that!" he thought watching the two men hurling cases onto the back of a trailer. Eventually, a large gap came up in the queue and Roger managed to hoick himself up and get off the plane. He was also getting hungry and needed to get some nutrition into himself, never mind a good flush of water down his stomach tube.

Once inside the terminal building, they found themselves on a crowded train platform. The crowd awaited the electric train that took them the short distance to the luggage pick up, customs and finally the exit. As the platform was so packed, Roger felt himself having to step back a couple of feet and leant against a wall. An electric train quietly came along, and Jess and Nick somehow ended up on it before they knew it. Nick cried back to Roger,

"Rog! See you at luggage!"

Roger nodded. Or at least Nick thought he did.

The train swept off leaving those who couldn't get on.

Roger took it in his stride. He edged forwards from the wall and patiently waited for the next train. Another plane must have landed as before he knew it, he was caught up in another crowd who were all of course going in the same direction. A train came in and he managed to get on it without breaking his neck. If only he could shout. No one seemed to care; it was not as if he looked safe on his legs. A doddery middle-aged bloke, dribbling mouth, gripping a small case, a suitcase, a rucksack on his back and a walking stick. He seemed to be invisible to everyone. He stood on the train and tried to hang onto one of the handles, the stick in his hand rose up as he raised it to hold onto the handle swinging in front of him. Unfortunately, it tapped an elderly lady on her lower back causing her to turn round sharply. She gave Roger a stern stare as Roger started dribbling causing the lady to look extremely repulsed. Roger shrugged. If he let go to wipe his mouth he'd go arse over bollocks. So he stood firm and allowed a small puddle of spit to form near his foot.

By the time Roger got to the first luggage carousel in the main airport, bags, and all sorts of different coloured cases were slowly building up. He saw Jess and Nick waiting at another carousel,

"Took your time Rog."

Roger ignored Jess's observation. Nick, on seeing his case coming around the carousel, moved forwards and managed to pull it off the belt as it went by. Roger's was the next case to come into view and be lifted off.

"Shitting-hell! I bet my case has gone AWOL! It will probably end up in China!" She went to the front of the carousel to wait for more cases to be put on it. Nothing happened.

The three waited for ten more minutes.

"Lost property then!" Nick sighed, his breathing starting to get faster, the nerves slowly getting worse. This was added pressure that they did not need.

"Damn!" Jess said, "Damn it!" she started to get

angry.

"It'll turn up, don't worry" Nick tried to reassure her, though was beginning to get stressed himself.

They walked off past the five or six luggage carousels to find the 'lost property office.' On the last carousel was a single pink suitcase, unclaimed and unwanted, going round and round in the ever-decreasing possibility of being picked up. Jess gave out a little scream as she saw it and ran over to claim it.

Nick sighed deeply. Thank God for that he thought. Now the difficult bit.

CHAPTER FORTY-SIX

The three were the last ones from the flight to walk slowly towards passport control. Reaching the passport desk Jess handed her passport to the border control officer. The officer quickly scrutinised the passport, looked briefly at Jess then returned it to her.

Jess was the first to walk through the green 'nothing to declare' customs corridor. It was empty. The crowds fighting to reclaim their cases in the collection area had long gone through and were probably free of the airport. Before she knew it, Jess found herself on the other side of customs and in the large Arrivals atrium. A few people were leaning over barriers waiting for friends, loved ones and customers for their taxis, from flights that were due in.

Roger shuffled through next. As he was walking, he glanced to his side and was shocked to see that Nick had gone. He was sure Nick was walking next to him after passport control. Roger stopped to look behind. Nick was standing just inside the opening of the corridor, leaning on the side of the wall next to a large photograph of a family splashing in the sea at some exotic location.

Roger flapped his arms about to try and get Nick's attention. Nick grimaced at him and motioned for Roger to keep walking. Roger reluctantly continued. He was struggling with his suitcase and the contraband case as well as his walking stick, wishing he had used one of the trolleys. As he staggered through the exit Jess grabbed him, guiding him to one side.

"What's going on Rog?" she whispered, "Where's Nick?"

Roger shrugged, pointing back to the corridor they had both walked through.

"This has got disaster written all over it Roger,"

Roger didn't acknowledge Jess. He had a bad feeling about the situation. This could NOT go wrong.

Nick was still standing at the entrance to the green channel corridor. He couldn't walk any further. His right foot had cramped. It had twisted itself inwards, pulling his ankle upwards in a dystonic rage. A contorted mess. He stupidly tried to move forward even though he knew it wasn't going to happen. The pain shot up his leg as he took a disfigured step, walking on the side of his ankle. He could not go anywhere. He was stuck. Stuck at Customs, smuggling £67 billion into the country. He was sure he had a case containing half the bonds.

He realised he hadn't taken his pill. "What an idiot!" he thought. All those times he had advocated for the Parkinson's community to get nurses to ensure they had their medication at the right time whilst in hospital, and here he was doing the scariest, stupid stunt he had ever been involved in.

His arms started to move wildly, stress and the fact his medicine had run out had ramped up his dyskinesia. With one unsteady hand, he pulled out his pills and managed to scoop one into his mouth. He was so dry and thirsty, but he managed to create enough saliva to swallow the pill. He could feel the horrible tasting powder of the pill stick to his dry lips and knew from experience that his tongue and lips were probably bright yellow, ensuring that he couldn't look more suspicious, like a dog with suspected rabies.

Nick tried to walk again but couldn't. Shit! He was well and truly stuck. It would take 20 minutes for his medication to start working enabling him to move again. Looking around he couldn't see anyone, no passengers or customs officers. Making him jump he felt his mobile vibrating in his pocket. He let it ring fearing that talking on a phone just before the most secure corridor in the United Kingdom might raise a few more eyebrows.

Jess took the phone from her ear, "He's not answering Roger! I bet he's been stopped! Shit Roger this is bad! He's the one who didn't want to do this!" she was getting stressed, "What if they come out and ask us to go back in to be searched?"

Roger looked at her. He couldn't get his letter sheet out as his hands were full. He guided her away from the arrivals entrance to a group of chairs. He sat down, put his bags down on the floor and pulled out his letter sheet.

"We don't know yet. Wait and see,"

"I've got a bad feeling about this" Jess didn't sit down. She started to pace up and down the length of the area. Roger could see her twitching start to escalate.

"He may not have the bonds" Roger pointed at each letter quickly, trying to get her eye as she walked back and forth.

"I bet he has. Do you think we should hang about?"

"Stay here." Roger used his letter sheet and nodded his head.

◆ ◆ ◆

Nick stood, still leaning on the wall, disabled by his twisted lower foot and ankle. He gripped hold of the bonds case and his bag strap and waited for his pills to do their magic. It needed to happen quickly.

Suddenly from out of nowhere came two customs officers, walking very briskly towards him.

"Sir, you can't stand here." one of them said sternly to Nick, "Sir you need to move on!"

Nick tried to speak. His dystonia got tighter, and his arms and trunk started to squirm, "I, I have..." he stuttered.

"Sir, we are going to have to move you, you need to come with us,"

"Parkinson's disease," he managed to spit out.

"Well we can talk about that in the office, now come with me please sir,"

"I can't walk!" Nick hissed through gritted teeth.

"Well, you got this far ok. We saw you!" one of them grabbed his arm.

"No, you don't understand. I can't physically bloody walk!"

"Sir do not use language like that!"

"Please, I can't walk, my pills have worn off"

The two officers looked at each other. The younger of the officers reached to his radio to ask for assistance. The other let his arms go.

"My foot cramps and I can't walk on it!" he pointed at his foot. Nick had calmed down and was able to talk normally.

Suddenly another Customs officer turned up.

"Sir, what's wrong? Why are you standing here?" asked the new Customs officer in a welcoming softer tone.

"I've got Parkinson's disease and I can't move, my foot had cramped. It's called dystonia!" Nick gasped.

The third, who was more of a senior official, asked one of his colleagues to get a wheelchair.

"Ok sir, we are going to take you to the office. We'll just wait for Dan to get a wheelchair,"

Nick started getting nervous, "But my friends are on the other side, they've just gone through," he looked at the man who was bringing the wheelchair "Can't you just take me through?"

"We'll take you through to the office first Sir." the wheelchair was positioned behind Nick, "What's your name?"

"Nick. Nick Goldsmith."

"Ok Nick, sit yourself down," as he was sitting down on the wheelchair seat one of the officials took his bag and the bond case off him. The Customs officer, on her Majesty's payroll, was carrying potentially $67 billion. Enough to change the inflation rate, interest rates or sink an economy in his hands! Enough to put Nick in prison for a long, long time.

Nick sat down. This was it. His life as he knew it was over. He was about to get searched, nicked, and would end up rotting in a skanky prison cell. Life would never be the same again. He'd lose everything. The fear started to gnaw at his stomach, he was sweating and felt dizzy as his pulse was racing. He could feel himself squirming in the wheelchair and tried desperately to stay still.

He was pushed through several doors and eventually ended up in a room, with no windows, with a table in the middle and chairs on either side, he guessed this was one of the airport's interview rooms. The man who had his bag and case placed them on the table and Nick was pushed up to the table.

"Coffee?"

"Er?" Nick didn't know what to say. Couldn't they just do this and get it over with?

"You might as well."

"Ok yes, yes, please. However it comes."

"Just ring your friends and tell them you won't be long," the man stopped, "Actually you look as though you may have problems with the keyboard, sorry, give me your phone and I'll do it."

Nick gave him the phone, his hands still moving uncomfortably, making obscure patterns in the air.

"Who do you want to call?"

"It's J."

The officer pressed "J" and gave the phone straight to Nick.

The three officers left the room, closing the door behind them.

"Nick what the hell is happening?" she answered the phone without it seemingly ringing.

"I've been taken to an office!" Nick whispered

desperately, "It's over!"

"Oh Nick" Jess whispered back.

"Just go Jess. You and Roger go." with that, he ended the call.

The officer came back with a coffee and put it on the table in front of Nick.

"You ring your friends?"

Nick nodded. He didn't know what to say.

"So how long do your meds take to start?"

"About half an hour, but I am a bit late taking them. I took it about 10 odd minutes ago."

"You're young for the disease."

"Yeah, I know."

"My father had Parkinson's. He had it for twenty years and I watched him decline, unfortunately." the man looked sad, "He fell and broke his hip, went to the hospital and then it went really wrong."

Nick sighed to himself. No one ever had any positive experiences with Parkinson's disease. It was all bad. He'd never heard someone say,

"My uncle had Parkinson's. He's fine! You'll be ok!"

"Oh, why? What went wrong with your dad?" Nick never thought he'd have someone telling him their Parkinson story whilst he was carrying half of a $134 billion load.

"They missed about two days of his medication. He never recovered. Couldn't move. So I know about the importance of your pills."

Nick smiled nervously, "Yes, it can muck you

up if you're late taking them."

"Well, you've shown us that today." the officer smiled.

Nick wondered what was going to happen. When are they going to search him? Are they investigating in Italy? Are they interrogating Roger and Jess right now? Did the man who looked at him at Rome airport have something to do with this?

"Finished your coffee?"

"Er yep." here we go, this was it. Within an hour he'd have some bloke wearing rubber gloves examining his bottom, searching for hidden gems.

"Right. I'll take you out if you feel you can walk."

Nick looked at him. "Sorry?"

"I'll show you how to get out of here, it can be a maze if you don't know where you're going?"

Nick grabbed the case containing the bonds first and then picked up his other bag.

"I'll just take you out and you can continue your journey home. How's it feel?"

Nick put weight on his foot, he felt it was back to normal as he lifted his foot up and down.

"Excellent. It's amazing what those pills can do. Do you know about that thing they can put in your brain? You going to have that done?"

"Trying to avoid it."

"Don't blame you. Bit weird having your head opened up."

Within minutes they were out in the main Arrivals atrium. The officer said goodbye and disappeared back into the inner sanctum of the airport.

Nick stood in the middle of the Atrium. He had the case containing the bonds in his hand and his main bag. Suddenly he felt someone grab him by the waist and kiss his cheek,

"We did it!" Jess laughed whispering closely into his ear.

"We flipping well did it!" Nick concurred.

Roger grinned from ear to ear. A tear flickered in his eye.

CHAPTER FORTY-SEVEN

Detective Inspector Craig Bullen walked quickly through the hospital. He wanted to get out of the building, get in his car and drive far, far away. He was still awaiting information on the smugglers. What he wanted to do was find a pub and get absolutely trollied. He wanted to get so drunk that any poison, unhappiness and tragedy would drown in his alcoholic assault.

Finally, he got back to the safety of his car. He sat at the driver's wheel and stared through the windscreen. All he could see was the brick wall in front of his car. He thought about his wife and kids. He had to tell his wife. He had been to all his hospital appointments on his own. She knew nothing. How was he going to tell his wife? He can't tell his wife! His brain suddenly kicked into panic mode.

How the hell was he going to tell his wife and kids he was soon to be in a wheelchair, going to need to be fed and washed by a carer? How was he going to explain to his wife that he was going to die? That he had motor neurone disease?

Suddenly he snapped, "Bollocks! FUCK! FUCK! FUCK!" he shouted, hitting the steering wheel several times.

He stopped hitting out and shouting as quickly as he had suddenly started. He closed his eyes, resting his head on the recently battered steering wheel.

Leaning back into his car seat he opened his eyes and whispered, "Bollocks" to himself.

The drive to the pub was quiet. The roads seemed spookily quiet, and he eased through every traffic light without stopping as they were all green when he reached them. Thirty minutes later he reached his destination.

Craig got out of his car and walked towards the pub. He'd been in the pub a couple of times during the day and knew that it would be quiet. Walking in he saw a few customers sitting around one of the back tables and an older man on a stool at the bar, a newspaper in front of him.

Craig ordered his drink, a pint of real ale, and walked over to an empty table, hidden by a wall from the rest of the pub. It was like a small snug that Craig felt he could hide in, away from any prying eyes. He sipped his beer and for some strange reason, after being told he had a terminal disease, he felt calm and relaxed.

He intended to have a couple of beers and go home. Maybe get a takeaway. Sit his family down and tell them what was going on. He had to tell them, and he wanted to do it openly and positively. Craig laughed sarcastically to himself at what he had just thought. Positive? Maybe not. He knew it would end up sad and teary. His wife would feel let down – he should have had her with him at his appointments. But he knew that he would get more stressed worrying about her stress as they went for each test and consultation. She'd need to be involved now. She'd have questions that he didn't want to have answered or had forgotten to ask the Doctor.

Craig finished his pint and bought himself another one at the bar. Looking around the pub waiting for his drink to be poured he noticed a few more of the tables had customers sitting at them. His eyes were drawn to one of the tables that had four people sitting around it. Looking at the profile of one of the men at the table he noticed he had very restless arms. The bartender put his beer on the bar. Craig paid the bartender. He could not place the man but knew he had met him before.

Craig's phone suddenly bleeped just as he remembered who the restless man was. It was that bloke with Parkinson's. He'd only sent him a text this morning! A weird coincidence. He didn't want to talk right now. He'd contact him another time. Craig felt his phone vibrate. With all the stress of being told he had motor neurone disease he had forgotten about work, the possibility of getting called to take some people into custody and any thoughts of criminals. He paused, took out his phone and saw that it was a colleague from work. He didn't want to answer it.

The phone kept vibrating in his hand.

Finally, he answered it,

"Yes Kelly?"

"Do you recognise them, boss?" Kelly sounded breathless on the phone.

"Recognise who?"

"I sent you the pictures through. The smugglers. They are on our patch. I've seen them before!" We've sent cars round to their addresses to pick them up." she took a deep intake of breath, "I'm five minutes away from one of their houses!"

Craig's mind suddenly went into override. For a second that felt like half an hour, he couldn't figure out what the hell she was on about.

"I'll have a look at the photo."

Craig opened the picture on his phone. It showed three people sitting together in what looked like an airport waiting area. He looked at the three. He couldn't believe his eyes.

The three were from the pub he raided a while ago, and they were sitting just across the bar with another woman!

"What on Earth?" dumbstruck and feeling faint at what he was looking at he muttered into the phone, "Ok keep me posted." he hung up the phone.

CHAPTER FORTY-EIGHT

Stan put his book on the table and took a sip of tea from the bone China cup and then rested it back down on the matching saucer with a gentle click. He looked at his watch. There should have been some news by now. He stood up and walked out of his cell onto the landing where he leant on the balcony that squarely flanked the walkways. Looking down through the protective netting he could see a group of men all dressed in grey tracksuit bottoms and mauve t-shirts playing pool. It had been a muggy day and most of the prisoners were trying to cool down in their respective cells or areas.

Stan meandered back into his cell, allowed the fan to slowly scan his face with cool air then sat back down at his table and picked up his book again.

Just as he was halfway through the page, he looked up to see a prison officer standing in the doorway,

"It's done, Mr. Tennant."

Stan put the book back onto the table and leant back in his chair, looking up at the freshly painted ceiling. He slowly smiled to himself.

"The bonds are safe as planned." the officer added.

"Problems?" Stan looked at the officer.

"The law knows who the smugglers are. A tip-off. They have been following them since they got there."

"Yes, I know. It's sorted. I've spoken to them, and it's sorted." Stan was a little annoyed that he was being told something he had already dealt with. "Anything else?"

"No Sir," the officer left the doorway.

Stan reached under his bed and pulled out a tiny mobile phone. Pressing a button on the phone he put it to his ear. The phone was smaller than his ear.

"It's done," he said when the call was answered.

"Good." the voice at the other replied, "And Matteo?"

"Dealt with."

"Completely?"

"Completely, slowly and comprehensively. I think others will heed the warnings...."

CHAPTER FORTY-NINE

Craig suddenly and accidentally locked eyes with Nick. Nick smiled and waved. Craig gave a small wave and then sat back down. He didn't want to do this right now.

"Hi" Nick walked into the snug, "You're that policeman aren't you, you know the one from the pub raid. You sent me a text earlier today."

"Yes, yes that's me."

"How are things? Did you or your 'friend' get any results? You told me someone was worried about some weird symptoms I think?"

"Yeah, I was having tests. It was me."

"I did think it maybe was yourself. So what's happening to you?"

"Erm, yeah they say I've got motor neurone disease or ALS."

Nick sat down at Craig's table, "Shit. I'm sorry mate."

The two men didn't know what to say to each other.

"I'm really sorry….would you like to come and

join us?" Nick broke the silence.

"No, no that's fine. Thank you."

"I don't know what to say."

"Snap." Craig took a swig of his beer.

"Are you sure you won't join us?"

"No. I have to go home."

"Yes sure."

Nick didn't know how to end the conversation. How do you get up and leave someone whose just been told such difficult, devastating news and who obviously doesn't want to talk?

"The doctor said I probably won't live past three years."

"Oh No! I'm so sorry. It's Craig, isn't it?"

"Yes and Nick?"

"Yes that's me."

"I probably will never see my daughter get married."

Neither spoke.

Nick again broke the discomfort of the silence, "I can't give you any advice Craig. My Parkinson's was scary, well still is, but not like the news you've had."

"It hasn't sunk in yet."

"No, I'm sure it hasn't."

"How long have you known?"

"An hour. I have to go back and see them again next week, well one of the nurses anyway."

"I'm so, so sorry Craig." Nick put his hand on the top of Craig's shoulder, "Come and join us."

"No, I need to get back. I must talk to my family."

"Well, I'll stay with you until you've finished your pint. You can't sit alone mate."

"Why did you do it Nick?"

"Do what?" Nick was a bit taken aback by the sudden change in tone of the conversation.

"Why did you and your pals bring those bonds into London?"

Nick felt the colour drain from his face. "What bonds?"

"Nick, you were being watched at Rome airport this morning!" he picked his phone up and opened the pictures app. "Look! It's a picture of the three of you taken this morning in Rome airport!"

"What on earth are you talking about?" Nick started to feel extremely uncomfortable.

"You smuggled in US bonds Nick. I've been involved in meetings with MI6 about this. Christ, they even had the FBI involved. It's major Nick! MI6 sent me your photographs literally just now." Craig grinned, "And I'm looking right at the gang of smugglers in front of me in my local bloody pub! It's a gift from heaven Nick!"

Nick looked away. Thinking.

"Cars are on the way to your homes! They'll go in and go through everything you own! Nightmare Nick! I should be taking you in!"

Nick coughed and returned his gaze to Craig. His dyskinesia started subtly to kick in.

"Why Nick?" Craig asked.

Nick looked at Craig, "Why? Why what?"

"Come on Nick! Why smuggle in that amount of cash?"

"I've no idea what you are talking about mate."

"Nick you were followed!"

"Well they got the wrong people – we were at a neurological conference in Rome! What the hell do we know about smuggling, never mind what your bonds are?"

"Nick, they don't want you necessarily. They want the people at the top. But you have to hand yourself in."

Nick looked at Roger, Jess and Liz at the table in the pub. They'd come here straight from the airport and picked Liz up on the way in a taxi. The three had come to debrief themselves on what they had just done and to try and get their adrenaline levels down. He was not about to let the last couple of days be a complete waste of time by handing himself in.

There was absolutely no way it was all going to fail at the bitter end. He had committed too much. He knew there was no actual proof of them carrying anything illegal. They'd received communication from Stan that all was good and the bonds were in a safe place. They would receive their payment at the end of the week and then they could get on with the rest of their lives.

Stan had also pre-warned them the police would come knocking due to a leak at Italy's end, but he promised he would "sort it." Jess had spoken to him by phone outside the airport. He had also given strict instructions to the three not to discuss it with anyone and deny all knowledge.

"Craig, I'm not going to admit to something I know nothing about!"

"I get it Nick. So where are the bonds now?"

"Craig. I've no idea!"

"You will be questioned, Nick. All of you. Your houses are being turned upside down as we speak."

"Well so be it. But we've done nothing." Nick started to sway as the stress started to hit home, "Are you going to take us in Craig?"

Craig looked down at the table and closed his eyes.

"Nick." he paused, "I've just been told I've probably got three years of shit in front of me. I need to be with my wife and kids." he lifted his head and stared at Nick, "Nick. I really don't care about some stupid bonds."

Nick sighed. He had mixed emotions of relief with incredible sorrow for Craig.

"Look, I've got to go. It's been a bad day." Craig stood up.

Nick put out his hand for Craig to shake it. "Look Craig, I'm sorry about your MND."

"Yeah, well…………cheers."

Craig left the snug.

"Craig!" Nick quickly called.

"Yes Nick" Craig turned round and walked the few steps back to the table.

"I hate to say Craig, but you'll soon find out why those three misfits did what they did."

"I think I can figure out why." Craig took out his phone and unceremoniously dropped it into the half-filled pint glass that he had left. "Leave it to me. Though I'm sure Tennant is already pulling strings."

"Thank you," Nick whispered under his breath, "Thank you so much."

Nick wiped his eye. They had been welling up with everything.

"I'm pretty sure it was done by three people who wanted more out of life." Nick spoke softly to Craig, "Three people who were fed up fighting. Three people who had so much to offer. Three people who just wanted to be a part of something."

Nick smiled,

"Three people who proved they can."

EPILOGUE

Jess impatiently waited for Nick to sign on to the zoom call. She had set it up to start at two pm and at five minutes past she started to get bored and irritated. It had been a good six months after the Rome job, and she had been staying in various five-star hotels with Roger for most of that time. Her chat with Nick was a weekly affair and she looked forward to gossiping about what was happening in their lives. Herself, Roger and Nick had built up a solid friendship with deep foundations due to their experiences in Italy.

The balcony she sat on overlooked the clear turquoise waters of the Mediterranean Sea, slowly lapping at the beach in front of her hotel. Jess's left shoulder twitched as she impatiently took a sip from the glass of water that was next to her laptop on the white table. Her Tourette's hadn't improved with a change in climate, which she hoped it would.

Suddenly Nick's face popped up on her screen. He looked a little harassed and started to speak. Jess couldn't hear a word he was saying, "You're on mute Nick." She coldly noted. The boredom of telling Nick the same sentence every time they spoke via Zoom was apparent in her tone.

"Can you hear me now?" he stuttered.

"Yes." Jess snapped back.

"How are you guys getting on? Looks hot!"

"We're good. It is hot and I love it!" Jess beamed. "How's that copper Nick? I've been meaning to ask."

"Craig? He's ok. Still working, but getting his head slowly round it all."

"Scary stuff, I don't know what I'd do if that was me."

Both paused for a brief moment of reflection.

"You on your own? Where's that cool bloke with all the bling?" Nick laughed, lightening the mood.

"He buys some hideous jewellery, it's embarrassing Nick!" Jess still hadn't recovered from the cringe-inducing gold sovereign chain necklace and ring set Roger wore out to dinner the previous week, "He's resting. We went for a walk this morning and I think I've worn him out! How's Liz?"

"Good. She's looking forward to travelling over there with me to see you both."

"Well, you both need to come soon 'cause me and Roger are off to mainland Spain next month"

"Oh ok, maybe we could catch up there. Do you know where you are staying?"

"I'll text you the details of the hotel and dates."

"Yes, thanks. Any news from Stan?"

"He's up for parole in late December I think." her arm flinched up in the air and she shouted something unrecognisable over her left shoulder.

"Do you reckon he'll get out?" Nick ignored the tics and noises that Jess had made.

"Good chance." Jess sipped her water, "He's got another job for us."

Nick didn't reply. He just looked at Jess.

"Nick I said he's got another job for us," she repeated. She knew that Nick would not be pleased. Before Nick could answer Jess cut in, "Oh and I spoke to…hold on a minute I've got his name written down on my phone," Jess scrolled through the contacts on her phone.

"Argh yes, Naoto Okano." she read the name out slowly.

"What the bloke from Chiasso?" Nick asked, recognising the name.

"Yep the one and only." she smiled, "he sent us his congratulations on getting further than he and that other Japanese bloke did."

"I think they were well and truly stitched up."

"That's what he said. He was amazed that they got away with it. Anyway, they made a few quid. Pity his mate died so quickly."

"Yes a shame. Did he say who they were working for? Who set it up?"

"No he wouldn't tell me. But he knew what they were carrying. I still think it was the Italian mafia. Especially with what happened to us!"

"Mm maybe. Doesn't make sense that they were set up though."

"Agreed." Jess took another sip of her water. The sun was getting hotter as the day went on, "Rome was fun wasn't it?"

"I definitely wouldn't put it in the fun category!" Nick coughed, disagreeing with Jess's idea of fun.

"I had fun! It was an experience."

"We were lucky Jess. It was the most stressful, scary, and the riskiest thing I've ever done! It was also too bloody hot!"

"We did it though."

Nick had to agree.

"Got a wedge of cash too" Jess added, "Well a lot more than a wedge." she quipped looking out to the calm, inviting sea in front of her. A view that she had always dreamed of that had now become her reality.

"Yes we did. I can't be grateful enough. But that's it Jess. You can't be lucky twice, and frankly, I do not want to end up in a prison cell!"

"I don't think you'd be locked up in prison for this one." her broad grin filled Nick's monitor screen.

"Well, I'm not doing it. Sorry end of."

"Time will tell Nick. Time will tell."

◆ ◆ ◆

Danny Giordano lay on his bed and gazed at the

pictures on the wall at the other end of the cell. He was wide awake contemplating what he had to do. Getting arrested for the post office job had been easy and ending up on remand was perfect. A court case for armed robbery was also welcomed. At least he'd get a long sentence.

On the wall that Danny was staring at was a poster of the back of a footballer, wearing an Italian team shirt, a ponytail part covering the name 'R.Baggio'. A large number '10' filled the rest of the blue shirt.

He had never been to Italy, experienced the passion of an Italian football game, or knew that much about Italian footballers. Danny was fully aware of the importance of football, Italian football to his family. His dad had often claimed that football was a close second behind being a catholic, and Baggio was an angel from heaven in his father's and his brother's eyes.

But his dad was dead, and Danny had to even the score. He had to take his revenge, and he had to do it himself. Once he was found guilty, bribes would be paid, violence would be used, and strings would be pulled resulting in his relocation to another prison.

Once there he would bide his time, groom his victim, become part of his crew, build trust and friendship before unleashing a bloody, horrific, vengeful, violent and fatal attack on the man who killed his father.

Stan Tennant was going to die.

A LITTLE MORE...

Thank you to my beautiful wife Kim for your patience and support. Thank you to those who helped, advised and understood – Zoe, Hills and Colin Dave K (photos), Jenny J, Gillian, Mairéad J and Clare S.

A massive thank you to Alison W. for your constructive support, endless read-throughs and marvellous suggestions. You played a very important part in this book.

Useful suggestions for advice :

UK
Parkinson's UK
The Stroke Association
Tourettes Action

USA
The Michael J Fox Foundation for Research

American Stroke Association
Tourette Association of America

"Employment rates of people with disabilities are lower than average, while their motivation to work is generally high. The combination of these two pieces of information alone would suggest that companies should be willing to hire people with disabilities. In addition, previous research shows that people with disabilities score higher in a number of efficiency-related metrics and assessments and not hiring disabled employees can mean companies are missing out on opportunities to increase productivity and economic success.

So why are so many people with disabilities still unemployed even though they are of working age? A reason why commitment to disability inclusive hiring is limited may be low employer knowledge, especially at the HR and management levels (Saleh and Bruyère, 2018), as well as social barriers resulting from a lack of social support (Naraine and Lindsay, 2011). If more companies recognize the potential of disabled workers and manage to recruit the right person for the right job, everyone could benefit. The Asperger Informatik AG calls it a win-win-win situation for the economy, society, and the individual."

Aichner, T. The economic argument for hiring people with disabilities. *Humanit Soc Sci Commun* **8**, 22 (2021). https://doi.org/10.1057/s41599-021-00707-y

"Employers have a duty to make reasonable adjustments if the disabled person has been put at a substantial disadvantage by a 'provision, criterion or practice' imposed by the employer compared to someone who is not disabled." United Kingdom Equality Act 2010

BOOKS BY THIS AUTHOR

Walking In Sand

Being diagnosed with a progressive disease is scary and life changing stuff. In the author's case it was "Parkinson's Disease" that the neurologist diagnosed him with as he was stood in the consulting room in his thread bare underwear. What do you do next? Who do you tell? How do you cope with it? Can I still work? Do I tell my loved one's and friends? What do I tell them? "Walking in Sand" is a moving, funny and practical story for all those affected by progressive diseases, especially Parkinson's disease. This short book is suitable for those who have been diagnosed with any sort of disease, for families of diagnosed patients and for health care professionals - so that they can really understand what makes some of their patient's tick. Its short, easy and quick to read, sad but with a smile. "Walking In sand" won't change your diagnosis but it may help fellow Parkinson's patients know they are not alone.

Printed in Great Britain
by Amazon